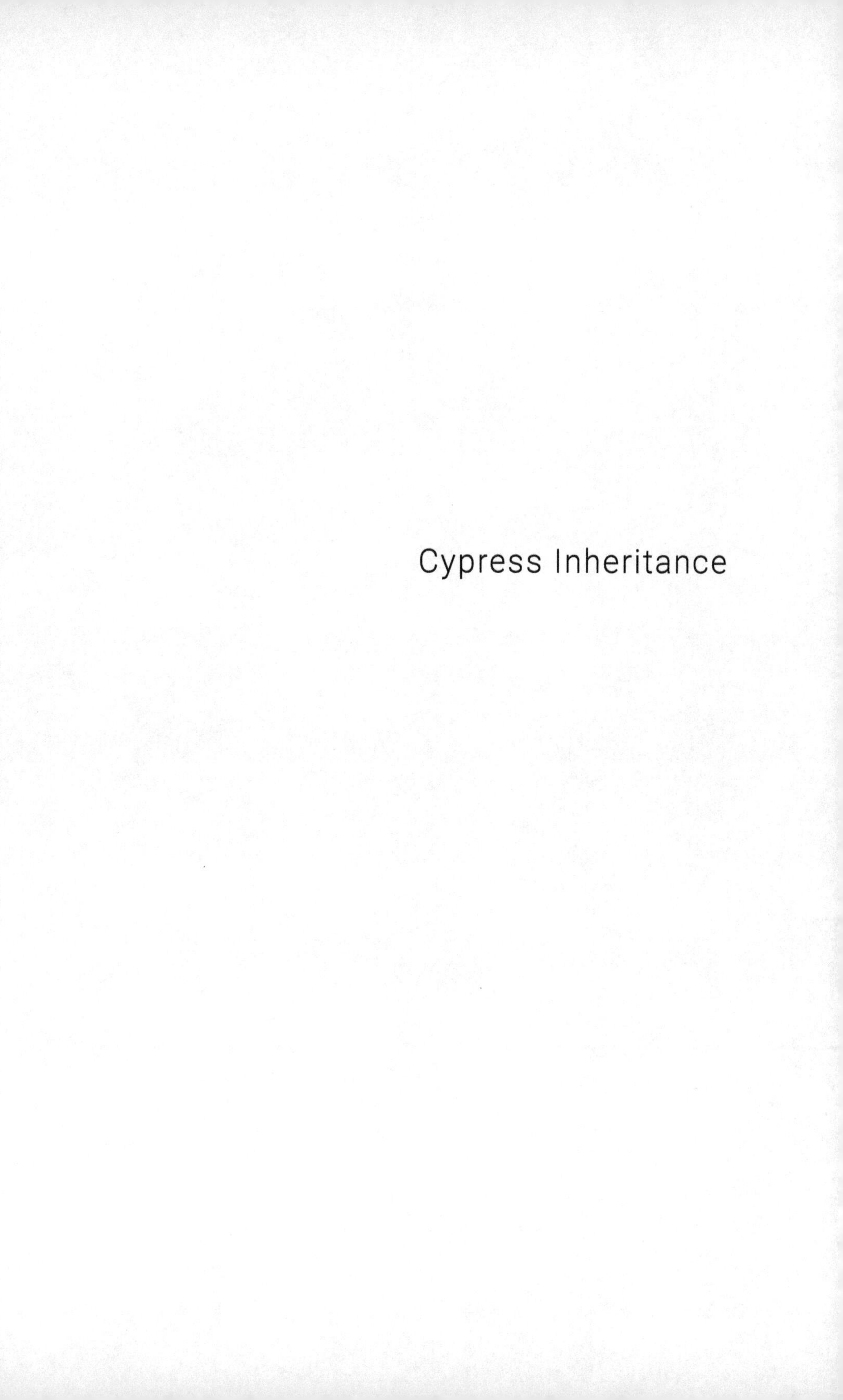

Cypress Inheritance

Cypress Inheritance

C.E. One Cypress

First Printing, 2025

Story By: C.E. One Cypress
Author C.E. One Cypress

Author David DeBorde

Summary: Lorna has always been driven to succeed and doesn't let anything stand in her way. But beneath her ambition lies an ache she can't figure out. Adopted as an infant, she's never stopped wondering why someone gave her away - who were her parents and what were they going through when they gave her up to an orphanage.

When a mysterious letter bequeaths her a massive estate, everything begins to change.

With secrets unfolding and responsibilities she never asked for falling squarely onto her shoulders, Lorna is about to learn just how important she is in the world and how far others will go to control what she's only beginning to discover.

Her inheritance is only the beginning...

1

Chapter One

The lateness of the evening brought a rich darkness settling over the landscape, and they moved accordingly with deliberation and caution. Their small boat drifted through a patch of still water, sprinkled with small rocks and stumps, barely visible, poking through the lake's surface. They had been fishing most of the day in one of Arizona's largest lakes and the moonlight had begun casting its lunar glow through the dense cloud cover making for somewhat of an eerie setting.

Frank, 30's and no stranger to fishing, country music and sodas, looks back to his buddy and fellow amateur fisherman, and utters in a low tone with no small measure of agitation, "Ray, I really wanna' get back soon! I can't see more than a few feet in front of us and I'm not too fond of the idea of smashing into something out here." Ray, also 30's, glances back at Frank with a smirk, "You gettin' a little skeered there, Princess?"

Frank mock chuckles and says, "Ha ha. Let's wrap this up."

From above, the enormous lake makes their 14-foot, small engine boat seem tiny. Ray sits at the back of the boat steering and listening to Frank complain. They have been fishing here more times than they can count, and always in the designated areas where the fish are teeming, but never in this area. The time has simply gotten away from them and now they are trying to get back to the dock, but they are a little turned around. Frank chimes in again, "Seriously, man. Don't feel like havin' to swim back to shore cuz you knocked into one of those rocks."

Ray finds his friend's reaction to the situation a little comical, but "Alright, alright. No one's swimming tonight. Gimme a second, I'll get us back." Ray is going as fast as he can safely go. They continue forward, not remotely prepared for what comes across next.

As they come around a small bend, the smoky mist separates just slightly revealing... Frank mutters, "You seein' this?"

"Yes I am." Never knew anything like this was out here."

...a small island in the distance. As they draw closer to the shoreline of the island, they notice a large structure in the distance. They cannot make out what it is yet, but they can see that it is huge. As they reach the shoreline of the small island, they realize there is a large mansion in the middle of the island.

It is nestled into the side of the mountainous island in such a way that unless you are almost on top of it, you wouldn't notice it, which is clearly part of the owner's intention. Just slightly overgrown with weeds, bushes and other foliage around the outside, it still looks as if it was once very well maintained. In addition to its gothically beautiful exterior, it is designed to make unwanted entry difficult like an old-fashioned European castle perched on a highpoint. There's no real beach to speak of, making it hard to get onto the island fortress, even if say, two fishing buddies were actually forced to swim to it because their boat hypothetically crashed on the surrounding rocks.

Ray eased back on the throttle as they neared the island, its towering mansion looming ahead like a fortress. The closer they got, the more imposing it seemed, casting long shadows over the water. Both men sat in silent awe, their eyes tracing the sprawling estate from its sprawling veranda to the steeply pitched roofs reaching toward the sky. It was a testament to wealth and power, standing defiant and unyielding against the backdrop of the darkening horizon. Ray speaks in a low voice... "You know this was here?"

Frank with his eyes glued on the sheer size of the mansion and his mouth slightly open simply replies with a similar tone as Ray, shaking his head at the same time, saying, "No..."

Frank was born, raised and did much of his living within an hour of that boat. Fishing has always been a part of this safe, comfortable existence. Not tonight, however, and his unease is slowly eclipsed by a feeling he hasn't experienced since he and Ray took a road trip to LA the summer after their high school graduation...

Frank is becoming intrigued with this mysterious fortress, "Looks deserted." He points, "Hey, there's a small dock," Pausing for a second after thinking about it he then says to Ray, "Pull up. Let's check it out really quick."

Ray just looks at him, "'Scuse me, weren't you just scared that we'd have to swim home and have to explain to Melissa why your clothes are wet and smell like a swamp?" Frank retorts, "Ray, you gonna bust my chops or pull up to that dock? I wanna take a quick look. Come on, man, ain't you curious?"

Ray sees the resolve in Frank's eyes, and slightly drops his shoulders in resignation. "This thing sinks, you're paying for a new one." "Deal!"

As they pull up to the dock, they notice a sign stating, "No trespassing" and another sign which is banged up and weathered, with markings indicating it is, or was, a government property at one time. They also notice what looks like a chain fence that has seen better days and once served as a barrier a few feet offshore going in a direction toward where they are landing. Ray says, "You sure about this? I mean I know it looks deserted but that looked like a government sign over there. And, that chain fence? If that is a barrier, I am fairly sure we are not supposed to be here."

Frank quickly jumps out onto the dock and after taking a few moments to take in the setting and says, "Come on, there's no one here, let's check it out." Ray isn't sure. Frank taunts him, "You coming, Princess?" Ray smirks at his own words being thrown back at him. Frank ties the boat to the dock.

Ray jumps out of the boat and starts up a small walkway to join Frank. "Look at this place. Can't believe I never knew it was here." As the two fishing buddies slowly move onto the front lawn taking in this massive secret place, they are unaware that they are being watched from inside the mansion. A pair of backlit eyes narrow as they peer down on Frank and Ray from an unlit upstairs corner room.

Frank leads Ray as they walk up a smooth grey stone path that guides them toward the castle-style front door. "Frank, you know what this reminds me of a little?" "What's that?" "It looks like what you would think a haunted castle would look like." Ray trying to catch up, "Great, now let's add getting scared to everything else!" Frank is still a good bit in front of Ray. Before Ray could say anything in response, a noise emanated from just left of the mansion coming from the woods.

Frank stops in his tracks as a sinking feeling hits his stomach. Ray speaks first, "You did hear that, right?" Frank, frozen in his tracks now, and in a low slow voice says, "Yeah, I did."

Lights that are reminiscent of streetlights, flash randomly, sending sparks of colored light breaking through leaves, branches and who knows what. The lights are followed by a sound coming from just beyond the denser trees. The sound of movement is similar to the first sound, except now, it is a little closer, a little clearer and most importantly – it sounds like footsteps coming toward Frank.

Frank has had enough, "I lost interest. Let's go!" Frank sprints toward the boat. Ray is somewhat amused as he watches Frank running to the boat!

Ray then turns to run after him laughing at how comical he looks running away but also scared himself!

Frank completely out of breath, "Let's get out of here, I've had enough of fishing, the lake, the boat, let's just get out of here!"

Ray, laughs, "You're schizophrenic! First, you're scared, then you're curious and now, you're scared again?"

Frank is not amused, "Not really wanting to get shot for being where we're not supposed to be. Let's get outta here okay!"

Ray replied, "Okay, ya big baby." Both now back in the boat, Ray cranks up the motor and quickly backs the boat out and heads it back the way of the protruding rocks and roots and then home. Ray faces forward, shining a light on the murky lake water. Frank doesn't want to look back, because he might see something that confirms and validates his fears.

However... He steals a glance back toward the island and sees... a silhouette. The boat rounds the bend and Frank's eyes are strictly facing forward.

When they do finally get back and are loading up, they see that the dock manager, Greg, a long-time friendly acquaintance, is wrapping up for the day. Frank walks up to Greg, separated by the counter. "Hey, Greg." Greg's head pops up, "Hey, Frank. You and Ray have any success? Exceed the limit?" Frank brushes this off, "Yeah, right. Uh, listen, Ray and I actually overshot that one spot you recommended and...well, we ended up at this island with a giant house." Ray walks up, "You're asking him about earlier?"

Greg immediately becomes less interested in wrapping up for the night and the blood drains a little bit from his face. "That is the Cypress Estate; very private. I don't recommend going back." Moving more quickly than before, he puts a few finishing touches on closing, "If you don't mind, gotta go." Ray apologetically backs away, "Of course. Come on Frank." Greg slings an old backpack over his shoulder and motions them out the door, "You guys have good night."

Standing outside the dock shop, Frank and Ray watch Greg walk quickly to his car and drive away. "Greg seem a little strange to you?" Frank asks, "Dude, we're not doin' this anymore tonight. We gettin' wings or you gonna call up the newspapers with a scoop on this mysterious island?" They have a quick staring contest, then Frank breaks, "Wings sounds good." The two buddies walk toward the car they came in and more importantly, back to the comfort and safety of the same old same old.

While the two buddies get in the pickup truck, back across the black water, past the protruding rocks and roots, past the dock, the rusty government sign, grey walkway stones, past the ornate, castle-like front door, past priceless works of art and old leather and dark wooded furniture, down the carpeted wooden stairs, into the lower parts of the mansion, in the dark and not doing very well, lies 25 year old, Lorna Ritten. She is a dark-haired beauty, athletic, confident, dangerously smart and currently trapped under a bookcase with no apparent way to get out.

As the dust and books that have fallen settle into their places, Lorna comes to a little groggy, involuntarily groaning from pain.

...

"Uhh...that hurts. Nicely done, Lorna. What did you do?" As she slowly regains consciousness, she realizes that she is pinned under the bookcase she was trying to climb, reaching for what she needed. Now, with several of the books it held, she has both of her legs pinned under the huge structure and is basically trapped knowing the time is running out.

She tries to lift it slightly to try and slide out, "Come on!" She can't move it at all. "Way to go Lorna." After a couple of attempts at trying to wiggle out from underneath and exhausting herself, she takes a second to just relax and thinks to herself, "How did I ever get to this?" Then she starts to think back to the events that brought her here to this place and point in time.

Five weeks earlier...

"Just five more minutes." A few more seconds pass and again she says, "Come on, just five."

2

Chapter Two

It's a beautiful sunny morning in a very nice development with newer homes just outside the downtown area in Sun City, Arizona. It's the kind of neighborhood that young, professional married couples buy and live in for at least the first few years of their marriage and maybe the first kid.

Inside one of these nicely coiffed homes is the beautiful woman from earlier...

Lorna, is in her smartly appointed study, taking her usual morning run on the treadmill and watching the morning business news. She loves this morning ritual – gathering her thoughts and planning the day while catching up on the market and politics. She made a decision two years ago, that she will learn about the stock market and how she can effectively use it to grow the profits she's bringing in from her real estate efforts. That's what rich people do and that's what she's going to do.

The beautiful long brunette hair was a gift, but her impressive athletic build is something she made happen. Lorna enjoys staying in great shape and as a person who is naturally driven and very focused, she handles both her career and personal fitness, with the same energy. She started her real estate investment business roughly five years ago, Ritten Investments Inc., and is investing in real estate mostly, but is always open to creating a new stream of income as long as it makes sense.

She was already gaining a reputation in the greater Phoenix area as competitive, tenacious, and according to some who have ended up on the short end of some deals, heartless. Her brown eyes are mesmerizing but fierce, revealing her tenacity and a strong level of confidence. She has a focus that is far beyond that of her few close friends, but she doesn't mind that they don't share her intensity; she is very happy they are in her life. She does not take the time to think about it that much, but if she took a moment to ponder, it's undeniable that they maintain balance by keeping her grounded in a "normal life," whatever that may entail.

After watching a TV talking head wax poetic about rumors of the Fed raising the rate by a half point and how that might impact house sales – something that might actually affect Lorna's business – she heads in for a quick shower. After throwing on an outfit she laid out the prior evening, she grabs herself a yogurt and some juice for a light breakfast.

Lorna takes a seat at her bar in the kitchen and goes over the paperwork on one of her real estate deals she is working on. Satisfied that everything is as in place as can be expected, she grabs her keys and is about to head over to her attorney's office to close on the deal. As she finishes up and is walking toward her front door, her phone rings. Looking at the caller ID, it is Steve, her attorney. His full name is Steven Reign, he's 37 and has been her attorney for the last three years for personal and business matters. Lorna trusts him, but they don't always see eye to eye on how business deals are to be handled. Still, they manage to make it work. He is not as aggressive as she is, which sometimes leads to a "good cop, bad cop" negotiating tactic, but he is a very good attorney.

Answering the call she says, "Hey Steve, I'm on my way."

Steve replies, "Lorna, I think you're going to really like this. I have the individuals who wanted the 5th block downtown property with the escrow deposit. Their attorney just called, and they will be coming over as soon as they can today for the paperwork!" Steve waits for her to be thrilled with this news.

Lorna closes her eyes and tilts her head back a little, taking a breath. After a few awkward silent seconds, "Steve, I told you that I had an offer on that property three days ago. I also told you since they had not come up with the deposit on time that the grace period had expired. You also know the whole reason for me meeting you this morning was to get all the paperwork done for the other buyer to go to closing!"

Steve replies, "I know Lorna, but the last time we talked about this, you didn't have a written contract on the new offer. These people are serious and have been working very hard to meet your deadline, they just needed a little more time. You also know why they want this property. I mean with it being for a children's home..."

"Steve!" She sternly stops him; this hits a nerve. "In case I wasn't clear before, I don't want to talk about this anymore."

Lorna believes that from a wholistic, overall viewpoint, she is a good person, some might say very good, and she does not like being made to feel guilty about something she believes is just business. Her best way to get around this is to control the conversation and not have to deal with these uncomfortable emotions. However, the tone of her voice made it very clear that her frustration is building.

Steve starts to speak again, hoping there is a way to help Lorna see his perspective, but she cuts him off, "Steven, Steven!" He stops and there is a moment's pause, and she continues, "Stop! I am not taking that offer at this point and I don't have time to talk about it. I have given you my decision on what I want to do and that is it!" The doorbell rings and Lorna ends the conversation, "Gotta go. I'll be there soon, and I do NOT want to talk about this anymore."

Lorna ends the call with extra pressure on the button, just to make sure that at least her phone understood how over she was with that conversation. After a quick, cleansing breath, she continues down the hall to answer the door. Still bothered by her conversation with Steve, she opens the door to see a non-descript uniformed delivery man holding a package, "Good morning. Lorna Ritten?"

Lorna replied, "Yes."

The delivery man delivers a line he's delivered a thousand times before, "This is for you. If you could please just sign right here on the pad..."

Lorna mumbles, “Sure.” signing and taking the large envelope letter from him and without looking up from the package, she mumbles, “Thank you” and starts to close the door. The delivery man exits and just before the door closes, a female voice reaches out, “Hey, don’t shut the--” The door shuts. Lorna looks up from the package, realizing, someone just called out to her and reopens the door with a smirking Chelsea, standing in the doorway greeting Lorna with a familiarity that comes from a solid friendship, “Morning to you too.”.

Chelsea, African American, is very pretty, athletic, and in her mid-20’s. She is one of Lorna’s few close friends and has been so since high school. She also moved into this young professional neighborhood briefly after Lorna bought her house, once her real estate buddy told her it was a great place to live. She only lives a few blocks down the street, so knocking on her door is a regular and expected occurrence.

Chelsea glances back at the delivery man, “Have a nice day!” The delivery man gives a half-hearted wave and continues on his delivery route. Lorna lightly jabs at Chelsea, “A friend of yours?” Chelsea lightly jabs back as she walks into Lorna’s house, “Ha. Ha. Someone around here needs to be nice to the delivery guys or you’ll make their list.”

Lorna looks up from the package, “I’m sorry, list? What list?”

Chelsea makes herself a cup of coffee and begins teaching Lorna about *The List*, “The List, Lorna. Every profession has them. Restaurants have the list for rude customers and then they secretly mess with the food. The DMV has it for people who complain about waiting for too long. And yes, Lorna, delivery guys have it for “Karens” who aren’t nice.”

Lorna grabs her cup of coffee, “Seriously, Chelse?” Chelsea plops on the living room couch, where it appears they are settling at least for the moment, “Look, girl, I’m just tryin’ to help you. If you don’t want your packages to be mysteriously delayed, ‘Oh sorry ma’am, it was right here in the back of the truck the whole time. Sorry for making you wait’, then you need to be nice, smile and wave at them, or you will make their list.”

Lorna stands by the door, "I really appreciate the lesson about lists, but are you just here to say hi or something more substantial?" Chelse gives her a sassy look. "Seriously, Chelse, I'm on my way out. What are you doing here?"

Chelsea replies, "Well, great to see you too!"

Lorna says, "I'm sorry I didn't mean it like that, I just had this aggravating call and was about to go out the door. Sorry, I just meant" smiling a bit too much, "What are you doing here? I thought you were going shopping with Brianna?" Lorna walks into her study.

Chelsea follows her into the study and replies, "That's too early, some of us have to work. We're gettin' together a little later today. I was on my way to work, saw your car still in the driveway and thought I'd stop by for coffee, contemplation and conversation. You know mornings are for coffee and contemplation, right?"

Lorna walks over to her desk, finds a large, silver letter opener that was a graduation gift from her adopted parents and starts to cut open the large letter envelope package and says, "I just have a minute, I'm actually running late for a meeting."

Chelsea doesn't seem particularly concerned about her being in a rush. She plops down in the large, well-worn leather chair in the study, the only piece of furniture that appears to have been used frequently. She lifts her feet onto the coffee table and settles in, making herself comfortable, "So how is the Lorna empire doing today?"

Lorna not entirely enjoying Chelsea's snark this morning, looks up from the contents of the package for a moment, "Sweet of you to ask, and the empire is doing just fine, thank you very much. Careful or you'll make the empire's *list*." Lorna continues and removes a thick set of documents from the delivered package.

Chelsea responds with, "Sorry, don't want to make the list. It's just... me and the girls have been talkin' and... you really need to enjoy life a little more. Maybe be a little less business focused all the time."

Lorna, reads over the first page of the paperwork, blocking Chelsea out to a degree. She does not look up as she is intently looking over the legal paperwork from the delivered package. Finally, she catches up to the conversation and slowly says, "So, that's what you and the girls are saying, hmmm? You know I like to build, keep things under control, and just be able to enjoy life in my own way." Lorna tries to be careful on how to position her words to not sound too self-centered.

Chelsea, feeling rather neglected, says, "Well, I'm glad we had this conversation. I can tell how you are now going to be a little less focused on business and more on your friendships. I'm delighted to witness your ability to pause and pay attention to other things, such as when someone is speaking to you." She says a little louder, as she sees that Lorna is not listening at all she then adds, "I'm also glad to see that at least you're not spoiled, selfish, non-caring...." Waiting for a reply and then picking up a magazine off the table beside her, as if in a waiting room.

Lorna, with a slight smile coming over her face, "This is unbelievable! Unless I just don't understand this legal real estate paperwork, which would just be super weird, it looks like I just inherited a mansion or an estate!" Looking up at Chelsea from the papers and now with a huge smile. "I'm gonna' own a mansion!"

Chelsea looking up from her magazine calmly says, "You're kidding." and she waits for something to follow from Lorna, but she still is smiling and just gestures with a turn of her head. Then Chelsea continues with a deadpan delivery, "Unbelievable, wow, stupendous, never been done before." After a brief pause, she puts down the magazine and walks over to Lorna puts her face in between the paperwork and Lorna's eyes, and says, "Hi, remember me? I'm in the room with you. What are you talking about, and who is that from?"

Lorna flips to the front of the pile of papers to read the sender information again and pointing to the main lines of interest, she says, "It's from the Law Office of Brown and Associates. Pretty sure I've seen that office before in a building downtown. I remember the office had a private, very elite look to it." She then points to the information that clearly states a few of the facts and then says again, "Wow, I mean, how about that!"

Chelsea just takes a step back and says, "Hold up! Who just gave you an estate and where is this magical mansion?"

Lorna walks around her desk and sits for a second, looking through more of the information intensely, she replies, "Apparently, it's on the outskirts of the city here in Phoenix, a little further out. They list some directions here, but I'm not sure exactly where it is. It's like longitude and latitude."

Chelsea asks again, only a little more assertive with her question, "Okay, but from whom? Last I checked, people don't normally just give out estates. Also, longitude and latitude?! Yeah, that doesn't sound suspicious."

Lorna retorts, "Well, according to what I've read so far, it seems that they prefer to remain anonymous."

Chelsea replies, "Uh huh. No, not suspicious at all. No one just gives away something this big."

Lorna pours over the paperwork with her trademark intensity, and then looks up at Chelsea, "Well..., they did! Chelsea grabs the paperwork and says, "Let me see that." Lorna responds, "Take a look."

Chelsea replying, "Well, it does look legit. Man, some people get all the breaks!"

Lorna grabs back the paperwork and without looking up, says, "It says that they were instructed to send me these papers if certain events took place. Don't know what that means. There's not really a lot on that in here from what I can see. Looks like I'm supposed to get these signed and notarized, then drop them off at that law office and that's about it from what I can gather. There will be some minor paperwork I would think, but essentially, it's mine"

Chelsea replied, "That's actually crazy!"

Lorna, now getting more excited about her new estate says to Chelsea, "Tell ya' what. I'll get these done and down there today after I stop by my attorney's and then... you said I need to spend more time with friends? Then, we can go check it out tomorrow." Lorna enters the coordinates into her GPS and continues, "It's not that far out of town from what I can tell. You could also maybe give Briana a call and see if she wants to go with us."

Chelsea replies, "Ok... never been to an "estate" before. Sounds cool, I guess." She turns to start to walk out and says again, "Unbelievable." They both head out the door.

Lorna quickly grabs her purse and rushes out to her car. "Be here in the morning so we can start early. I'm running late for a meeting."

Chelsea responded with a slight roll of her eyes, "Yes, boss," as they were leaving. Lorna, now in a great mood, just smiles back and says, "Gonna ignore that, cuz, I love you Chelse" and gets in her car. Chelsea, knowing Lorna can't hear her now, mutters, "Um hm."

Later that morning, Lorna arrives at Steve's (her attorney) office. Over the past few years, Steve has gradually come to terms with her assertive nature and has learned that she isn't afraid to express her differing viewpoints when she has them. They've had a few challenging conversations in the past, but they've always managed to overcome them and move forward.

Steve has very strict principles that come from his Christian upbringing and believes in keeping his word to a fault. He was raised and greatly influenced by his grandmother, and she would bean him if he didn't act with integrity.

As they sit in his office at a large meeting table, they are still slightly arguing about the real estate deal that they were addressing earlier. His office is large and has a contemporary design. One of the features is the glass walls that separate the office from the receptionist area. This is a very useful feature, but it's not particularly pleasant at the moment, with anyone who may try to read lips and body language.

Steve sees the very clients that he is tussling with Lorna about, walk into the wide waiting area at Steve's receptionist.

The clients are two modestly dressed women in their 50's, they are clearly sisters, and one man in his 50's who is obviously married to one of the sisters. They are trying to get the property to provide a permanent residence for homeless children and have been trying to get something done for a while. The reason they have been trying to obtain this place is because it is set at a reasonable price and really meets all the practical needs for the orphanage between usable kitchen, location, and what they can afford.

Steve, slightly bothered by Lorna's position says, "Lorna, I understand the other offer is a good deal for you, but those people on the other side of this glass, the folks with the orphanage, were assured that if they get the down payment, they could have the property."

Lorna, looks out the window, watching the clients as she paces around, unsettled by all of this. Finally, she says, "Yes, but as you are well aware, they did not get it until the day after this newer and more lucrative offer came in. Now, I'm acting in my own interest and sticking to the rules of the agreement, which happens to be to my advantage. The facts are that they were late, and I have every legal right to go with this offer." She turns and looks directly at Steve, making eye contact that reflects her intensity and current emotional state of mind. She continues, "I have no connection to them, and I'm not contractually obligated to honor this handshake deal."

Steve, feeling the desperation and need with the three orphanage representatives, replies, "Do you really want to tell them that they will have to start all over and lose the time and money they spent to get this far? So close to being able to help those kids?"

As he concludes his questions, he gazes at Lorna in almost disbelief that she could be so withdrawn from wanting to help these people. Especially considering the potential use of the property to benefit children.

Lorna pauses for just a moment sits back down across the table and then replies to Steve's question with, "No, not at all."

Steve with a quick change to his expression just before she continues and says to him more firmly and speaking a little faster, "That's your job to tell them, not mine. This is business and it's that simple. I am done with this conversation. I have a new estate to go check out tomorrow, so handle this. I left a copy of the paperwork on the estate I mentioned, with your receptionist." Lorna gets up and pushes her chair back under table, then stops and looks directly at Steven. She says very plainly, "Are we clear on what I want done?"

Steve still sitting and looking up at her across the table is completely deflated, but maintains a professional demeanor and says, "Yes..., I understand."

As Lorna gets her briefcase and walks out the door. She must pass by the clients waiting in the lobby area. She walks quickly, hoping to put this behind her, but as she passes them, the gentlemen stands up and says to her, "Thank you so much for being patient with us. Helping us get to this point. We are thrilled to finally be able to move forward and help these children."

As kind and appreciative as the gentleman is acting toward her, Lorna does not want to be in this situation. She tries her best to put on a poker face and not seem uncomfortable, but she is not doing very well. The fact, she has already sold the property to someone else, and this man is so relieved and appreciative, is making her miserable. She simply smiles and says, "Steve is available, now." Lorna turns and points back at the door, directing them to go in and see him.

Then she says, "He will go over the details with you."

The gentleman responds with, "Thanks again!"

The two women stand and with gratitude say, "Yes, we can't thank you, enough!" Smiling at her, they then turn and go into Steve's office.

Lorna, knowing they are not getting the property, as they joyfully walk into the glass walled meeting room to hear the bad news from Steve. She looks back at Steve who holds the door open for the three clients to come into his office.

As they stand halfway between Steve and Lorna, they turn and smile at Lorna before proceeding past Steve and entering his office. Steve and Lorna maintain eye contact for a moment. She made a decision in her best interest, and now it's his responsibility to clean up the aftermath.

Lorna starts to walk down the hall, but as she turns the corner, she stops and fights with herself as to whether or not she'll keep walking or actually take a peek. She loses that internal fight and stops. She turns back slightly to steal a look. She sees them take their seats. She pauses for a moment as she sees Steve sit down at the table across from them.

She can see him saying a few words and before very many are spoken, the trio's posture seems to melt. The married sister bursts into tears.

Lorna looks down at the floor and for just a second thinks about what if... and then quickly the thought of "It's nothing personal, it's just business" slaps her mind. She regains her resolve and with a little more starch in her resolution, she continues down the hall and out the building.

Lorna gets into her car with a new resolve and does her best to put the misfortune of some, behind her. The focus is now on her newfound asset – this mysterious estate. She turns on her car and rifles quickly through the paperwork, just to make sure that it's all there and even to make sure that she didn't dream up all of this. Time to get those documents signed and submitted.

3

Chapter Three

As she pulls out of the parking lot, she is so completely absorbed in all things "Mystery Estate" that she is unaware of the sedan that pulled out to follow her at an unnoticed distance.

Enroute to this elite law office, Lorna considers all the possibilities this new property might offer her. She has no clue what's on the property, what it's zoned for or what its resale value is, but it must offer some value. That is... unless it's underwater with a ton of liens gumming up the title. Wait a minute! Maybe Chelsea was on to something earlier...? Perhaps she's being too optimistic, too naïve. Why would someone just give her a property?

OK, she's got some questions to ask of this elite law firm. But she still thinks it must be above board with how the property is briefly described in the paperwork; she was pretty sure there was mention of a residential structure. From the earlier GPS search, she knows a little about the area from past listings near this location.

Lorna rolls up to the downtown address and pulls up to the valet area, where a valet approaches her. She greets the valet, "Hi, I'm, Lorna Ritten. I've got an appointment with Brown--" the valet interrupts, "Oh yes, Miss Ritten, they called down and told me to expect you. Your valet is completely validated including gratuity." He leans in with a friendly tone, "It means you don't need to tip." He straightens back up, "Here's your ticket and take as long as you need." The valet politely waits for Lorna to exit her vehicle. She responds, "Well. OK, then. Thanks, I guess." Lorna's immediate thought was, *This is either gonna be really good or really bad. Time to go in and find out which one of those this is.*

As Lorna ascends to the pinnacle of the city's skyline, entering what is likely the most ostentatious and expensive skyscraper downtown, the sedan from earlier drives by with its dark-tented windows, looking mysterious.

Lorna passes by a uniformed security guard and decides not to bother him with silly questions like, where's this elite law firm? She can read. She'll just figure it out, which is exactly what she does. Which floor is the home to the Law Offices of Brown and Associates...? Ah, the top floor, naturally.

The elevator was polished and nice with marble flooring and dark wood paneling. Why does this feel like a set up? She could just kill Chelsea for making her paranoid. Or, maybe hug her neck...? Let's see how this goes.

The elevator doors slid open, encouraging Lorna to emerge from the elevator and enter this dark, sophisticated office with... no one at the front desk. Now, her suspicion is going into overdrive, *Why would the valet say they're waiting for me and not have, well, anyone waiting for me...?*

The office is sophisticated but simple; there wasn't an office manager with a big budget who went crazy with the decorations to show off for clients. It has a very secure feeling to it, almost as if you walked into a bank. As she stands alone in the lobby, she is not sure what to do, there is no call button and so she decides to just wait for a few minutes to see if someone does come out. She mumbles to herself, "Yep, nothing suspicious about this." A few moments go by, and an executive looking lady comes around the corner and says, "Can I help you?"

Lorna then replies, "Yes, my name is Lorna Ritten, and I received this yesterday..."

Before she completed her sentence the lady takes a few steps to a side credenza, and she cuts Lorna off saying very directly, "Yes, Miss Ritten I have everything here for you ready to complete the transaction.

Lorna is taken back slightly at how everyone down to the valet seems to be well aware of her and that she should indeed be there right now. Yeah, she might have some questions, but she'd like to see this play out a little bit more; let them play their hand and show what they are about first. The lady then says, "Do you have everything that was requested in the documentation for finalizing this transaction?"

Lorna replies, "Yes, here it is." she hands the paperwork to the lady, and she responds in her professional manner, "Thank you, please have a seat? This will only take a few moments."

Lorna says, "Sure." Then turns to find a comfortable seat – they all look comfortable. The lady walks back through a door behind her, and the thick door shuts in such a way that it would make you think it was a refurbed vault door.

Lorna selects the dark leather chair in the middle and pulls out her phone to check emails; perhaps there's an update from Steve on how the orphanage people reacted, what they might have said. Or maybe she'll find an email from him with his tendered resignation because they are too incompatible to do business together. Let's hope not... Nah, he wouldn't do that, not over email, anyway.

Lorna's thoughts drift back toward this mystery estate. She cannot help but wonder what is going on and who in the world may have left her something, especially an "estate" and maybe most importantly, WHY? Who would do such a thing? As an orphan, you always wonder who might be out there in the world that could surprise you with who they are, what they are like, and what, if anything, do they have to do with you...?

As Lorna goes down this *What If* cerebral rabbit hole, the door opens and the lady walks back behind her desk and says, "Thanks so much for your patience. Here are your documents, verification was successful and everything is now official. There is nothing more you need to do regarding paperwork. Here is a folder with your signed papers and a few more land and deed documents that have been included, marking that this is official and recognized by the state of Arizona."

Lorna is taken back by the strangeness of this entire process, "Thank you very much. I was also wondering if you could give me..." As Lorna is about to try and get some answers, the phone at the receptionist's desk buzzes, and the executive lady promptly picks it up, listens attentively, and responds with, "I will be right there."

Then she looks at Lorna, controlling the moment, saying, "Thank you for coming in promptly. All the information you need to visit and perform any transactions are in that folder and are also registered with the state. And, since I regrettably cannot stay and answer questions, you should know that there are no liens or debts associated with this property. The taxes are all current and have been pre-paid for the next year." The executive lady walks around the desk to the door and opens it for Lorna to exit.

Lorna is really caught off guard with the last several moments and is almost in a daze as to what she should do, especially with her usually being the one controlling the moment; she had questions. Lorna simply turns and walks to the door and as she is walking out says, "Thank you. Miss...?" The lady looks at Lorna and with very little emotion says, "You are welcome, Miss Ritten." Then after Lorna is out, she shuts the door, and Lorna hears the thick door lock behind her.

Lorna reaches the outside valet area and the valet from earlier already has her car waiting for her. Lorna reflexively pulls some cash out of her small purse and tries to tip the valet, but he holds up his hand and reminds her, "Miss Ritten, that's kind of you, but as I mentioned earlier, they've already compensated me. Please drive home safely." "OK, thanks" is all Lorna could get out.

Lorna slips into her car in somewhat of a daze still unsure of how to decipher the way everything just went down. However, she is holding a fat folder from this high-end law firm, which is supposed to hold a lot of answers. She throws it onto the passenger seat, as if to prove that this wasn't some bizarre dream. There's a thick legal folder sitting on the passenger seat, so this must have happened, right?

As she goes back to the idea of what she has just acquired she decides that ultimately it doesn't matter. She somehow inherited this estate. The taxes are current and even pre-paid for the next year, giving her ample time to decide whether to sell it. The person who orchestrated all of this is irrelevant, at least for now. It's official: she's the owner of this enigmatic property, and that's all there is to it.

She starts up her car and drives away. Normally, she would work a little later but after today's events, after this episode with this elite attorney's office, she is ridiculously preoccupied and wouldn't be able to focus on work anyway. Time to head home and absorb this new venture while wearing sweatpants and chilling at her desk.

With all that has transpired and being more distracted than usual, Lorna completely fails to realize the sedan that has followed her most of the day, is still following unnoticed, a block behind her.

Meanwhile, back in Law Offices of Brown and Associates, Silhouetted figures sit in a highly secure back meeting room, monitoring surveillance footage of Lorna driving home and having a conversation about her. As three of them carry on an active conversation, the younger gentleman says to the executive lady and older gentleman, "I guess now we wait and see."

The impact of these words, obvious though they might be, stops all conversations for a moment. Then, the older gentleman stands up and walks over to an electronic map on the wall, staring and studying it, he says, "Yes, I suppose we do. Much to be realized very soon." He turns around, still silhouetted in the dimly lit room, looking at the young man and the executive lady with a heavy concern.

Later that evening, Lorna returns home, wearing comfortable sweats and a university T-shirt. She sits at her desk, diligently studying the documents in a large folder, determined to extract as much information as possible. As she reads and takes everything in, she imagines the estate and what it may be like. It is described as an enormous residential house. Some might go so far as to think of it as a mansion.

She can't help but imagine the people who once called that place home and ponder why it was entrusted to her. Unfamiliar with the region, her mind races with curiosity about its appearance and character. The state is a tapestry of contrasts, each area boasting its own unique identity, making her wonder about the vibrant differences she might discover. You can find diverse landscapes in Arizona, ranging from the arid and Martian-like terrain of certain areas to lush regions with vibrant flowers and abundant vegetation. The mountains offer snowfall at certain times of the year, and the Grand Canyon is a natural wonder that cannot be missed.

She can only imagine what these answers might be, but her main thoughts are on just the simple fact that however she came to own this property, this asset, it is hers, now. Deeply absorbed in her intricate world of information, documents, and designs, she absentmindedly reaches for her cup of tea, savoring the warmth as a brief reprieve. Suddenly, with a careless flick of her wrist, the cup tips over, sending a cascade of tea across her desk. "Brilliant," she mutters with a sarcastic chuckle, shaking her head at her own folly. Papers in hand, she dashes to the kitchen, her feet barely touching the floor, in search of paper towels to rescue her beloved workspace from the aromatic flood.

As she retraces her steps towards her study, her gaze is drawn to the grand expanse of the front window. Its blinds, left open in a moment of absent-mindedness spurred by the day's tumultuous events, offer an unrestrained view of the street. There, across the way, sits an enigmatic sedan that has been shadowing her movements.

Although she dismisses it as a mere coincidence, a flicker of unease stirs within her, for she can't quite remember ever seeing it parked there before. It lingers in her mind, a fleeting whisper of mystery in the quiet evening air. “OK, crazy, don’t start getting paranoid on me.” She dismisses this and returns to her desk and the documents to her mystery estate that now live rent-free in her mind.

Meanwhile, across the street, the man in the sedan receives a call. He answers plainly, "Still here. Nothing significant to report yet, but I'll alert you if anything noteworthy unfolds... Understood." With a quiet click, he ends the call and resumes his vigil over Lorna's house. Aware of the need to stay undercover, he starts planning his next move to remain hidden in plain sight.

Lorna cleans up the mess, but she does walk back to the window slowly and stands a few feet short from it, thinking, *Remember, just because you're paranoid, doesn't mean they're not really out to get you.* She chuckles at her attempt at being witty with her internal dialogue, but she still peers out for just a few seconds. The car turns on its lights and at the same moment her phone rings, which causes her to jump!

As the adrenaline subsides, she feels her energy waning, drained by the sudden startle. She turns toward her desk to grab the phone, noticing it's Steven on the line. Still irked by the events earlier in the day and now by his impeccable timing, she answers with a tinge of irritation. As she half-listens to his voice, her gaze drifts back to the window, only to find the mysterious car has vanished. Distracted by this, she barely registers Steven's words and replies absentmindedly, "I'm sorry, could you say that again? I was distracted."

Steven sighs and says, "I just wanted to call and ask one more time could you reconsider the situation with that property. Those people in the office just...,"

She interrupted him sharply, "Stop right there!" Her words were clipped and firm. Pausing, she shook her head with disbelief, as if chastising a child, "I've already made it clear. Don't make me repeat myself. My decision is final. Now, if there's nothing else, I need to go." A tense silence lingered in the airwaves, thick and suffocating. After a moment, she pressed on, "Is there anything else?"

Steven, feeling utterly defeated, like a dog who had been kicked one too many times, muttered, "No. Nothing else."

"Great, I'll talk to you tomorrow sometime. Goodnight." Lorna hung up her phone, her voice still echoing in her mind. She stood there, frozen in the moment, trying to piece together the whirlwind of the past few minutes. Had she been too harsh with Steven? Or perhaps she hadn't pushed hard enough. The uncertainty gnawed at her. But one thing was certain: she wanted to keep working with him. Yet, her patience had its limits, and he needed to align more closely with her vision.

With a decisive nod, she sank back into her chair and stared at the papers scattered across her desk. The energy had drained from her, leaving her with no choice but to call it a night. Tomorrow would be another demanding day, and she needed to be ready for it.

...

Lorna was jolted back to reality by a sharp pain in her leg. Reality was grim – she was pinned under a hefty bookcase, a consequence she mused, of having been so harsh on Steve. Despite the dire circumstances, she fought to maintain a positive outlook. Yet, the pain in her leg was just a prelude to the larger threat that loomed over her. The injury seemed trivial in the grand scheme of her predicament.

In her introspection, Lorna realized that her recent experiences had inflicted more than just physical pain. A deeper, more emotional wound had been carved into her heart, a sensation unfamiliar and unwelcome.

Her contemplation was abruptly cut short by the ominous sound of footsteps above. The silence that followed was even more unnerving than the footsteps themselves. She froze, listening intently, but no further noise came. Reality settled in, a sobering clarity – she might not escape this ordeal!

Caught in her helplessness, Lorna's mind drifted back to the sequence of events that had led her here. She clung to a serene memory, a morning following a restless night. She had gone for a brisk run, savoring the tranquility, before indulging in a hot shower in anticipation of her friends' arrival. The memory was a brief respite from her current, stark reality.

...

4

Chapter Four

It was an unusually crisp, Arizona morning and Lorna was up and at 'em, getting her morning going. Meanwhile, Chelsea parked in Briana's driveway, and Briana eagerly came out of her house to get into her friend's car, displaying even more enthusiasm than usual.

Briana is meticulous in her approach to fashion, ensuring every detail of her attire, hair, and makeup aligns with her signature style. Each ensemble she adorns not only meets but elevates the mark of elegance and sophistication. Ever since she reached her teenage years, she's frequently been asked, "Are you a model?" or "Have you done any modeling?" This line of inquiry follows her consistently, a testament to her captivating presence. Interestingly, her friends Lorna and Chelsea share this experience, creating a dynamic trio that commands attention. When they grace a public space with their presence, they become the focal point of admiration, causing heads to turn and eyes to widen in appreciation from those fortunate enough to witness their chic entrance.

Despite all of this, Briana's most endearing quality is being a down to earth girl. She is very witty and has been friends with both Chelsea and Lorna since they were in elementary school. She slides into Chelsea's car with an almost over the top cheerfulness, saying, "Good morning, how are you doing this fine day, my most beautiful friend?!"

Chelsea replies, "Uh, good. Boy, are you in a good mood!"

Briana says, "I'm always in a good mood. What're you talkin' about?"

Chelsea, "I have to say you usually are. Just tired, and your perky nature is harshing on my mellow. I need coffee!"

Briana replies, "You need to get some sleep and stop staying up late with all your social media."

Chelsea, "Yeah, yeah, I know already. More sleep. Less social media."

Briana, looking at her and nodding her head in total agreement. Then Briana says, "Soooo, what are we doing exactly? Lorna had some new real estate deals, blah, blah, blah. What's the big deal here?"

Chelsea replies, "Well she inherited this one, a mansion, and are you ready for this? No idea from whom!"

Briana looks at Chelsea with her mouth wide open until she says, "What!? She inherited this huge place, and doesn't know who just gifted her this thing? Uh, that's suss."

Chelsea says, "I know! I know! Listen, don't make this a big deal. Just be cool about it."

Briana says, "You know she's always wondered about her real parents. Maybe she sees this as a path to find answers for some of those questions. This should be a unique day, to say the least."

Chelsea just nods and then quickly says. "Yes, but do not bring it up. I am telling you it's just not a good idea. If she wants to talk about any of that or really anything, let her bring it up, OK?"

Brianna simply replies, "I understand."

Then Chelsea kind of gives her an "I mean it" look.

Brianna says, "I do. What's that look for? I get it."

Chelsea just says, "Okay." Then smiles but still obviously serious about what she said. Chelsea's car weaves through Lorna's neighborhood and finally...

...they pull up to Lorna's house. Lorna is just walking out to her car. Chelsea parks and they quickly get out and go over to Lorna as she is putting her bag and briefcase in her back seat.

Lorna says, "Hi guys." As she shuts her car door.

Briana says, "Hey good morning!"

Chelsea says, "Are you excited?"

Then Briana awkwardly mutters, “Yeah, so... do you think this may be a blood relative or someone who may know stuff about your past, who you are...?”

Chelsea shoots a look of *You have got to be kidding me!* and barks, “Bree!”

Lorna briefly cuts her eyes at Chelsea and Brianna, but tries to project that she’s not really bothered by the comment, “First of all, I know exactly who I am. Ummkay?” she asserted, her eyes locking with theirs, daring them to challenge her self-awareness. "Secondly, it’s no big deal," she continued, brushing off any hint of drama with a wave of her hand. "I’ve never wanted to dwell on this, and I’m certainly not going to start now." Her voice, firm yet playful, cut through the charged air like a blade.

But beneath the steely exterior, there was a flicker of excitement. "I am, however, thrilled about this estate," she confessed, her voice softening as a smile crept onto her lips. "So... let’s go!"

The three women exchanged glances, a silent agreement passing between them. They had been friends too long to let an awkward moment linger. They piled into Lorna’s car, the awkwardness dissipating like morning mist as the engine roared to life. The road ahead was open and promising, just like their bond.

As Chelsea and Briana get into the passenger seats, Chelsea gives Briana a look that was a combination of *Thanks a lot!* and *What was that??*. She whispers to Brianna, “Be a little more careful, please...”

Brianna chimes in, “Alright, positive vibes from here on out. Right girls?” Chelsea and Lorna tepidly agree and with that, they back out of the driveway and away they go on their journey.

It’s a pleasant day and the drive seems effortless as the trio of friends quickly get past their awkward moment and enjoy each other’s company. They talk about politics, food, the latest fashion trends, etc.

Finally, the conversation veers back to the focus of this little trip.

Briana chimes in, "So, Lorna." Lorna, in a mocking, but friendly way echoes back, "So, Brianna." Brianna ignores this and continues, "What's the deal with this place we're going?"

Lorna strips away the snark and answers honestly, "I really don't know that much about it or about him. Yeah, I did figure out it was a man who gave this to me. I went through some of the information last night and it was really kind of interesting. Just fragments of information. This may sound weird, but I even got the feeling that it was a little sad and this man, whoever he is, was a little, older and maybe even lonely. With the information being so singular and with what few notes there were, they seemed like there was pain. He did seem extremely driven by all the ambition that seems to be there. I mean there was always building and adding on to the estate. Also, innovative and seemed very smart, but empty. I dunno, my thoughts are all over the place on this."

The car was cloaked in an uneasy silence, the kind that stretched and shifted like a shadow on a long summer evening. Chelsea and Briana exchanged a glance, a silent communication that passed between them as Lorna recounted her thoughts on the man who left her the estate. Her words hung in the air, heavy with unspoken meaning, and the look on their faces didn't escape Lorna's notice.

She shifted in her seat, eyeing them with suspicion. "What? What's with the look?" she demanded, her voice slicing through the tension.

Briana forced a smile, shaking her head in an attempt to deflect. "Oh, nothing," she replied, eager to steer the conversation away from the unvoiced suspicions. "Did you tell anyone else about this? I bet your parents were curious, especially your mom. What did they say?"

Lorna sighed, leaning back with a look of resignation. "I haven't told anyone else," she admitted. "I haven't really talked to my parents much lately. We're not exactly seeing eye to eye on a lot of things, especially business matters. What would I even say? There's too much uncertainty. That's why we're doing this."

Briana hesitated, her natural curiosity and concern for her friend warring with her caution. Why was Lorna so secretive? It baffled Briana, an open book herself, as she longed for Lorna to share more about the mysterious documents. But Briana knew when to push and when to wait, and this was the fine line she walked now, her questions held in check by the fear of saying too much.

Brianna pushes, but gently, "Yeah, we understand but Lorna when you talk about this person, do you kind of see a little of you maybe? I mean you're great. You're our sister, so please take this the way I mean it, but...all you do is work and try to get a little bit more. We're your closest friends on planet earth, unless you've got a double life going on in Tucson, and you hardly let anyone in."

This hit a small nerve. Half kidding and half serious, Lorna replies, "Hey, you wanna' walk back home? I've got my trusty GPS, so I really don't need you to read a map to get there. I hear the coyote population is really thriving in this area."

Briana tries to cool things down, "Easy, Tiger. We're just saying you are very driven and focused. You don't leave a lot for personal or even any fun it seems, although, this little road trip kind of counts, so there's that."

Another awkward moment with only the faint sound of the radio filling in the silence. She continues, "Lorna, we do care about you that's all."

Lorna, knowing they both do care about her says, "I... I know you do and whether or not I think now is the time to address it, I understand where you're coming from. I'm fine, and this does makes me happy for the record. So, if we could not be so dramatic and just relax and stop analyzing me, there may be a free lunch in it for you, mmkay?"

Briana responds, "I do like free lunches." At this moment, she feels relieved that her inquiries didn't escalate into a bigger issue. She's delighted to move forward, fully aware of how Lorna can be at times.

They share a chuckle laugh. But as Lorna laughs, she also has a slight concern about the conversation. She knows there is truth to what was said about her character flaws and for a person who prides herself on being in control, that is not comfortable for her at all. She has to admit to herself that there was a time she viewed things differently and this is really highlighted by the heated exchange at Steve's office. She knows deep down that she would not have been so cutthroat just a few years ago.

Brianna then says, "Okay, I'm thrilled to be here and going with you on this little epic adventure but, I'm getting hangry. So, about that lunch..."

Lorna realizes she's a little famished herself, "Actually, food doesn't sound too bad."

Maybe it's the alure of fried things with gravy, but Lorna has always had a soft spot for diners and greasy spoons. She spots one, *DJ's Diner*. That sounds good.

The trio gorge on highly caloric and tasty foods, no salads on this day. Lorna does, however, through the course of this go back in her mind to the conversation that took place and the things that do still bother her more than she will let anyone really know.

But she again pushes this out of her mind, and they wrap lunch and continue. Then as they are getting closer to the address and as Brianna is looking around and a little nervous says, "Why would anyone want to live way out here? Everything seems so spread out. It just seems old out here.

Lorna replies, "I think it is kind of cool. I mean I guess they were very private people, whoever they were. I know I like my privacy. I like this a lot! It has a peaceful feel out here.

Chelsea then says, "You mean a 'why am I here feeling?' don't ya?

Lorna, rolling her eyes and slightly kidding but not completely, replied, "Please stop! You're freaking Briana out!

Then Brianna, in all seriousness, says, "Yeah, stop before you freak Brianna out!"

As they approached their destination, Lorna reassured everyone, saying, "I think it'll be fine, just relax!"

They drive through neighborhoods and past shopping areas, eventually, finding themselves on the outskirts of town, arriving at the address where the estate is located according to the legal documents Lorna received from the law firm.

Brianna begins to answer, "I am re... Whoa!" as they reach a clearing and catch sight of the mansion positioned on the estate. It looks massive and elegant from the road. Brianna then continues, "Is that it? I mean, are you kidding me?"

Chelsea, gazing on in astonishment, “No way that’s it.”

Lorna, “Uh, according to this address... Yes, that is it. Wow! And, uh, that is...amazing!” Lorna maneuvered her car down the road, a sense of anticipation building with each passing mile. The towering gate loomed ahead, both inviting and foreboding. She brought the car to a halt, her fingers nervously tapping the steering wheel. A look of excitement rested on her face as she reached for the manila envelope resting in her glove compartment.

Within it lay the papers she had reviewed countless times, each glance reinforcing the improbability of their mission. Yet, here they were, on the cusp of stepping into the unknown. Lorna’s heart raced as she double-checked the address written in bold letters, her eyes flicking back and forth between the paper and the imposing barrier ahead.

Taking a deep breath, she retrieved the code from within the package, her hands trembling slightly. She entered the numbers with deliberate precision, conscious of the weight of each keystroke. The final digit clicked into place, and for a heartbeat, time seemed to suspend.

Then, with a mechanical groan, the gates began to part. Lorna and her companion sat transfixed, the car idling quietly in the shadow of the opening portal. The reality of gaining entry, of stepping into a world veiled in secrecy and power, washed over them. They were no longer outsiders, mere spectators from the periphery; they were about to cross a threshold into uncharted territory, with all its promises and perils.

Chelsea then says as they are pulling through the gate, “I cannot believe how easy it seems to be for you. Things just falling into place. Unbelievable.”

Lorna just smiles speaking mostly to herself, "This is going to be incredible!"

They crept up the long driveway, tires crunching on the gravel, until they reached the imposing double doors of the mansion. Exiting the vehicle, Brianna and her companions stood in awe, dwarfed by the sheer magnitude of the estate before them. Brianna broke the silence. "Shall I assume you have a key?" she asked, her voice tinged with both excitement and incredulity.

Lorna smirked, brushing her hair back with a nonchalant wave. "Actually, no need for a key. I read in the paperwork that the place is set up with a coding system. The gate code gets us access to everything we need inside," she replied, her eyes scanning the towering facade.

Chelsea, taking in the grandeur of their surroundings, let out an excited gasp. "Well, seeing it in person is something else. Wow!"

Brianna nodded in agreement, her eyes wide. "Yeah, wow is right!"

Chelsea turned to Lorna, her expression a mix of admiration and playful envy. "Lorna, does anything ever not go your way? This is unbelievable! And honestly, maybe just a tad unfair. Send some of that luck my way, would you?"

Lorna chuckled, a satisfied smile playing on her lips. "Come on, let's go in and check it out."

As they approached the doors, Brianna's cautious nature resurfaced. "You think it's safe, right?" she asked, her voice tinged with concern.

Chelsea waved off the worry with a light-hearted laugh. "Oh, don't start with your scary movie fears!"

Lorna came to her friend's defense, her tone gentle. "Hey, give her a break."

Chelsea, still teasing, grinned back. "You, telling someone to give a break! Where's the mirror? Quick, I need a mirror for Lorna to use in front of her big ole mansion!" she quipped, a mischievous glint in her eyes.

Lorna rolled her eyes with mock exasperation. "Ha, ha. Such a comedienne," she said dryly.

As they finally reached the entrance, the air around them was charged with anticipation and awe, broken only by a sudden, resounding crack of thunder that made them jump, then laugh nervously at their own reactions.

Chelsea gave an exaggerated eye roll, while Lorna merely smiled and reassured them. "Come on, it's okay," she said, leading the way with a confidence as grand as the mansion that loomed above them.

5

Chapter Five

Brianna then asks, “So, I do not see a keypad, or anything. How are we getting in?”

Lorna replies, “Well maybe it’s not locked.” She then reaches for the door, and it opens for her with ease. She just turns and looks at them and says, “See, no problem.” Chelsea chimes in, “Kind of expected it to creak open all creepy-like.” Lorna ignores this and enters.

The trio walk a few feet into the foyer looking around, amazed by the level of extravagance with which the mansion is furnished. It just reeked of old-world opulence, but not gawdy. Dark wood furniture carefully placed and large, Renaissance style paintings adorning large walls.

BANG! The door slams shut, startling Lorna and her friends. They were all are a little startled, and again, Briana was visibly jumpy and screamed, then apologetically mumbled, “Uh, sorry.”

The trio stood in the grand foyer of the mansion, Chelsea attempting to mask her apprehension with a facade of confidence. "It was just the wind," she asserted, though her voice hinted at uncertainty. "Right?"

Brianna, puzzled, responded sharply, "Wind? What wind? There’s no wind! I didn’t feel any wind."

Lorna chuckled softly, trying to diffuse the tension. "Come on, calm down. She's right; I did feel a slight breeze. There must be a window open somewhere, and it just caught the door. Relax."

Lorna's eyes scanned the ornate surroundings as she pressed on. "Help me find the office in this place. See if there are any papers or records that might offer some answers. Anything could be helpful.

When I was going through the papers last night, some things seemed relevant."

Brianna looked around, taking in the vastness of the mansion. "I've seen regional malls smaller than this place. How do you plan on finding it?"

Chelsea interjected, "Better question: what do you expect to find? Looking for anything in particular?"

Lorna sighed, a mix of determination and uncertainty in her tone. "I don't really know. I want to look around and see what I can find. My instincts tell me there's something here. I just need to find it. Come on."

"Anybody bring a flashlight?" queried Brianna. Without missing a beat, Lorna reached into her bag and pulled out three compact, yet powerful flashlights. "A soldier always prepares," she quipped.

Chelsea smirked at the remark, "So now, you're a general?"

Lorna handed out the flashlights, her expression turning serious. "Take these and stay sharp."

The three cautiously proceeded down the hallway, their flashlight beams cutting through the dusty air like lasers. The sheer scale of the house was staggering as they passed opulent vases, oil paintings, and sculptures. Lorna's gaze lingered on the rows of knights' armor lining the hallway. "Well, that's interesting?" she mused, the armor appearing even more imposing in the focused light.

The grandeur of the mansion was undeniable, its imposing presence magnified by its eclectic mix of tapestries and art – a testament not to the refined tastes of the elite, but to someone with an eye for the curious and the cash to indulge it. As Lorna and her companions wandered through its maze-like halls, more exotic treasures lay in their path until they stumbled upon a slightly ajar door. It led them into what could only be the office.

Lorna stepped inside cautiously, the beam from her flashlight slicing through the dimly lit room. Around her, high shelves groaned under the weight of hardcover books, walls dominated by photographs and accolades, but it was the massive mahogany desk that caught her focus. She circled it carefully, her eyes scanning over the official documents strewn carelessly across the leather desk mat.

As she sifted through the papers, a name emerged repeatedly – a foundation unfamiliar to her. Her companions, meanwhile, remained oblivious to the eyes that had tracked their every move since they set foot on the estate's gravel drive.

“I want to check out some of this stuff,” Lorna said, breaking the silence. “There should be a generator we can start up somewhere, from what I saw in the papers last night. Let's see if we can find it and get some power on. This place is too..."

“Spooky?” Brianna suggested, her voice breaking the tension.

“Yeah, a little spooky,” Lorna admitted, casting a reluctant smile Brianna’s way.

Chelsea, meanwhile, was equally distracted, her gaze drawn to a large portrait on the wall. “You think that guy was the owner?” she asked, pointing at the photograph.

Lorna spared the portrait a fleeting glance. “I suppose. Who else would have their photo hung up this prominently?” she shrugged, returning to the papers. The man in the picture had an air of authority about him, his gray hair lending him an aura of wisdom, a hunting rifle slung over his arm.

Lorna replied, “Not really sure but maybe so.” Then she continues rummaging through the papers she found on the desk.

Brianna watching Lorna says, “You seem so...I don’t know...uncaring.”

“Brianna,” Lorna called, still engrossed in her task, “It's not about caring. It's about understanding. Besides, I’m curious about what this place is worth. Maybe it sounds harsh, but it’s business, you know?” Her voice trailed off, knowing she sounded cold.

“See if you can find that generator,” she said, shaking off the momentary guilt.

“Fine, but we're not staying long, right?” Chelsea turned to Brianna, unease creeping into her voice.

"Relax, we won't be much longer," Lorna assured them distractedly. "See if you can find it and meet back here in thirty minutes tops."

"Yes, boss lady," Brianna teased, though her eyes were serious.

With a determined nod, Chelsea and Brianna left the office, fanning out through the mansion's shadowy corridors in search of the elusive generator. Lorna lingered a moment, her eyes catching a glint of something familiar in the portrait's glassy eyes, but she pushed it aside, engrossed in the papers sprawled before her.

Chelsea and Briana, motivated by a mix of curiosity and necessity, ventured through the mansion. Their steps echoed through the vast corridors as they searched for the generator room, which Lorna believed to be crucial to their exploration. Meanwhile, Lorna was immersed in her own investigation within the confines of this old-wood office that seemed untouched by time.

The office exuded an air of quiet authority, its walls adorned with towering bookcases that reached proudly from the polished hardwood floors to the ornate ceilings. Each shelf was a treasure trove of literature and curiosities, an eclectic assembly that seemed to whisper forgotten tales. Lorna scanned the collection with a discerning eye, her fingers trailing along the spines of books that whispered secrets of the past.

Her search among the orderly chaos of files and drawers yielded little of consequence—until her gaze fell upon a peculiar ceramic sparrow. Nestled incongruously among the tomes, it stood about five inches tall, its unusual build hinting at something more than mere decoration.

Drawn by its incongruity in the otherwise conventional space, Lorna reached out tentatively toward the sparrow. As her fingertips grazed its surface, the sparrow's eyes flickered to life with an unexpected glow. Startled, she pulled back just as a book jutted slightly forward from the shelf, as if nudged by an unseen hand.

She hesitated, then, fueled by curiosity, examined the book more closely. It wasn't a book at all, but a clever façade concealing a hidden compartment. Within this secret space lay a cache of aged letters, their brittle paper and faded ink a testament to the passing years. Lorna's heart quickened with a blend of reverence and curiosity as she delicately unfolded the letters. She sank into the leather chair at the desk, immersing herself in the intimate revelations of a mysterious figure from the past.

She begins to read the journal which starts with an entry in 1980:

Journal Entry – October 17, 1980

I am sitting here at my desk; it is getting late. The room is quiet except for the soft ticking of the clock. I miss you so much! It has become increasingly hard to focus; and all I can think about is you. I keep waiting for you to come in and tell me it's time to stop working and come to bed. But the realization sets in that you are not here, you are not coming in to get me, and I just feel a little more weighted down and alone. It hurts so much!

There is so much to do, so much more responsibility now, I need you so much! It has only been a few months, but it feels like everything now that I remember was just a dream. I do take comfort in knowing where you are now and that does at least help for a moment or two before I start to miss you again.

Tonight, the only thing I wanted to do was be able to talk to you. To have the comfort of your presence. Since I cannot and since there is no one that I feel, I can really trust talking to, I thought maybe writing this may help. I started to do a Journal entry, but my mind just goes to you. I took your letter out and read it again, it was the first one that you wrote to me. It does help in some ways too. It helps me remember the love we had and how special you were.

Vonya, I am going to do my best to raise her. It will not be easy I know, but I am going to do all I can to give her a great start. I am also still trying to put a plan in place to move forward our vision on helping children the way we talked about. I am going to do my best to be a man you would be proud of.

I will try to get some rest now; I know that is what you would say. I love you Vonya and I always will, there will never be another.

Yours always, Alfred

Lorna paused, her eyes lingering on the letter as she absorbed the depth of emotion it contained. Clearly, it was a profound declaration of love, a testament to a significant loss. Her curiosity piqued, she wondered about the identity of the person mentioned as needing to be raised.

Compelled by her discovery, she turned her attention to the letter mentioned. Despite its aged and worn appearance, the handwriting remained clear enough to read. Eager to uncover more, she began to delve into the faded words, each line pulling her deeper into the mystery of the past relationship it chronicled.

To My Sweetheart,

I know that we have only been dating for a few months, but these have honestly been the best in my life. You are the most beautiful person I have ever known. I don't just mean outside, but also inside. I never dreamed I would meet someone who has the heart you have, the patience and someone who makes me feel like I can achieve anything! I never would have imagined that I would meet someone like you and certainly not be blessed for someone like you to be with me. I love you so much and am so looking forward to our future together. I feel so loved by you and I love you so much.

Yours Always,

Vonya

Lorna sank into the cushioned embrace of the wingback chair, her eyes glazing over the faded ink of the letter in her hand. Each word seemed to echo within the confines of the dimly lit study, imbuing the air with a tender, almost haunting resonance. The letter, filled with raw, unguarded emotion, stirred something deep within her as if whispering secrets from a bygone era, weaving tales of love that seemed too pure to be real.

She was lost in the winding narratives when a sudden sound pierced the silence, startling her back to her senses. Instinctively, she snapped upright and restored the book—her discreet cover for the letters—to its rightful place on the ancient mahogany shelf.

With measured care, she folded the letters, their aged paper crinkling softly, and slipped them into a folder on the cluttered desk. Artifacts and knick-knacks from an era past jostled for space, adding to the room's aura of mystery. Lorna cast a quick glance to ensure the book was securely placed, then turned her attention to the shadowy corridor.

6

Chapter Six

"Chelsea? Brianna?" Her voice carried through the cavernous room, rippling softly against the darkened walls.

After what felt like an eternity, the shuffle of footsteps signaled the approach of her friends. "Why didn't you answer?" Lorna asked as Chelsea and Brianna materialized from the shadows.

"What do you mean? We came straight down the hall," Chelsea said, her brow furrowed with confusion.

Lorna hesitated; her mind briefly entangled in a web of confusion before dismissing it as another quirk of the mansion's acoustics. Eager to gloss over the unsettling moment, she steered the conversation back towards their objective. "Did you find the generator?"

"Sort of," Brianna replied, her voice a mix of awe and laughter. "We stumbled onto something like... NASA."

"What...?" Lorna's curiosity was piquing.

"It's not just a generator; it's like a full control room from a sci-fi flick," Brianna explained, attempting to capture the enormity of it.

Chelsea jumped in, "And starting it up is another thing—all the controls have labels, but they're complete gibberish."

Lorna's mind raced, her imagination painting vivid images of the hidden complexities within the mansion, each mystery darker than the last. This place was more than it seemed, and she could feel the intrigue pulling her deeper into its enigmatic embrace.

Unfazed by the potential challenge, Lorna asserted confidently, "It can't be that hard. Come on y'all. Show me this over-the-top control room."

Together, they retraced their steps to the enigmatic room. Along the way, Brianna asked, "Did you find anything interesting?"

"Not really," Lorna admitted, her thoughts still partially lingering on the contents of the letters. "I really need to explore more of it when I have more time."

Upon re-entering the room, the complexity of what confronted Lorna hit her like a jolt. The place was far more than just a generator room; it was an intricate control center loaded with novel technology and cryptic labels.

Chelsea gestured towards a vaguely marked switch. Lorna approached, adjusted it with a skillful twist, and to their collective astonishment, the room was suddenly awash in light, unveiling an extensive array of panels and screens.

"How about that," Chelsea remarked, clearly impressed. "Just needed the right touch, I guess."

As they ventured further, the room offered more enigmatic data and technology. Lorna's attention snagged on a framed section of the wall, featuring a panel with recessed holes suggesting some unspecified function.

Checking her phone and realizing the time, Lorna suggested, "Let's quickly Look around this area and head out for dinner."

They agreed and started towards the exit when a sudden clap of thunder halted them in their tracks. After a brief, cautious pause, they continued their exit, unaware of the shadowy figure observing them from a staircase.

Lorna led the way to one of the mansion's main libraries, a lavishly appointed room filled with an impressive collection of books and artwork. Her eyes were immediately drawn to a striking portrait of a woman above one of the fireplaces, possibly the woman mentioned in the handwritten letters. Intrigued by a potential connection—did she resemble the beauty in the painting? —Lorna pondered the woman's identity. Yet the room's opulence quickly reclaimed her full attention.

Near the fireplace, a neatly stacked pile of wood and a box of matches suggested recent activity, hinting that the mansion might not be as deserted as they had thought. Meanwhile, Chelsea and Briana, positioned at the rear of the house, debated their next move. As they decided on a direction, Briana glimpsed a fleeting figure in the doorway, sending a shock through her system and deepening the mystery surrounding the mansion and its elusive occupants.

In that charged moment, Brianna, visibly shaken, seized Chelsea's arm, her voice thick with panic. "Chelsea! Chelsea!" she cried urgently, her eyes wide as she pointed frantically behind them. By the time Chelsea turned, the source of Brianna's alarm had vanished into the shadows of the dim corridor, leaving no trace.

"What's wrong with you?" Chelsea asked, her tone a blend of concern and confusion as she tried to comprehend Brianna's distress.

"I swear I saw someone standing by that door," Brianna confessed, her voice trembling, echoing her frayed nerves.

Sharing a sense of unease, the group swiftly made their way to the front door, eager to escape the unsettling atmosphere of the grand estate.

Unbeknownst to them, a shadowy figure loomed on the second floor, silently watching their hasty departure through the dimly lit hallway. As they exited through the front door, a gust of wind, like a whisper, signaled their exit.

Once they settled into the car, an unexpected silence hung in the air, each woman waiting for the other to break it. Suddenly, the trio shared a chuckle and a collective sigh of relief. "Man, let's go get dinner," Lorna suggested. Her two friends nodded in agreement, and the car pulled away from the imposing mansion.

As they left, a shadowy figure, the vague outline of a person, watched from an upstairs window.

7

Chapter Seven

Their evening plans led them to a quaint restaurant nestled between the estate and the bustling town center. Lorna maneuvered her car into a parking space with practiced ease. "Have you been here before?" Chelsea asked. "No, this is my first time," Lorna replied, her mind still tangled with the strange happenings at the mansion and the unsettling letter she had discovered. As they approached the restaurant, Brianna commented hopefully, "This looks promising."

Approaching the entrance, Lorna noticed a young girl, no older than fourteen, sitting alone on a bench. Her sad eyes and disheveled appearance suggested homelessness, tugging unexpectedly at Lorna's heart.

Inside, the doorman welcomed them warmly. "Welcome to Rosa's," he greeted with a wide smile. They thanked him, but his attention soon shifted to the young girl outside. As they perused the menu, Lorna watched as the doorman approached the girl, speaking sharply and gesturing for her to leave. Reluctantly, she stood and walked away, and he returned to his post with a strident demeanor.

After dining, Lorna paused to ask about the girl. The doorman's response was dismissive. "Oh, she's just one of the local teens. She and her sister have been told not to loiter. Sometimes patrons give them food. I apologize for the problem."

Brianna, unable to hide her irritation, was ready to challenge him, but Chelsea sensed her friend's anger rising and intervened. "They are not a problem," Chelsea stated firmly. "Perhaps showing a little compassion would be better." The tension lingered as they left, leaving the doorman to ponder Chelsea's pointed words.

As they exited, Lorna interjected, "Well, this has been fun. Time to go,"

Back in the car, Lorna remarked dryly, "I think that went well."

"I was just trying to make my point without making a scene," Chelsea explained. Brianna belted, "Well, if Chelsea hadn't stopped me, I would've gone off. That's not cool!"

"Some people are just like that. Not much you can do," Lorna added, trying to ease the tension. Brianna chimed in once more, "He didn't have to be rude to that girl. He has no idea what their lives are like." Then Lorna cut her off, "Let's just enjoy the ride home."

Brianna and Chelsea just look at each other and then Brianna says, "Well glad to see you are so compassionate. You used to really be so..."

But before she could finish, Chelsea jumps, "Yeah, let's all just enjoy the ride home." Trying to lighten things once again.

Lorna, choosing her words carefully, added, "I'm just saying, that's how some people are. It's frustrating, and I do care but we shouldn't let it ruin our evening." Brianna, seeing the pointlessness of continuing the argument, relented. "Sure, I guess I get it." Chelsea tries to break up the tension, "So, what's next?"

The mall loomed ahead like a haven as Lorna took a steadying breath. "How about we hit the mall for a few things?" she proposed. Chelsea nodded, welcoming any excuse to shift gears from the current awkward air between them. "Sure, why not," Brianna agreed, her enthusiasm barely flickering.

With a destination programmed into the GPS, they set off. Upon arrival, Lorna declared her plan to stop by the office supply store. "You all go on. I'll catch you later," she told them. "Alright," Brianna said, dismissing the notion. "Chelsea, let's look at those shoes. Lorna, meet us back here later."

Lorna stood amidst the extensive aisles of a sprawling department store that seemed to house an eclectic mix of everything one could imagine—from the latest fashion in clothing and elaborate home furnishings to a colorful array of toys and games. As she navigated through this commercial maze, her attention was drawn to a poignant scene unfolding in the toy section. There, under the bright fluorescent lights, a young boy accompanied by an older man—possibly his grandfather or perhaps his father—stood contemplating a collection of model cars and ships.

The older man's demeanor was commanding and stern as the boy deliberated each option with a seriousness that seemed too mature for his age. It was evident from their interaction that a strict rule was in place—only one item could be chosen. This rule highlighted not just the scarcity of these moments in the boy's life but also the weight of the decision he had to make. Lorna, trying not to watch, but cannot help but notice the situation. The young boy's significant choice was under the scrutinizing gaze of this no-nonsense older man, who looked as if he did not really want to be there but had to.

This scene struck a chord within Lorna, she thought, "I have so much to look forward to and here this boy is, with having only a few brief moments to make the best choice he can. This ignited a cascade of memories that transported her back to her own childhood, which, although different, resonated with deep emotional undertones. She remembered vividly the day her adoptive parents had revealed the origins of her beginnings. Lorna was twelve years old when they told her that they had found her in an orphanage without any personal records—no name, no medical history, no birth certificate. She was a child without a past, and the realization that she could have faced a life devoid of family, much like the countless other children she had left behind, was overwhelming.

In that moment of revelation, overwhelmed by a profound sense of gratitude, Lorna remembered looking into her adoptive parents' eyes, her own brimming with tears, and thanked them earnestly. She thanked them for choosing her, for giving her a family, a home, and an identity. She remembered pausing and just looking at them for a moment and saying, "Thank you." Her voice thick with emotion, deeply aware of the extraordinary life she had been given—a life that many orphans could only dream of.

Now, observing the young boy in the store finally make his selection, Lorna felt a sudden surge of guilt wash over her. This emotion starkly contrasted with her usual detached demeanor, which was/is a byproduct of her relentless pursuit of success. Her achievements and ambitions had often blinded her to the simpler, more heartfelt aspects of life—those genuine, unguarded moments like the one she was witnessing.

Her thoughts then drifted to the earlier encounter of the young girl she had seen sitting alone on a bench outside the restaurant. The girl's desolate expression haunted Lorna, stirring a rare flicker of compassion that was both unfamiliar and unsettling. The image of the girl's loneliness juxtaposed sharply with the boy's dilemma, highlighting the pervasive themes of need and nurture that threaded through the tapestry of human experience.

Feeling increasingly suffocated by the materialism of the store—a consumer showcase that seemed to mirror the internal turmoil she was experiencing—Lorna decided it was time to leave. She sought out her friends, Chelsea and Brianna, and suggested they head home. Her voice was steady, though it thinly veiled the chaos stirring within. "If you don’t mind, let's go. I really need to get some paperwork done," she stated, her words more abrupt than she had intended.

Chelsea and Brianna exchanged puzzled looks but agreed without further inquiry; they had become used to their friend’s occasionally abrupt nature. The ride home was enveloped in silence, each mile deepening the introspective weight bearing down on Lorna.

8

Chapter Eight

Once home, after briefly saying goodbye to Chelsea and Brianna, Lorna retreated to the solitude of her bathroom tub, hoping the warmth of a bath might calm her nerves. However, relaxation eluded her. Later, as she changed into comfortable clothes and tried to immerse herself in the routine of reviewing paperwork in her study, she found no peace. The events of the day, particularly the letters she had unearthed, wove a complex tapestry of emotions that left her feeling profoundly conflicted.

That night, rest was but a fleeting visitor. Lorna tossed and turned, her mind racing with the revelations and reflections that had surfaced throughout the day. By dawn, she felt adrift, disconnected from her usual routines and perspectives.

Seeking some semblance of clarity, Lorna decided to forego her typical morning routine and opted for a reflective walk in the nearby park. She tossed on some sweats, donned her ear pods and she was out the door with a flourish.

Seated on a bench, with the backdrop of the city's hum and the occasional laughter of children playing nearby, she found a brief respite from her inner tumult. Here, in the simplicity of the park, surrounded by the ebb and flow of everyday life, Lorna pondered the profound shifts in perspective the previous day's experiences had provoked.

As she sat, the distant sound of a child's laughter mingling with the rustling leaves, Lorna reflected on the significant changes she might need to make to align her life with the new values that had emerged from her recent experiences.

Lorna was sitting alone on a park bench, immersed in a deep moment of self-reflection. She pondered deeply about her adopted family, her two best friends, the mysterious mansion she just inherited and even her stinker of a cat. She took a swig of cool water from her tumbler and then something jostled her out of this reflective state.

An unexpectedly poignant scene captured her attention in the park. A young mother was there with her son, who looked to be about seven or eight years old. They were sharing a small treat together. The mother handed her son an ice cream cone and with a gentle caution said, "Be careful and don't drop it." Before she could even finish her sentence, the ice cream toppled to the ground.

The boy's face crumpled with anguish, and he softly muttered, "I'm sorry." The mother, trying to hold back tears as she struggled to maintain her composure, bent down slowly and said, “It is okay, son; we just don't have enough money to buy another one.”

In a touching display of maturity, the little boy placed his hand on his mom's shoulder, smiled, and said, “Don't worry, I still have the cone to eat.”

Just then, another child, a little girl who had been watching, approached them. She had just received an ice cream cone and offered it to the boy, saying, "You can have mine." The boy looked at his mom for approval to accept it. His mom glanced at the little girl's mom, who had a tear in her eye as she nodded with a warm smile.

The boy's mom smiled at her son and said, “It's okay.” The boy, now beaming with excitement, said, “Thank you!”

This simple act of pure generosity moved everyone involved, profoundly touching them.

This exchange, filled with innocence and kindness, struck a deep chord within Lorna. It sharply contrasted with the complex web of emotions and decisions entangling her own mind, reminding her of the genuine connection and simplicity she felt was lacking in her life.

As Lorna stood frozen, watching the scene unfold, she could barely contain the emotions clutching at her heart. Memories flooded her mind, vivid and unyielding. Her thoughts drifted back to a day that had reshaped her entire existence—a day when her parents sat her down in their familiar living room, their faces a mixture of tenderness and resolve.

They had spoken softly, yet their words reverberated through her being. Lorna had discovered she was an orphan before she ever had a name. She was a child born from mystery—a child found in the sterile silence of an orphanage, devoid of any identity. No birth certificate, no medical records, just a nameless start in a world that often overlooked the voiceless.

For a 12-year-old, it was a truth both vast and intimate, a revelation that pressed heavily on her young shoulders. But in that moment of weighty silence, a wellspring of gratitude surged within her. She turned to her parents, her voice steady and filled with a newfound resolution. "Thank you," she had whispered, "For giving me a family, for granting me a life."

That seed of gratitude had grown within her, blossoming into a drive to aid those left behind in the shadows of orphanages. Yet, as adulthood wrapped her in its relentless embrace, the sharp focus of her altruistic intent blurred. Success became the beacon she chased, and somewhere along the path, she found herself drifting from the promises she had made to her younger self.

Lorna felt the weight of her choices, the ghost of her past whispering to her. Could she reclaim the purpose that once burned so fiercely within her? The answer lay somewhere in the tangled web of her journey—a journey still unfolding.

Now, witnessing the selfless act of a child, Lorna realized just how far she had strayed from her former self. It was a painful but necessary realization—a poignant reminder of her past ideals and the person she hoped to become again. With a renewed resolve, Lorna decided it was time to reevaluate her priorities in life. She needed to reconnect with her core values, those that had driven her before her pursuit of material success overshadowed them.

Feeling a mix of sadness, hope, and determination, Lorna stood up from the bench and left the park. She dials Steve as she is walking and says, "I need to meet with you this afternoon, what time can you be available?" Steve, taken back a little by the surprise meeting says, "I'm available after 1:30 today."

She replies, "Great I'll see you then." She hangs up the phone and heads home to change and think through exactly what her new plans will look like.

9

Chapter Nine

As Lorna walked home to prepare for the meeting, her mind buzzed with plans and possibilities. She was so absorbed in her thoughts that she failed to notice a man who had been observing her from a distance. Unbeknownst to her, this man had been watching her for the last ten minutes, and even as she headed home, he continued to follow her, maintaining a cautious distance.

Upon arriving home, Lorna quickly changed clothes and organized her papers. She was about to leave for her meeting with Steve when she briefly noticed a car that seemed oddly familiar. It was the same vehicle that had been trailing her from the park. Brushing off the coincidence, she drove off, focused on the significant changes she was eager to implement.

Lorna barely let the wheels of her car come to a stop before she shifted it into park. In a hurry, she slammed the door and strode purposefully into the office building where Steve's office was located.

Once inside, she made a beeline for the receptionist's desk, but catching sight of Steve, she noticed him motioning for her to come in. She bypassed the desk without a word and entered his glass-walled office.

As Steve closed the door behind her, a question hung in the air. "Are you okay?" he asked, scanning her face for answers.

Lorna paused, her chest rising and falling as she caught her breath, but she didn't reply right away.

"What's going on, Lorna?" Steve pressed, confused by her anxious demeanor. "Earlier you sounded nearly in tears, and now you're so anxious I don't know what to think. What's this about?"

"Those people we talked to a few days ago—you can reach them, right?" Lorna shot back, hardly letting her words settle.

"Yes... I can reach them, but..." Steve began, his confusion growing.

"Then call them. Now," Lorna interrupted. "Tell them there's an option they might really appreciate."

"Wait a minute. Weren't you committed to selling that property to someone else? Alright, you gotta' clue me in. Just hit me with it," Steve persisted, trying to keep up with her pace.

Lorna nodded, determination glowing in her eyes. "Yes, I'm still going through with that sale as promised, but I've come up with a solution that could work even better for them than what they were thinking originally."

Steve, thrown by her sudden strategic shift, searched for clarity. "I'm utterly confused and—"

"Are you going to call them, or should I?" Lorna cut him off again. "I'm sorry for being abrupt, but we don't have time to waste."

Taken aback by her apology yet intrigued, Steve nodded, a chuckle escaping despite his puzzlement. "Okay, alright, give me a minute." He signaled his secretary, "Could you try to get the Jacobs on the phone? It's urgent."

Within minutes, Steve's secretary buzzed back, informing him she had Mr. Jacobs waiting on line 2. Steve thanked her and then promptly picked up the receiver. "Mr. Jacobs, thanks for taking my call on such short notice. I have potentially significant news for you and was hoping you could come down with your wife and her sister to discuss it."

Mr. Jacobs, intrigued, responded, "Yes, we can make it down. Can you give me an idea of what this is about?"

Steve hesitated, choosing his words carefully. "I'd prefer to explain in person if that's alright."

"That's fine. We'll be there in about 45 minutes," Mr. Jacobs replied, his tone reflecting a mix of curiosity and readiness.

"Thank you, and we'll see you then," Steve concluded the call, hanging up with a heavy sense of anticipation. Turning to Lorna, he couldn't hide his bafflement. "NOW, can you please explain what this is all about?" His voice held a mixture of frustration and confusion.

Lorna took a deep breath, realizing how her sudden change of plans must have seemed abrupt and mysterious. She knew she owed Steve a proper explanation, especially given their partnership and his unwavering support in past endeavors.

"Steve, I've been doing a lot of thinking," Lorna began, her tone earnest. "What we're doing in business is great, but I've been feeling like we could do more—something that truly makes a difference. After seeing the Jacobs and knowing their situation... Well, I believe we have an opportunity to get started with making that difference."

Steve listened intently, his initial confusion slowly giving way to understanding. Lorna's shift wasn't just a business maneuver; it was a moral decision, a paradigm shift, an attempt to align their work with deeper values.

Lorna sat across from Steve in his office, her expression serene yet resolute as she began to explain the sudden shift in her priorities. "I know this all seems abrupt and perhaps contradictory to what I've said before, but yesterday, something changed for me," she began, her voice steady and sincere. "I realized just how blessed I am and how little I've really done to help anyone else. I mean, I care, of course, but it's always been from a safe, convenient distance. I've never truly acted on it. I realized I need to try to do more, to make a real difference where I can. Today, I am certain of one thing: I can help those people and their children."

Steve looked back at her, astonishment written all over his face. This was not the Lorna he had known over the past five years. Her words and the conviction behind them took him completely by surprise. After a moment of silence, during which he simply stared, trying to reconcile this new version of Lorna with the one he knew, he finally spoke, "I just want to say how proud I am of you. I know this isn't about me, but what you're planning to do is truly commendable, and I'm honored to be a part of it."

A broad smile broke across Lorna's face, her eyes glistening with unshed tears as she absorbed Steve's words. "Thank you, Steve," she said softly, then added, "Let's wait for them to get here and discuss everything together."

Steve, now intrigued and somewhat excited about what Lorna might propose, nodded and instructed his secretary to bring in the guests the moment they arrived. "Please make sure they come straight to my office," he said.

Lorna then turned her attention to a file in front of her. "Here's what I'm thinking," she began, spreading out the paperwork for the estate she had recently inherited. "This property, by my estimates, is far more valuable than the downtown property I sold. It's larger, comes with more land, and frankly, it has greater potential. There's even some tech in it that has to be worth something."

She paused, placing both hands firmly on the table and looking intently at the documents before her. "I want those people who were interested in the other property to have this one," she declared, looking up at Steve with a determined gaze.

Steve, still in a state of shock, tried to process her words. "Wait, you mean to sell them this property for the same price as the one they lost?" he asked, trying to find logic in her proposal.

Lorna shook her head. "No, that's not what I'm saying," she clarified, causing Steve to slump slightly, bracing for what he thought was coming next.

"I don't intend to sell it to them," Lorna continued, her voice calm yet firm. "I want to give it to them."

Steve's eyes widened in disbelief. "Give it away? As in, for free?"

"Yes, that's generally what give away means. This government still gives tax write offs for donations to charities, right?" Lorna teased, a mix of disbelief and resolve in her own voice. "I want to donate the property, with certain stipulations about its use, of course. It should serve a purpose--help those in need."

Steve, struggling to grasp the magnitude of her decision, finally found his voice. "You're serious about this, aren't you? You're really going to give away a valuable piece of real estate?"

"I am," Lorna affirmed with a slight smile. "And believe it or not, I'm happy about it. It's a big step, and it feels a bit overwhelming, but it's the right thing to do. I'm happy. There, I said it. I'm happy."

The room fell silent for a moment as both contemplated the significance of the decision. Lorna broke the silence, her tone now brisk with urgency. "Let's hurry and get the necessary documents signed. I've wasted enough time; I don't want to waste any more."

She began rifling through the papers, organizing the documents needed for the donation. "They can't get here quickly enough. Let's get these signed."

Lorna continued to pour over the paperwork, her actions swift and determined. It was clear that this decision was not just a momentary impulse but a profound shift in how she viewed her responsibilities and her ability to impact the lives of others positively. As they waited for the Jacobs to arrive, a new chapter was beginning, not just for Lorna but for all those her decision would touch.

"Thank you for trusting me with this," Steve said finally. "Let's see what we can do for the Jacobs. It's a bold move, but it's one I think could redefine what our business stands for. Will you hit me if I say I'm proud of you?" Lorna smirked, "Maybe."

Lorna sat at the head of the conference table, the freshly signed documents spread out before her, each bearing her signature next to the clauses she felt were most crucial for the future of her recently inherited estate. "I do have one main stipulation," Lorna began, her voice firm but calm. "I want the estate to be renamed Vonya's Children's Home."

Steve, looking up from the paperwork, asked, "Okay, why that name?"

"There's a lot behind it, more than we have time to get into right now," Lorna replied quickly. "Just ensure the name is established and prominently displayed on the sign outside of the estate."

"Okay, no problem," Steve nodded, making a note.

Soon after finalizing these details, the Jacobs arrived and were promptly escorted to the conference room. They entered cautiously, sensing the significance of the meeting but uncertain of its specifics. As they settled into their seats, Steve greeted them warmly, "Thanks for coming in, please have a seat." He gestured towards Lorna, adding, "I think you remember meeting Lorna the last time you were here."

They nodded, their expressions somber and they were trying to be polite despite the last, hurtful encounter with Lorna. Steve continued, "Well, she has something important to discuss with you today."

Lorna looked around the table, taking in the faces of those she had last met under less-than-ideal circumstances. "First, I want to apologize for how I behaved during our last meeting," she began, her voice sincere. "I wasn't very friendly and certainly didn't engage with you in the business manner you deserved. I am sorry, and I ask for your forgiveness."

The room's atmosphere shifted from puzzled curiosity to compassionate understanding. Mr. Jacobs responded with a gracious nod, "Of course, we forgive you. It's so rare for anyone to have the bravery to ask. Thank you, Miss Ritten!"

Encouraged by their response, Lorna felt a wave of emotion but continued, "That means a lot to me, thank you. Recently, I received news of an inheritance—a significant estate. Initially, I was thrilled, I mean who wouldn't be? But after visiting the property and reflecting on recent events, I've had a change of heart and perspective."

She paused, gathering her thoughts. "I've realized many things about myself—flaws I had ignored and truths I had avoided. And, during this introspection, I saw a clear path to begin making amends. This estate is much better than the property you first thought about purchasing from me. I now view it not just as land, but as a chance for redemption and to truly make a difference."

The room fell silent, the room hanging on her every word. Lorna leaned forward, her hands pressed against the table, "I've decided to transfer ownership of this estate to you. Furthermore, I intend to assist in setting up a plan to cover the estate's taxes for the next five years, to ensure a smooth transition."

A hush fell over the room, the magnitude of her announcement sinking in. Suddenly, Alise Jacobs, overcome with emotion, stood up and walked around the table. With tears streaming down her cheeks, she embraced Lorna tightly. "Thank you, thank you so much," she emoted.

Mr. Jacobs and his sister-in-law, Seline, also stood and joined in the embrace, expressing their gratitude with warm hugs. Even Steve, moved by the scene, found himself wiping away tears, hoping no one saw him doing it.

After a few moments of emotional exchanges and the group regaining their composure, they began to discuss the logistical details of the transfer. Lorna provided them with contacts and legal advisers who could facilitate the process, ensuring that the transition of the property would be as seamless as possible.

As the meeting drew to a close, Lorna stood up, her heart lighter yet filled with a new sense of purpose. "Look, I've gotta' get going, but please don't hesitate to reach out if you encounter any issues or need further assistance," she said, her voice steady but gentle.

The Jacobs family reassured her of their gratitude once more, promising to honor the spirit in which the gift was given. They watched as Lorna exited the room, a trail of hopeful gazes following her departure.

Lorna walked out of Steve's office with a profound sense of peace, knowing she had not only changed the trajectory of her own life but had potentially transformed the lives of others through her actions. As she stepped outside, the weight of past missteps felt lifted, replaced by the promising weight of future possibilities. She was ready to embrace this new chapter, where success would be measured not just by wealth and accolades but by the positive impact she could have on the world around her.

10

Chapter Ten

Lorna adjusted the rearview mirror briefly before stepping out of her car and into the bustling atmosphere of the plaza where they had dined the night before. Her mind was on a mission—to find the little girl she had seen sitting alone, looking desolate. The large plaza was busy, thronged with shoppers meandering in and out of the numerous shops. Lorna walked purposefully, her eyes scanning each face, hoping to spot the young girl among the crowd.

As she passed a busy café, her focus momentarily diverted from her quest, she accidentally bumped into a woman, sending the contents of her bag sprawling across the sidewalk. "I am so sorry," Lorna blurted out, bending down to help gather the scattered items. As she did so, her gaze inadvertently caught a man sitting in a car across the parking lot, staring intently in her direction. Noticing her observation, the man quickly pretended to fiddle with his phone. Lorna stood up, apologized again to the woman, who reassured her with a kind "It's okay."

Lorna's attention snapped back to the mysterious man in the car, just as he started his engine. At that moment, a familiar harsh voice rang out. "How many times do I gotta' tell you? Get outta here! Leave now!" It was the same restaurant doorman from the previous evening, reprimanding the little girl she had been searching for.

Without hesitation, Lorna started walking toward them, calling out "Hey!" in a firm, assertive tone. The doorman looked up, startled by her intervention. As Lorna approached, she could see the little girl's face, a mixture of fear and resignation.

Lorna approached the scene with a determination fueled by righteous indignation, her heels clicking sharply against the concrete walkway. She fixed her gaze on the doorman, whose demeanor shifted from authoritative to uncertain under her scrutiny.

"Excuse me!" she declared, her voice slicing through the ambient noise of clinking cutlery and murmured conversations of outside dinning. "I understand the need to maintain order, but does that justify berating a child? This is the best solution you could muster? Perhaps, if you harnessed a bit of empathy and some basic decency, you could maybe show a little bit of mercy."

Rendered speechless by her words, the doorman stood, his expression faltering.

Lorna's tone softened as she continued, her eyes now gentle. "In the future, aim for a little more compassion. Please."

Turning her focus to the young girl, Lorna's expression melted into a warm smile. "Hey there, what do you say we grab some pizza?" she suggested, her voice inviting and kind.

The little girl's face lit up with a hopeful smile, and she nodded eagerly. Lorna reached out her hand, and the little girl glanced at it for a moment. Time seemed to slow down for a moment. Just as Lorna was beginning to think this was not turning out like she hoped it would, the little girl stood up from the bench and took Lorna's hand.

As they turned to leave, the doorman, perhaps moved by the scene, murmured, "I'll try."

Lorna gave him a slight smile and nod, then focused all her attention on the little girl as they walked toward the pizza place. Across the parking lot, the man who had been watching Lorna resumed his observation, his interest piqued by her actions.

Inside the pizzeria, they chose a cozy table by the window. The waitress approached with a cheerful, "So, what would you two ladies like to have?"

Turning to the little girl, Lorna asked gently, "And, what're you thinkin'?"

"Is pepperoni okay?" the girl asked tentatively, her voice barely above a whisper.

Lorna grinned, exchanging a glance with the waitress, "Absolutely! Matter of fact, how about double pepperoni, and make it an extra-large."

The girl's smile widened, lighting up her face, filling Lorna with a sense of fulfillment, albeit momentarily. As they waited for their pizza, Lorna couldn't help but feel a mix of emotions. She was genuinely pleased to bring a moment of joy to the girl, but she was also acutely aware of the long list of responsibilities waiting for her—decisions and tasks that, while important, suddenly seemed less pressing in the face of this simple act of kindness.

Despite this, Lorna couldn't shake a lingering feeling of unease. Even as she prioritized helping this child today, she knew that her professional and personal goals still loomed large, challenging her to find a balance she hadn't quite mastered yet. This moment of charity, profound yet simple, was a step, perhaps a small one, toward reconciling the woman she was with the woman she hoped to become.

The waitress reapproached their table, "We'll have it out shortly."

Lorna then turns to the little girl and asks, "So, what do they call you?"

The girl smiles sweetly and replies, "My name is Amy." Amy, though petite, had a radiant smile and long light brown hair that added to her charm.

Lorna responds warmly, "Amy, I'm Lorna. It's very nice to meet you. How old are you?"

Amy answered, "I'm 12."

Lorna gently probes, "Does your family live nearby?"

Amy hesitated for a moment, her expression betraying some nervousness.

Lorna reassured her, "It's cool, I just wanna' help."

Amy finally responded, "I live with my sister, not too far from here."

"It's just the two of you?" Lorna asks.

Amy nods. "Yeah. Been that way for a couple of years now."

Lorna hesitates before asking, "And, your mom and dad?"

Amy's face grows serious as she explains, "I don't really know. As long as I can remember, it's mostly been me and my sister. We've stayed with different families, but nothing for too long. A few years ago, we managed to get a small apartment. My sister works hard, and I do what I can. We get by. She always tells me that God will take care of us—and I believe He does."

Amy's words strike a chord with Lorna, causing her to pause. Lorna's parents were devout Christians, but Amy's unwavering faith is something Lorna herself has struggled to embrace.

Trying to shift the focus, Lorna asks, "Is your sister at work now?"

Amy nods. "She's at her other job. Usually gets home around 10 p.m. Sometimes I come here, and people feel sorry for me and give me food to bring home."

Lorna feels a wave of compassion stirring—a sensation foreign to her in recent years. She's spent so much time focused on her own desires, getting what she wanted without much thought for others. When their steaming pizza arrives, Lorna orders another for Amy to take home.

As they finish eating, Lorna offers, "Can I drive you home?"

Amy beams. "That would be great! You can meet my sister too. We don't usually have visitors, so this would be awesome!"

Lorna smiles. "Sounds awesome to me!"

Amy directs Lorna to her home, a modest apartment in a rundown area. Lorna says nothing about its condition but takes in the effort the sisters have put into keeping their home tidy and organized.

Inside, Amy points to a chair. "That's the good one. You sit here."

Lorna sits, touched by Amy's hospitality and lack of embarrassment about her humble surroundings. Before she can dwell on her own materialism, the door opens, and Amy's sister, Cindy, enters.

Cindy, almost 19, looks tired but determined, with long brown hair like Amy's. Cindy, shocked to see a stranger in the apartment, exclaims,

"Hello! Hello?" She smiles at Amy, who runs to hug her and exclaims, "This is Lorna! She helped me tonight and bought us pizza!"

Cindy, cautious but polite, says, "Uh, nice to meet you," looking at Amy for clarification.

Amy explains, "Lorna helped me with that man I told you about—the one who hasn't been very nice. She also got us pizza!"

Cindy smiles warmly. "Yeah, you mentioned that. Thank you so much, uh, Lorna, is it? How much do I owe you?"

Lorna waves it off. "Nothing. I enjoyed spending time with Amy."

Cindy's gratitude is evident. "That's incredibly kind of you."

Lorna, feeling a mix of emotions, hesitates before saying, "Actually, there's something I'm working on that might interest you. It's a new project—a children's home opening nearby. I'll have some influence over how it's run, and if you're interested, there might be a position for you."

Cindy stares at her, then tears up. "I've been praying for something like this. Been applying to a lot of places, but you know, it's a tough job market. You have no idea how much we've needed this kind of chance. It could change everything—help me finish school and give Amy a better life. Thank you!"

Amy interrupts with enthusiasm, "How about a group hug?"

Cindy laughs, and Lorna chuckles too. The three embrace, and Lorna feels both joy and an inner turmoil.

As they pull away, Lorna's thoughts race: *What is happening to me? I've given away a massive property, and now I'm in a strangers' home trying to help them. I don't even understand their level of faith. I'm glad I helped, but I need to process all this.*

Lorna says, "I'm so glad I got to meet y'all! Unfortunately, I really gotta' get going, but someone will contact you tomorrow to get things started with that position, Cindy. They'll go over the details and help with the transition."

Cindy and Amy thank her again and hand Lorna a sticky note with her contact information. As Lorna steps toward the door, Amy runs over to give her one last hug, “Thanks for the pizza and ride home and everything. Goodnight!”. Lorna hugs her lightly and says, “Goodnight to you both. Now, let me get out of here before I start crying.” Tearing up, she leaves as they wave goodbye from the doorway.

Back in her car, Lorna feels the comfort of familiar surroundings. She begins the drive home, unaware of the same car from earlier trailing at a safe distance. What she doesn’t know is that a second car has now joined the pursuit. Lost in thought about the evening’s events, she pays little attention to her surroundings.

At the stoplight, Lorna glanced into her rearview mirror, catching sight of a car she vaguely recognized. She usually didn’t bother checking if anyone was tailing her, but as the night stretched on, she wondered if she should start. When the light turned green, she dismissed the notion, especially as both vehicles turned in different directions.

When Lorna pulled into her driveway, she stepped out of the car and instinctively scanned the surroundings. Everything seemed normal; nobody was following. She chastised herself silently, "Stop being paranoid and get on with that bath!"

Once inside, Lorna indulged in the hot bath she had craved all day, seeking a reset to gear up for tomorrow. But as the minutes ticked by, though she tried to clear her thoughts, her mind kept wandering back to the wonderful, but also unsettling encounter with Cindy and Amy.

The following morning, Lorna reached out to Steven, facilitating the connection between the orphanage she had pledged her estate to and Amy’s sister, Cindy. Initially taken aback, Cindy expressed her astonishment and gratitude to Lorna for the unexpected opportunity that could alter the course of her and her sister’s lives. Cindy confided in Lorna that while people often talk grandly to boost their own egos, they seldom deliver on their promises.

Lorna diligently liaised with the management team at the children's home, securing herself a seat on the board to ensure the property was used appropriately. Everything seemed to be unfolding smoothly on that front.

While satisfied with the progress related to Cindy and the orphanage, Lorna frequently found herself lost in thought about her own adoption. She grappled with reconciling the empathy she felt for the two sisters with the lingering pain of her own relinquishment.

...

Suddenly, a loud thud snaps her out of her thoughts. She freezes, holding her breath, straining to hear. Footsteps approach, and a wave of fear paralyzes her. She knows the situation is dire. Her emotions flood in—fear, confusion, and the raw vulnerability of the unknown. Just as she's about to scream, a loud banging echoes elsewhere in the mansion, diverting whoever or whatever was coming toward her. Time is running out, and she's stuck, unsure of what to do.

...

11

Chapter Eleven

"Focus!" she commands herself. Dangling from the indoor climbing wall at the gym, her left-hand struggles to maintain its grip. The ground seems dangerously close as she searches for a better hold.

"Hey, you good?" comes a familiar voice.

Lorna looks over to see Chelsea climbing beside her, clearly enjoying the challenge. Chelsea thrives on competition, especially with Lorna, and uses the moment to distract her rival. Lorna shoots her a sharp look, regains her grip, and climbs with renewed determination. Chelsea smirks and tries to find a quicker route up the wall.

The indoor climbing wall is one of their favorite activities at the "All American Gym" (AAG), a sprawling fitness center downtown. Known for its extensive facilities, AAG is also a haven for kids from a local children's home, who often jog on the treadmills or play basketball. The gym makes a point to create a welcoming space for them, and Lorna has recently taken an interest in improving their experience.

"Are we done climbing plaster yet? I'm starving!" shouts Brianna from below.

Lorna and Chelsea exchange an exasperated glance. Lorna calls down, "Can you not? We're climbing here!" Chelsea adds, breathless, "Yeah, unless you're going to join us, enough with the talking thing!" Brianna snarks back, "We need more of the eating thing!"

Brianna, seated on a folding chair, doesn't even look up from her thick Victorian novel. "Climbing? Is that what you're calling it? Seems more like a metaphor for your struggle to get to the top." Her voice drips with playful sarcasm. "You should try being more secure, independent and confident. You know...like me."

Lorna and Chelsea shake their heads as Brianna quips, "This doesn't even count as shopping. Thanks, Chelsea."

Chelsea had invited Brianna to shop for iPad covers and protein bars but detoured to the gym. Uninterested, Brianna buried herself in one of her fashion magazines, that fuels her disdain for elitism and privilege.

Two 12-year-old girls stroll by, wearing government-issued middle school gym shorts and T-shirts with their school's name emblazoned across the front. Brianna, catching sight of them in her peripheral vision, looks up just as they pass and smiles before returning to her book. Lorna, watching the moment unfold from above, smiles faintly and resumes climbing. Brianna's bluntness sometimes irks her, but Lorna appreciates how much Brianna understands and supports AAG's mission.

On another section of the climbing wall, a fit blond man in his mid-20s pauses midway, checking his harness and rope. Lorna notices him, and for a brief moment, their eyes meet. Embarrassed, she looks away and refocuses on her climb.

"Not bad to look at," Chelsea teases, catching the interaction while also vying to outpace Lorna.

"Um..." Lorna mutters, struggling to deflect the topic.

"He's not the worst-looking guy I've seen. What do you think?" Chelsea adds with a sly grin as she hunts for a new hold.

Lorna sighs. "Look, you know I just broke up with... well, he-who-shall-not-be-named. I'm not ready. Too much going on."

"He's been watching *you*," Chelsea quips, smirking as she edges upward. "Caught him glancing over a few times. You're so Lazer-focused you don't notice these things."

Lorna shrugs. "Should I find that creepy or flattering?" She quickens her pace, leaving Chelsea scrambling to keep up.

"Take it however you want. He's fit," Chelsea says with a grunt as she struggles to match Lorna's progress.

Determined not to lose again, Chelsea bites her lip, coils her body, and leaps upward, skipping a few holds in a bold move to catch up.

Lorna freezes, eyes wide as Chelsea's risky maneuver unfolds. *What is she thinking?*

Chelsea stretches, her hand brushing the edge of a crevice near Lorna. "Yes!" she exclaims.

But the victory is short-lived. Her grip falters, and her momentum slams her against the wall. Her hands slip entirely.

"No!" Chelsea yells as she falls, the safety ropes catching her just before she hits the ground.

"Well, that was dumb," Lorna calls down, lowering herself to where Chelsea dangles.

"Yeah..." Chelsea grumbles, a mix of frustration and embarrassment on her face.

"It's cool. I'd probably try a flying squirrel move too if I were losing," Lorna teases, helping her out of the harness. "But you're buying appetizers tonight."

Chelsea groans. "Yeah, yeah. Maybe I let you win." Lorna busts out laughing. "Thanks, Chelse, I needed that!" Lorna derides.

From below, Brianna chimes in. "Okay, hungry over here—ready to go."

The trio heads toward the locker room. Lorna changes quickly while Chelsea gets dressed, and Brianna scans the bulletin board, clearly eager to leave.

"These kids can't just 'do something else.' They need Phoenix Children's Home, and the city commissioners should back it," Lorna says, tossing a gym towel into the laundry basket.

Chelsea counters, "Fair, but who's paying for it? A run-down children's home isn't exactly a tourist attraction for Phoenix. 'Come visit! We gots homeless kids!'"

Brianna, pacing by the locker room door, retorts, "So a community needs profit to have a conscience?"

"Come on, Bree," Chelsea replies. "You know what I mean."

Lorna interjects. "I get it, but everyone should help—corporations, governments, communities. It's not just one group's problem."

"That's nice in theory, but what does that look like in reality?" Chelsea asks.

Brianna sighs. "This is just *fascinating*, but I need some dinner."

Lorna checks her watch. "Yeah, let's go. Don't want to hold up Brianna's appetite, even though she eats less than a bird. See you both at Rembrandt's."

Chelsea heads out first, calling back, "See you there!"

Brianna lingers briefly, turning to Lorna with a playful grin. "Hurry up, us birds are hungry." She exits, leaving Lorna alone in the empty locker room.

There's a faint noise—a shuffle, a small echo.

What was that?

"Hello?" Lorna calls out, walking to the end of the lockers. She glances around but sees nothing out of the ordinary. Just as she's about to dismiss it, four older women enter, grumbling about how the new squash court's polished floor is unsuitable for "women of their advanced experience." Lorna chuckles softly, grabs her belongings, and heads to the door.

In another part of the AAG...

Two larger, middle school girls have cornered a smaller girl, about 10, who's wearing a faded pink tracksuit. One bully, with unnaturally bright orange hair, dribbles a scuffed basketball while taunting the smaller girl. The other, tall and solidly built, smirks in agreement.

"Hey, Pinkie. Nice outfit. Are you a piggy bank? If I crack you open, do quarters fall out?" The Orange-haired girl sneers.

The smaller girl, "Pinkie," looks down, her insecurity growing. She feels the weight of being from the children's home and having no family. She just wants to fit in.

The taller girl grabs the basketball and bounces it off Pinkie's head. Orange-haired laughs loudly as the taller one catches the rebound, smirking as she passes the ball back. Pinkie, near tears, mutters, "Cut it out! Just leave me alone."

"Oh, come on, Pinkie. I know you've got quarters in there!" Orange-haired sneers, pulling the ball back to throw again.

But she doesn't get the chance.

Lorna, exiting the locker room, sees the scene unfold. She steps up behind Orange-haired, grabbing her arm before she can throw. The ball drops to the floor. "Really? Lydia?? Whad I tell you about this kind of thing?" Lorna says firmly.

The bully steps back, a forced grin on her face. "Lorna, my home girl! Wassup?" She raises her hand for a casual high five.

Across the gym, Dennis and Susan Wright pause to watch. The gym owners, they're well-known for their generosity, especially toward less fortunate kids. Dennis, at 6'2", carries his 52 years with athletic ease, while Susan, elegant at 5'8", is a picture of fitness and poise.

Lorna narrows her eyes. "I think it's time for you two to go."

Lydia and her friend, Becky, turn to leave.

"Hey, Lydia," Lorna calls. Both girls turn back. "You should be setting a good example, not causing pain. Try helping someone feel welcome here instead of making them afraid."

Lydia shrugs. "Sure, I'll think about it real hard," she replies sarcastically.

"Great," Lorna says. "You'll have two weeks to reflect. You're both on probation. No gym until then."

"Two weeks?! for this?!" Lydia protests, but Lorna's stern expression ends the argument. With half-hearted apologies, the two bullies slink away.

Lorna approaches Pinkie, who's still teary-eyed, staring at the floor. She kneels beside her, placing a comforting hand on her shoulder. "You okay?"

"Yes," Pinkie whispers, wiping her tears.

"Don't let them bother you. It's going to be okay." Lorna gently wipes away the remaining tears.

Pinkie looks up, offering a timid smile that melts Lorna's heart. Memories of her own lonely childhood flood back.

"Thank you," Pinkie says softly.

"You're welcome. What's your name?"

"Sam," the little girl replies.

"It's nice to meet you, Sam. I don't think I've seen you here before."

"It's my first time," Sam explains. "I just moved to the Phoenix Children's Home from another place. One of the ladies said I'd like it here. I thought it'd be fun, but... I don't know anyone. I just wanted to watch TV." She grins shyly.

Lorna feels a pang in her chest. Sam's story stirs memories about her own adoption, and how she never knew her real name or birthday. She recalls how blessed she felt to be chosen by her adoptive parents.

"Well, Sam," Lorna says, "how about you hop on a treadmill, and I'll join you after I change?"

Sam's face lights up. "Really?"

"Really."

"Okay!" Sam exclaims, dashing off toward the treadmills.

Lorna quickly texts Chelsea to push their dinner reservation back by 45 minutes. As she turns, Dennis and Susan approach her.

"Don't worry," Lorna says preemptively. "I handled it calmly. I just wanted them to see they were wrong."

"We saw," Susan says, wrapping an arm around Lorna's shoulder. "You did great. Couldn't have handled it better myself."

Dennis nods. "I'm sure that kind of thing hits close to home for you."

Lorna smiles faintly. "Yeah. Guess it does."

Lorna looks at Dennis and Susan, "I know I don't say it enough, but I really love being a part of this. I appreciate it."

Dennis and Susan exchange a pleased glance. Susan hugs Lorna warmly, and Lorna smiles. "Well, I gotta get ready for dinner soon, but see you both tomorrow."

"Enjoy your dinner. See you tomorrow," they replied cheerfully.

Lorna meets Sam for their run, followed by watching cartoons. Mrs. Matthews, a volunteer from the children's home, arrives to pick up Sam. Approaching them, she asks, "Did you have a good time?"

Sam hesitates for a moment and Lorna is concerned for a flash and then Sam beams, "Yeah! Definitely!"

Lorna smiles at Mrs. Matthews. "We had a blast running and watching TV." Turning to Sam, she adds, "I'm here all the time, so I'll see you around for sure. There's an indoor gym league for 10- to 12-year-olds with different activities. You should check it out next time."

Sam grins. "I will! Thanks for running with me."

Mrs. Matthews thanks Lorna, then gently nudges Sam toward the car. Sam waves enthusiastically as they drive away, her face still lit with joy.

Lorna quickly changes, exits the gym through the glass doors, and heads to her car. She tosses her duffle bag into the back seat and sinks into the driver's seat. The parking lot is thinning as the Arizona sunset bathes the scene in warm, golden hues.

As she prepares to drive, she notices a car passing. The driver, silhouetted in the fading light, turns and stares at her longer than expected. Lorna shakes her head, dismissing the moment.

She starts the engine, then glances at her blue binder on the passenger seat. Putting the car back in park, she opens the binder. It contains research she's collected about her past: hospital documents, state certificates, name searches, and photos of people resembling her, with handwritten question marks on the glossy prints.

One page is a printout of the Armstrong Library homepage, featuring its mix of old wood, ancient texts, and advanced technology. Another page shows Lorna's handwritten notes:

- *Why was I put up for adoption?*
- *Why are there so many dead-ends?*
- *Tonight, I'll look for old, unscanned records.*

Her phone beeps. It's a text from Brianna: *Are you still going to make it by 7?*

Lorna replies, *No, I told Chelsea I'll be late. Just a quick shower, check on Tigger, and I'll be out the door. Sorry!*

Brianna responds immediately: *Great... Thanks for making me wait... Hurry up I'm hungry!*

Lorna smiles and shakes her head, amused.

She drives home and entering her house, she pauses, expecting a greeting from her cat, Tigger, but is met with silence.

"Tigger?" she calls.

No response.

Her home is cozy and organized, with decor that hints at her travel dreams: a poster of hikers in the Swiss Alps, a coffee table book on Old England, and antique finds from estate sales.

In the kitchen, she notices a dirty coffee cup in the sink—a remnant of her rushed morning—and an oatmeal-caked lid lying on the tiled floor.

How did I not see this earlier?

She picks up the lid and places it in the sink. "Tigger?" she calls again, reminded of his skittish nature.

Tigger, a tiger-striped stray, had walked into her home and refused to leave when she first moved in. She'd wanted a dog, not a cat, and spent a week trying to shoo him out while brainstorming dog names. But Tigger never got the hint—and he won her over despite herself.

Lorna walks into the bedroom, her thoughts elsewhere, when a sudden meow breaks the silence. Startled, she bends down to peek under the bed and spots Tigger curled into a fluffy ball.

"Hey, Mr. Dummy. What are you doing under there?" she says, scooping him up. "Since when do you hide under the bed, huh?"

She places Tigger on the bed and heads to the bathroom for a quick shower. Afterward, she changes into a black skirt and a flowy blue top. "Have an interesting day?" she asks the cat as she brushes her hair and hurries to finish getting ready before Brianna texts again complaining about her hunger.

12

Chapter Twelve

Sitting on the edge of the bed, she slips on a pair of heels, touches up her makeup, and gives Tigger a parting command. "You're in charge while I'm gone. Keep an eye on the place." She heads out the door, chuckling to herself at her little routine.

Lorna gets into her car and sets off to meet her friends for dinner. The Arizona night sky is stunning, with stars twinkling brightly above. As she drives, her thoughts drift to her earlier time with Sam. The little girl's words still echo in her mind, pulling at her emotions and leaving her with a deeper resolve to uncover answers about her own past. She looks forward to the next visit at the library to continue her search.

Arriving at Rembrandt's, a chic restaurant in the revitalized merchant district only ten minutes from her house, Lorna admires its modern stone façade and the stylish crowd bustling in and out. The restaurant's high demand makes reservations a must, and outings like this are a rare indulgence for her and her friends.

Stepping inside, Lorna exudes a calm confidence, even knowing she's late. She wouldn't trade her time with Sam for anything. After scanning the busy dining room, she spots Chelsea and Brianna seated at a cozy table near the back.

"Look who finally decided to join us," Brianna quips as Lorna approaches.

"Took a few extra minutes, chill," Lorna replies, sliding into her seat with a playful smile. "Something came up at the gym last minute. Sorry…" Her grin softens the apology.

Brianna smirks and fakes waving an invisible palm frond absolving Lorna of her tardiness, "Yeah, yeah, you're forgiven."

Lorna looks around. "So... Anna? Where is she?"

"She texted me that she couldn't make it," Chelsea says, glancing up from her menu.

"Aww, I was looking forward to catching up with her. It's been weeks since we talked," Lorna says, frowning slightly. "Does she seem distracted to you lately?"

Chelsea flips a page in the menu. "Maybe. I mean, she's been busy. Lots of work, I think."

Lorna nods. "She probably misses home. She's from Ukraine, remember? That must be tough."

Brianna adds, "I bet it is. I love her accent, though."

"Me too. She's such a sweet person," Lorna says warmly.

Just then, their waiter approaches, dressed in sleek black slacks, a dark blue button-up, and a gray tie. "Good evening, ladies. I'm Donald, and I'll be taking care of you tonight. Have you decided on appetizers?"

Chelsea flirts lightly. "What do you recommend?"

Donald smiles. "The stuffed mushrooms are a favorite."

"Sounds perfect," Brianna agrees, and Lorna nods in approval.

"Great, I'll get those right out," Donald says, disappearing toward the kitchen.

Lorna turns to Chelsea with a sly smile. "By the way, you're paying for that, remember?"

Chelsea groans sarcastically, "Oh, yes... I haven't forgotten."

Brianna teases, "A little flirty there, Chelsea. I thought you swore off men for now?"

"I don't need the distraction," Chelsea fires back, deflecting the comment. Then, turning to Lorna, she asks, "So, when are you getting rid of that annoying cat of yours? What's his name again? Felix?"

"Tigger," Lorna corrects with a laugh.

"Like from the cartoon?" Brianna asks, smirking.

"Exactly," Lorna replies with mock exasperation. "And to answer your question, I have no idea when—or if—I'll get rid of him. Honestly, I've tried everything short of throwing him out of a moving car. He's like feline superglue."

Chelsea chuckles at the comment, then suddenly remembers, "Oh, by the way, Sean said to say hi."

"Oh, you saw him?" Lorna asks, curiosity piqued.

"Yep," Chelsea replies casually, shaking her head.

Brianna grins mischievously. "So, Chelsea, when are you two finally going to admit the obvious?"

"The obvious what?" Chelsea volleys back, a slight edge of suspicion in her voice.

"You know," Brianna presses with a Cheshire Cat smile. "When are you two going to admit you *like-like* each other?"

"Not my type," Chelsea retorts without missing a beat, looking down at her menu in an effort to end the conversation.

Sean, a mutual friend, had been hinting at an interest in Chelsea, and the three of them knew it, though Chelsea seemed determined to dodge the topic.

"Oh, you have a type now?" Lorna teases, winking at Brianna.

The three women laugh, the conversation light and full of camaraderie. Lorna glances around the bustling restaurant, taking a sip of water. Her eyes drift toward the bar, and she freezes when she catches sight of the blond guy from the gym. Sitting alone at the far end of the chicly designed bar, looking at the menu. For the second time today, their eyes lock briefly before he looks away.

"Hey, Chelse," Lorna whispers, her voice carrying an exaggerated air of mystery.

"What?" Chelsea whispers back, mirroring her tone with playful cheesiness.

"It's that blond guy from the wall," Lorna says, leaning slightly closer.

"What?!" Chelsea exclaims, her volume rising significantly.

"Shh!" Lorna hisses, hiding her face behind the menu in embarrassment. "Thanks for not being loud or obvious."

Chelsea smirks, peeking over her own menu. "Yep, that's him. How about that?" She looks over at Brianna, who is already forming a mischievous grin.

"Well, now," Brianna chimes in with perfect timing. "Look who has an admirer."

Both Lorna and Chelsea turn to her, unimpressed by her smugness. Chelsea raises a brow. "Maybe it's just a coincidence. Or, hey, maybe he's interested in *you,*" she suggests with a teasing nudge at Lorna.

Before Lorna can respond, their waiter arrives with a large, steaming plate. "Ladies, here's your appetizer," he says as he places the dish on the table. The smell of stuffed mushrooms wafts invitingly, distracting Brianna and Chelsea just as Lorna glances back at the bar. The blond guy is still there, though he looks deep in thought.

Interesting coincidence... or something more?

"Excuse me," Lorna says suddenly, standing up. "I need to use the restroom."

Chelsea tosses down her napkin. "Want me to go with you?"

"No, thanks. I think I can manage on my own," Lorna replies, rolling her eyes playfully before walking toward the restrooms.

As Lorna leaves, Brianna turns to Chelsea, leaning conspiratorially across the table. "Why do we always go to the bathroom in pairs? Is it some societal thing to distract women while men sneak bites of food?"

Chelsea shakes her head, giving Brianna a *you-did-not-just-say-that* look. Their waiter, trying not to laugh, says, "I'll leave you ladies to enjoy your appetizers," before retreating.

Meanwhile, Lorna weaves through the crowded restaurant, doing her best to avoid eye contact. She's acutely aware of the blond man's possible gaze and quickens her pace toward the restroom

Inside, she finds a woman putting the finishing touches on her eyeliner. The stranger caps the eyeliner, tosses it in her purse, gives herself a wink in the mirror, and exits, leaving Lorna alone.

Lorna washes her hands and glances at her reflection. She offers herself a small smile, shaking her head in amusement. *What am I even doing?* With a deep breath, she collects her tiny handbag and steps back into the hallway.

Just as she's about to turn the corner, she nearly bumps into a tall, dark-haired man who seems to appear out of nowhere. He smiles politely.

"Excuse me," Lorna says with a quick nod, stepping aside.

But before she can move on, he speaks. "I'm sorry to bother you, but... you look really familiar. Lorna, right?" His New York accent adding to the intrigue.

"Uh, yes," she replies, turning to face him fully. "Do I know you?"

"My name's Vincent," he explains. "I dabble in real estate, and I saw one of your cards at an office earlier today." He pauses, momentarily distracted by something behind her.

"Yes?" Lorna prompts, curious.

"Sorry," Vincent says, refocusing. "I was saying I'm learning about the market here and could use some advice. Maybe you could help?"

Lorna nods politely. "Here's my card. Feel free to reach out. I need to get back to my friends now."

"Of course," Vincent says with a charming smile. "Nice meeting you."

As Lorna walks back to her table, she glances over her shoulder and notices Vincent looking in the direction of the blond guy, who now appears to be getting up from his seat. Turning back, she realizes Vincent has vanished from the hallway.

Must've gone to the bathroom.

When Lorna returns to her table, she sees the blond man leaving the restaurant. *Maybe he was too shy to say hello.* The thought lingers as she reengages herself in the lively conversation with her friends.

Later during dinner, the conversation turns serious. "I know someone has to pay for it, Chelsea. And I completely agree that we don't want to overburden the city council with yet another group looking for a handout," Lorna says, leaning forward slightly as she interjects.

"Wait a second! 'Another handout'?" Brianna counters, clearly irritated. "Some of those so-called handouts are the only lifelines people have."

"Are they all necessary?" Chelsea challenges. "The problem is, over time, we've become increasingly dependent on the government for these things. Even efforts like the Phoenix Children's Home are hindered because they don't have enough buy-in from individuals and communities to really be effective."

Brianna's eyes narrow. "Okay, Chelsea, so tell me this: how exactly do we pay for 'things' like helping single moms below the poverty line or homeless kids living on the street?"

Chelsea finishes chewing her bite of food and shifts gears with a smile. "First of all, this food is incredible. Great choice coming to Rembrandt's," she says, prompting a round of agreement from the others. Then she continues, "Secondly, people forget that historically, a lot of these services weren't provided by the government at all. They were managed by local churches or charities."

"That's a nice thought," Brianna retorts, crossing her arms, "but let's be real. We're too far gone to go back to that system. People are overwhelmed as it is, and nonprofits are stretched thin. We have to figure out how to help people within the system we actually have."

Lorna jumps in, her voice firm. "I don't have all the answers to Phoenix's problems, but I do know this: something has to be done for those kids at the Phoenix Children's Home. The city council's hands-off approach is infuriating, especially since their reason for not helping is that the home is faith-based. It's ridiculous!"

Chelsea raises a brow. "But you're not even part of that church or denomination."

"No, I'm not," Lorna admits, her voice softening. "But the Rittens didn't care about that when they gave me a chance. Two individuals—not the government—chose to step in and make my life better.

I wouldn't be here without them." Her voice cracks slightly, and she stops, taking a deep breath.

A quiet pause settles over the table, heavy with unspoken thoughts, until Chelsea breaks the silence. "You know," she says gently, "I've always thought of the Rittens as your real parents. It's hard for me to imagine it being any other way. I can't begin to understand what that must feel like for you."

Chelsea looks at Lorna with admiration. "And for what it's worth, I really admire how you handle everything, especially not knowing the full truth about your past."

The tension dissolves into a mutual smile among the three friends, just as their waiter, Donald, arrives with the check. "Here you go, ladies," he says cheerfully, placing the bill folder on the table. "I'll pick it up whenever you're ready."

The women pull out their credit cards as Lorna continues. "Chelsea, I appreciate what you said, and I agree individuals need to step up. But I also believe the government has a role to play. That's why I've set up a meeting next week with some city council members."

"Really?" Brianna asks, intrigued. "Think it'll work?"

Before Lorna can answer, the waiter returns. "All set here?" Chelsea hands him the folder with a smile. "Here you go, Donald," she says.

"I'll take care of this for you," Donald replies, heading off to process the payment.

Brianna shifts the conversation to something lighter. "Anyone up for a late movie? That one with the guy and the... thing? You know, it's like attached to him, but not really. And it stars that cute actor who went to rehab a couple of years ago... What was his name?"

Chelsea rolls her eyes. "Bree, you just described half the movies released in the last decade."

Lorna laughs. "Sounds tempting, but I think I'm going to head to the library and then home."

"The library?" Chelsea asks, surprised.

"Yeah," Lorna says, her tone more serious. "Lately, I've been trying to dig deeper into my past. It's been bothering me more than usual."

She hesitates, clearly nervous. "I just don't understand why I ended up for adoption. The more I try to find answers, the more questions I uncover."

Donald returns with their cards. "Here are your cards, ladies. I split everything except the appetizer. So, who's Lorna?"

"That's me," Lorna says, raising her hand.

"Chelsea?" he asks, handing over the next card.

Chelsea grins. "Present."

"And that leaves Brianna," he finishes, handing her the last card.

"Thanks. Great service," Brianna says politely as she tucks her card away.

Donald smiles. "My pleasure. Hope to see you ladies again at Rembrandt's."

As he walks away, Chelsea turns back to Lorna. "So, what were you saying?"

Lorna exhales, gathering her thoughts. "I just really want to know. It's that simple. The reality is, there are two people out there who brought me into this world and left me. I've made peace with the family I have now, but not having closure about *why* is hard. I need to find out."

Her friends nod, the conversation momentarily heavy again as they finish signing their receipts.

As they leave the restaurant and head to their cars, Chelsea stops and turns to Lorna. "I'm really glad you told us. I hope you get the answers you're looking for."

Brianna adds warmly, "Me too. You know we love you, girl."

Lorna smiles, pulling them both into a hug before climbing into her car.

Lorna pulls open the door, and slides into the driver's seat with a soft sigh. The blue, three-ring binder she had been carrying rests on the passenger seat, catching her eye. She reaches for it, flipping it open to a section of handwritten notes and photocopied documents she has carefully collected over time.

13

Chapter Thirteen

Her eyes scan the pages, her brow furrowing slightly as she revisits the same unresolved questions that have haunted her for years. Each bullet point and scribbled margin feels like a whisper from the past, urging her to uncover the elusive truth about her origins.

Frustration bubbles up as she taps her fingers against the steering wheel, wishing for even the smallest breakthrough. The silence of the car is comforting, but Lorna remains oblivious to the fact that she is no longer entirely alone. Unseen, someone in the distance has fixed their gaze on her, observing her movements with a quiet intensity.

Unaware of the presence, Lorna eventually exhales deeply and closes the binder, setting it back down. She starts the ignition, and the soft rumble of the engine hums against the quiet night. Shifting into gear, she eases out of the parking lot, merging onto the main road. Ahead of her, Phoenix glimmers under the cloak of evening, its skyline a tapestry of twinkling lights that only reveal their full magic once the sun dips below the horizon.

As she drives through the city, the buzz of nightlife begins to surround her. Neon signs flicker, casting vibrant hues onto the sidewalks where groups of people laugh and stroll. Phoenix feels alive in a way that only the night can evoke—a glittering, electric version of itself that seems worlds away from the bustling heat of the day. Lorna, however, barely notices the beauty around her. Her mind is occupied, churning with thoughts about the avenues she might explore once she arrives at the library.

She mentally reviews her plan of action: old microfiche archives, directories, genealogy databases, and unscanned documents that might hold a sliver of new information. She hopes against hope that tonight will yield something—a name, a clue, a connection she hasn't yet considered. Determined, she tightens her grip on the steering wheel and presses on, the shimmering cityscape reflected in her windshield as Phoenix stretches out before her, full of possibilities and secrets yet to be uncovered.

...

The sound of footsteps echoes through the hallway, louder and heavier this time. Lorna's heart races as she realizes it's more than one person—or thing—approaching. The steady thud grows ominous, reverberating off the walls, signaling the arrival of something significant. Fear tightens in her chest, her mind spinning with possibilities. After everything she's already witnessed, she can only imagine what might come next.

The rhythmic pounding crescendos, accompanied by an unsettling noise, like garbled communication in a language she cannot understand. Then, they appear. Not one, but three massive, metal-clad figures emerge from the shadows. They look like futuristic knights, their armor sleek and reflective, their forms towering and menacing. Each holds a rifle, the barrels gleaming under the faint hallway lights, and all three raise their weapons in unison, pointing them directly at her.

The tension is unbearable. Lorna braces herself, convinced this is the end. The silence between the heavy thumps of her heartbeat is deafening. Just as it feels like they're about to fire, a commanding voice cuts through the air with startling clarity.

"STOP!"

The voice, firm yet feminine, holds undeniable authority. From behind the armored figures steps a strikingly beautiful woman. Her appearance is unlike anything Lorna has ever seen. She is dressed in a sleek, futuristic jumpsuit that clings to her form, clearly functional yet elegant, with subtle panels and illuminated lines suggesting advanced technology. Her poise is confident, her movements fluid and purposeful.

The knights lower their weapons immediately, snapping to attention as the woman strides past them. Without hesitation, she approaches Lorna, who is still pinned beneath the heavy bookcase.

...

Arriving at the historic Armstrong Library, Lorna can't help but admire the grandeur of its design. The exterior looks like a massive red-brick fortress, rising four stories tall and bordered by ornate granite stonework that lines the roof and frames the building's corners. It stands as an architectural ode to a bygone era, blending strength and elegance in equal measure.

Lorna ascends the broad stone steps leading to the entrance, her heels clicking rhythmically against the polished surface. Each step resonates with purpose as she approaches the enormous double doors, crafted from weathered oak and reinforced with black wrought iron. These doors, imposing and steadfast, creak slightly as she pushes through them, welcoming her into the hallowed halls of knowledge.

Inside, the library is a study in contrasts compared to its blocky exterior. Dark, polished wood dominates the interior framework, giving the space a warm, timeless elegance. The bookshelves, meticulously lacquered, stretch endlessly toward the ceiling, and the walls are lined with real wood panels, adding to the ambiance of stately refinement.

For some, the smell of aged wood and leather-bound books might seem stuffy, but to Lorna, it's intoxicating. The aroma mingles with the faint scent of old paper and the polished leather chairs scattered throughout, creating a sensory experience that invigorates her love of history and learning.

As she steps further into the library, the sheer magnitude of its design never fails to amaze her. The entrance atrium opens to reveal a four-story-high ceiling, capped by an awe-inspiring stained-glass skylight. The circular window, undoubtedly the work of a European master craftsman, depicts Moses standing on a boulder, holding the Ten Commandments before a gathering of the children of Israel. The vibrant hues of the glass are brought to life by the soft glow of the moonlight outside. Below the image, an inscription reads: *May those who seek knowledge, seek the Giver of knowledge.*

Lorna makes her way to the spiral staircase that ascends to the second level, marveling at the library's enormity as she climbs. With its unparalleled collection of books and resources, the Armstrong Library boasts the largest inventory in the state of Arizona, surpassing even the libraries of the University of Arizona and Arizona State.

This library is a haven for scholars, students, and seekers like Lorna. The library's subscription to virtually every public and private database available ensures a steady stream of visitors, especially college students on weekends. This is precisely why Lorna prefers her weekday visits, when the library is quieter, and the atmosphere more contemplative and serene.

Reaching the second floor, she passes the reference desk, a beautifully lacquered oak structure where Mrs. Velez, a kind and cheerful librarian, often works. Tonight is no exception. Seeing Lorna approach, Mrs. Velez waves warmly. "Hello, beautiful!" she calls out.

"Hi, Mrs. Velez," Lorna replies with a smile.

Mrs. Velez chuckles. "I'm always surprised to see you without a couple of fellas following you around. You're so stunning; it's a wonder you're not constantly being chased!"

"You're the beautiful one, Mrs. Velez," Lorna replies sincerely, causing the librarian to blush a deep red before returning to her work with renewed vigor.

As Lorna moves further along the floor, a set of oaken double doors catches her attention. A large sign above reads: *New Addition! The Armstrong Library's Art Collection.* Curious, she pauses, looks around, and then steps inside.

The room is a treasure trove of artistic expression. Paintings, sculptures, and multimedia installations line the pristine white walls and fill the space, each display carefully curated. Paintings from different eras are arranged chronologically on one side, while sculptures dominate the central area. Toward the back, a sleek metallic door bears a sign: *Rare*

Collections. Viewing by Appointment Only. Lorna has never noticed this door before.

Her curiosity piqued, she wonders, *What could be behind that door? The Ark of the Covenant?* Smirking to herself, she takes one last glance around the gallery before returning to her mission.

Finally, she makes her way to her usual spot in the lineage and biography section, which has become her second home in recent weeks. She noisily sets her belongings on a large wooden table, collapses into one of the sturdy leather-backed chairs, and scoots forward with a determined sigh. "Alright," she mutters under her breath. "Let's get busy."

Opening her blue binder, she flips to the page containing a photocopy of her birth certificate, leaving her belongings at the table as she ventures a few rows over in search of a specific book. Spotting her target, *Birth Records – Phoenix Vol. XIV,* she returns to her table, adding the hefty book to a stack of local magazines. Methodically, she begins her work.

The *Birth Records* volume contains photocopies of every birth certificate from area hospitals. Lorna compares her document—one given to her by her adoptive mother—to the records, flipping page after page. The same question beats relentlessly in her mind: *Why can't I find my birth certificate? Why can't I find my parents' names?*

Hours pass as she combs through the pages, her frustration mounting. Each photocopy is another dead end. Her efforts to trace her lineage have yielded nothing but more questions, and the familiar wall she keeps hitting feels taller and thicker than ever.

The section of the library is eerily quiet, with no one else around. She's tempted to let out a scream of sheer exasperation but resists. It's not her style, and besides, she wouldn't want to alarm Mrs. Velez.

Instead, Lorna takes a deep breath, refocuses, and flips to the next page. *One of these records has to hold some answers,* she tells herself. *It's just a matter of time, right?*

As the clock ticked closer to closing time, Mrs. Velez approached Lorna's table, her soft-soled shoes nearly silent on the polished wooden floor. "I'm sorry, sweetheart, but it's time," she said with a warm, apologetic smile.

"Thanks, Mrs. Velez," Lorna replied, her voice tinged with weariness. She began gathering her belongings, shuffling papers back into her blue binder. Another long, tedious evening of research had passed, but the gnawing hunger for answers remained. The same questions echoed relentlessly in her mind: *Who were my parents? Where do I come from? Why did they give me up?*

Descending the grand staircase to the first floor, Lorna noticed how much quieter the library had become. The emptiness amplified the sound of her heels clacking against the floor, the faint echo bouncing off the towering walls. As she walked beneath the stained-glass window depicting Moses, she felt the weight of his steady gaze, his figure standing as a timeless reminder of the search for knowledge.

Pushing open one of the heavy wooden doors, Lorna stepped into the cool night air, gripping her backpack tightly. She descended the wide stone steps and headed toward her car. The parking lot was sparsely populated, with a handful of patrons still getting into their vehicles. She glanced around, her eyes sweeping the area. Everything appeared ordinary at first glance.

As she clicked the keyless entry to unlock her car, a gray sedan caught her attention. Its windows were tinted so dark that nothing inside was visible. The car rolled slowly through the lot, moving just a hair slower than what seemed natural. Lorna's stomach tightened as her gaze followed it. She squinted, trying to make out anything through the windows, but all she could see was a shadowy silhouette. The figure inside seemed to be watching her.

The car's unnerving presence sent a flutter of unease through her. Butterflies churned in her stomach as she watched it finally roll out of sight. Despite its departure, the unsettling feeling lingered. Across the parking lot, she noticed another figure moving toward a car. She couldn't make out their features in the dim light, but their calm and deliberate movements didn't ease her anxiety.

"Yeah," she muttered sarcastically under her breath, "Yeah, that's not creepy."

Sliding into her car, she started the engine and headed home. As the night deepened, Lorna lay in bed, her thoughts racing. She briefly wondered about the blond man from the restaurant. Had he wanted to talk to her but been too shy? The thought flickered for a moment before giving way to the pressing questions that had consumed her in recent weeks. Her mind returned to the endless documents, the elusive records, and the unanswered questions as she drifted into a restless sleep.

Unbeknownst to her, a car idled down the street, its driver surveying the area. Another vehicle approached slowly, and its arrival seemed to prompt the first car to leave abruptly. The quiet neighborhood returned to stillness, but an undercurrent of mystery remained. Lorna's mind raced, but aided by her white noise machine, she finally drifted into slumber.

The following morning greeted Lorna with an overcast sky. Pulling into the office building of Aztec Realty, she took a moment to appreciate the familiar structure. A.R., as it was commonly called, was one of the largest and most respected real estate brokerages in the Phoenix area, located in the upscale suburb of the Highlands. Built by Larry and Mitzi Gronberg three decades earlier, the company had weathered the highs and lows of the real estate market. Despite recent challenges, Lorna had thrived in this environment, carving out a name for herself as a savvy and successful entrepreneur underneath this corporate shell.

Dressed in tailored slacks and a stylish blouse that exuded professional polish, Lorna carried a soft leather briefcase in one hand and a box of fresh bagels in the other. Her ensemble struck a perfect balance between business practicality and runway sophistication.

As she strode through the front doors, the cheerful receptionist, Claire—Mitzi's bubbly 19-year-old granddaughter—greeted her with a wide grin. "Morning, Lorna!"

"Good morning to you!" Lorna replied, placing the box of bagels on the desk. "And, I brought these little guys to keep that smile on your face."

Claire's grin widened, if that were possible, "No way! Are these from Linamens?"

"Oh, yes. The one and only," Lorna said, opening the box and handing Claire a bagel along with a tub of cream cheese shmeer.

"You're the best!" Claire squealed, already spreading cream cheese with glee.

Mission accomplished. Lorna smiled and made her way to her office. Once inside, she set down her briefcase, unpacked her laptop, and began checking her voicemail. The first two messages were forgettable: one about office supplies and another from a political campaign seeking her support.

The third message, however, caught her attention. A man's deep voice with a New York accent filled the room.

"Hello, Lorna? It's Vincent Burrell. We bumped into each other last night at Rembrandt's. I wanted to follow up with you about what we discussed. I'm in the market for some prime retail real estate, and since your company lists a lot of properties I'm interested in, I was hoping you could give me a call..." BEEP.

The message cut off abruptly. Moments later, the fourth message began, Vincent chuckling as he continued. "Guess I got cut off there. As I was saying, I'd love to discuss my needs with you. Here's my number..."

Lorna jotted down the number, leaning back in her chair to think. She hesitated for a moment before dialing.

After a few rings, Vincent's familiar voice answered, "Uh, hello?"

"Hi, Mr. Burrell. This is Lorna Ritten, returning your call."

"Oh, yeah, yeah! Great. Thanks for getting back to me," he said, his tone enthusiastic.

"I'd be happy to show you the properties you're interested in," Lorna offered. "What's your schedule like next week?"

Vincent hesitated briefly. "Next week? Hmm, well, I guess Tuesday works. That's five days away. Does that work for you?"

"That'll work," Lorna replied, sensing a faint urgency in his voice but deciding not to press further. "Yes, that works for me," Lorna replies, her tone professional yet accommodating. "But I'll need to know which properties you're interested in. Some are only available for viewing at specific times."

"Tell you what," Vincent says, his voice steady with confidence. "Why don't you meet me at my house on Tuesday at 9 a.m.? From there, we'll head out to see whatever properties are open. I'll email you the ones I'm interested in, and you can decide which ones we visit."

"That sounds fine," Lorna replies. "I'll plan to meet you then, Mr. Burrell—"

"Vin," he interrupts smoothly.

"Excuse me?"

"Most people just call me Vin," he clarifies.

"Alright, Vin," Lorna says, adapting easily.

"And don't worry, I'll have some fresh bagels for us," he adds casually. "I know a guy who gets them shipped in from back east. Keeps me stocked so I can have one for breakfast a few times a week."

"Bagels from back east? Sounds tempting," Lorna replies with a light laugh. "I doubt indulging in some bagels will ruin my diet too much. See you at 9 on Tuesday."

"9 it is," he confirms. Click.

Lorna sets the phone back in its cradle and opens her laptop, scrolling through her email to check for his list of properties and to review her schedule.

Her thoughts are interrupted when Mr. Gronberg, the co-owner of Aztec Realty, leans his head into her office. "Hey, kiddo, got a minute?"

"Always have one for you, Mr. Gronberg," Lorna replies warmly.

He steps inside, taking a seat in one of the guest chairs. Larry Gronberg exudes a seasoned charm—a blend of sharp business acumen and the affable demeanor of someone who's spent decades navigating the Phoenix real estate market.

"How are things going?" he asks, his voice carrying the familiarity of a mentor who genuinely cares. "You've been absolutely tearing it up in sales lately. Mitzi and I couldn't be happier. But, I wanted to check in with you about this meeting downtown."

Lorna sets her laptop aside, turning her attention fully to him. "I'm excited about it," she says, a hint of enthusiasm in her voice. "In fact, I was just about to head out." She starts gathering her things, slipping her laptop into her leather bag.

"That's what I wanted to talk to you about," Larry says, his tone shifting slightly. "You're going to be around some very powerful people. Speak your mind but be careful not to ruffle too many feathers. Aztec Realty has a strong reputation in the community, and we want to keep it that way. We've been supportive of this project, but politics can be tricky, and you know, perception matters."

Lorna pauses, sensing a rare vulnerability in her typically composed boss. "Mr. Gronberg," she says with a reassuring smile, "I promise I won't tip over the mayor's apple cart—or anyone else's for that matter. Besides, I'm an independent contractor, so you've got plausible deniability if I accidentally stir up trouble." That gets a smile out of him.

She lets her tone turn sincere. "But really, I appreciate you and Mitzi supporting the Phoenix Children's Home project. It means a lot to me."

"Thanks for saying that," Larry replies, his shoulders relaxing slightly. "You know we trust you completely. I guess being a father—for my kids and this business—makes me a little paranoid sometimes."

Lorna, now standing with her bag in hand, steps toward the door. Before leaving, she places a comforting hand on Larry's shoulder. "Don't worry, Mr. G. I'll kill them with kindness. We'll make you proud."

Larry chuckles softly, nodding his appreciation.

With that, Lorna strides confidently out of the office, ready to face whatever challenges await her downtown.

14

Chapter Fourteen

Lorna hops into her car gripping the steering wheel tightly as she maneuvers through the maze of downtown Phoenix traffic. Her mind is laser-focused on the meeting ahead, the most important of her career thus far. She weaves through the bustling streets with practiced precision, eventually pulling into the parking garage adjacent to the municipal building. Finding a spot on the third level, she grabs her bag and binder and steps out, her heels clicking rhythmically against the concrete floor as she makes her way toward the exit.

Crossing the busy street, she bounds up the wide concrete steps of the historic municipal building, her pace quickened by nerves and excitement. The building looms above her, its stone façade a symbol of authority and power. Inside, she navigates the security checkpoint, placing her bag on the conveyor belt and stepping through the metal detector. The guard waves her through, and she glances at her watch. One minute to spare.

"Wait!" she calls out as the elevator doors slide shut just as she reaches them. Her shoulders sag in frustration as she watches the elevator ascend without her. Looking around frantically, she spots a sign that offers a lifeline: *Stairs.*

Wasting no time, she pushes open the heavy door and begins sprinting up the stairwell, her heels echoing off the walls. Skipping every other step, she ascends three flights in record time. By the time she bursts through the door onto the third floor, her breathing is labored, and a sheen of sweat has formed on her forehead.

Standing in the corridor, she scans the signs on the doors until she spots it: *The Groutsen Conference Room.* She glances at her phone to check the time. Barely made it. Straightening her posture, she smooths her hair, adjusts her blouse, and takes a deep breath to steady herself. She wipes the perspiration from her forehead and plasters a confident smile on her face.

The Groutsen Conference Room is modest, to put it kindly. It's a clean, institutional space with white walls and fluorescent lighting that hums faintly. A long table dominates the room, surrounded by wheeled chairs that are just comfortable enough for short meetings. At one end of the table, a rectangular cutout reveals tangled A/V cables, and a large projector screen has already been pulled down for her presentation.

Lorna steps into the room, her smile unwavering. "Good morning!" she greets the room warmly.

The only occupants are County Commissioner Paul Adams, a seasoned politician of 61, and his young assistant, Dave, who looks barely older than 22. Both rise to shake her hand.

"Good to see you, Lorna," Commissioner Adams says with genuine friendliness. "Please, have a seat."

Lorna sets her materials on the table and glances around the room. "Uh, where is everyone?"

Adams chuckles. "Business leaders are rarely on time for these things. They like to blame it on the security downstairs. Can you believe that?"

Lorna laughs politely. "Hard to imagine," she replies, though she suspects he's not entirely joking.

The door swings open, and in stroll four business leaders, their chatter filling the room as they take their seats. Trailing behind them, exuding charm and authority, is Phoenix Mayor Plaxico Brown. At 55, Plaxico's background in private-sector business has translated seamlessly into his political career. He's every bit the politician, effortlessly commanding attention with his polished demeanor and quick wit.

Once everyone is seated, Commissioner Adams stands to introduce the attendees. “Ladies and gentlemen, we’re joined today by an impressive group. We have Julian Hegel, owner of our largest local chain of car dealerships. Matt McKoncle, founder of a prominent construction firm and a significant landowner in and around Phoenix. Barbara Lopez, CEO of the Southwest’s top PR firm, Stride. And Jeremy Hodges, a senior VP at IGHD Mobile, part of the larger IGHD corporate umbrella.”

After a round of pleasantries, Adams turns the spotlight to Lorna. “Now, I have to say, this young woman deserves a round of applause for managing to get all of you into the same room at the same time. That’s no small feat. How’d you pull that off, Lorna?”

She smiles and shrugs modestly as Adams continues. “Without further ado, Lorna Ritten.” He offers a golf clap, joined by a smattering of applause from the room.

The butterflies in Lorna’s stomach intensify, but she channels her nervous energy into the presentation she’s meticulously prepared. She steps to the head of the table, clicks the remote, and begins.

“First, I want to thank all of you for taking time out of your busy schedules to hear this proposal,” she says, her voice steady and clear.

Before she can fully dive in, Mayor Brown interjects with a teasing remark. “It’s a miracle she got all of us here! Last time I saw this group together was at my inauguration. Well, everyone except you, Jeremy. Remind me again, where were you that day?”

Jeremy offers a tight smile, gesturing for Lorna to continue. “We’re here for her, Mayor.”

Plaxico smirks but falls silent, allowing Lorna to proceed.

She dives into her pitch, her passion for the Phoenix Children’s Home evident in every word. Slide after slide showcases compelling images of the home’s work over the years, highlighting its impact on the community and the dire need for funding. She outlines her vision: repairs to the historic building, an annual budget to sustain operations, and programs to support education and job training.

Her proposal includes turning the home into a hub for adults seeking GEDs, as well as building a professional-grade kitchen that could serve both the children and the city's hungry while offering culinary training programs for the unemployed.

The room is silent, the audience captivated. Lorna's confidence and dedication shine through, but the lack of immediate feedback unnerves her. *Do they hate it?* she wonders, her mind racing. *Just finish strong, shake their hands, and leave.*

Fifteen minutes later, Lorna wrapped up her presentation with the slide every PowerPoint user knows well: *Thank you for coming. Any Questions?* The words glowed on the screen as she turned to face the room with a bright yet slightly nervous smile.

Lorna nodded at Dave, who flipped a switch to bring the lights back up. She scanned the room, her hands clasped in front of her. "So... any questions?" Her voice was steady, but her heart raced.

The room fell silent. No one moved.

Then, from the far end of the table, a slow clap broke the tension. Lorna turned toward the sound, her breath catching as she saw it was Mayor Plaxico Brown. His applause was deliberate, his face showing emotion he could barely contain. His eyes were red-rimmed, and it was clear he had been moved during her presentation.

The applause spread, first tentatively, then growing in volume and enthusiasm. Soon, everyone in the room was standing and clapping, their faces a mix of admiration and respect. The small, sterile conference room, so institutional and bland just moments before, now radiated warmth and energy.

"Young lady," the mayor began, his voice thick with emotion. "I grew up in the poor part of town, not far from Phoenix Children's Home. My mother raised me by herself, and we didn't have much. Many of my school friends were kids from that home."

The room fell silent, everyone visibly moved by the mayor's vulnerability. His words hung in the air, heavy with sincerity.

"I know that a lot of people at this table feel the same way I do," the mayor continued, his tone growing sharper. "But some of them will still find excuses—reasons why they or their companies can't get involved. I'm looking at you, Jeremy."

Jeremy Hodges, a senior VP at IGHD Mobile, bristled at the comment. "Plax, give it a rest," he shot back. "IGHD Mobile has a long history of philanthropic efforts—"

"Oh, you mean like that downtown playground your company pledged to build? The one that's still a vacant lot?" interrupted Matt McKoncle, the construction mogul.

"Please, Matt," Barbara Lopez, the PR executive, cut in. "It's not like you ever donate to the arts programs or—"

Before Lorna could process what was happening, the room dissolved into a cacophony of bickering voices. Arguments overlapped, tempers flared, and accusations flew across the table. Lorna's eyes widened in disbelief as she watched her carefully planned meeting spiral out of control. Dave, the young assistant, pressed himself against the wall like a frightened kitten, his wide eyes darting between the combatants.

"ALRIGHT, ALRIGHT!" Commissioner Adams's booming voice cut through the chaos. "EVERYONE, CALM DOWN! NOW!"

The room stilled, though a few muttered jabs were exchanged as the attendees grudgingly settled back into their seats.

"Thank you," Adams said firmly, his tone leaving no room for further interruptions. He turned to Lorna, his expression softening. "Miss Ritten, I want to thank you again for coming and presenting today. Please know we'll coordinate with your team in the next 24 hours to schedule a follow-up meeting. Now, I believe you have something for everyone as they leave?"

Lorna nodded, still rattled but determined to maintain her composure. "Yes, thank you all for attending," she said, her voice quieter than usual.

As the attendees began to leave, Lorna handed each of them a glossy folder from her briefcase. The materials detailed her proposal in greater depth, complete with financial breakdowns, timelines, and testimonials from those impacted by Phoenix Children's Home.

Most of the attendees took the folders without much acknowledgment, clearly eager to escape the room and their rivals. The mayor was the last to leave, pausing beside Lorna. He took his folder, leaned in, and said softly, "Don't let this little spat discourage you. I believe in what you're doing. Give it time, and we'll make this happen." He gave her a reassuring wink before stepping out.

When the door closed behind him, Lorna turned to see Dave still pressed against the wall.

"You okay, Dave?" she asked, a slight smirk playing on her lips.

"Uh, yeah. Fine," he mumbled, his voice barely audible.

Adams approached, clapping Dave lightly on the shoulder. "Don't worry about him, Miss Ritten. Ole Davey here's been with me for two weeks. He's not quite used to the political world yet. Are you, Dave?"

"No, sir," Dave replied sheepishly.

The commissioner shifted his focus to Lorna. "Listen, you did great in there. This is a bold initiative, and I respect the heck out of you for pursuing it. But I won't sugarcoat it—this won't be easy. There'll be more meetings like this, with more yelling and grandstanding. It's the nature of the beast. But if anyone can push this through, it's you."

Lorna took a deep breath, nodding. "Thank you for all your support, Commissioner. Couldn't have done this without you."

Adams smiled. "My pleasure. We'll be in touch soon about the next meeting. Have a good day."

As he and Dave gathered their belongings and headed for the door, Lorna called out, "Mr. Adams?"

He turned back, raising a brow.

"I WILL get everyone back. Even Jeremy Hodges."

The commissioner's smile widened. "If anyone can do it, it's you."

15

Chapter Fifteen

With that, he disappeared down the hallway, leaving Lorna alone in the now-empty room. She packed her materials, turned off the lights, and locked the door behind her.

Outside, the weather had turned gray and damp, a reflection of her mixed emotions. She crossed the street to her car, climbed inside, and sat for a moment, replaying the meeting in her mind. Despite the tensions, she felt a flicker of hope.

She decided not to drop by the Phoenix Children's Home just yet, opting instead to send a text to Marie, the home's director: *The meeting went well. More to come soon.* She didn't want Marie to sense any worry she might be feeling.

After returning a few business calls, Lorna decided to call it an early day. She drove to the gym, eager to clear her head and process the events of the morning.

As she entered the gym, she spotted Sam on a treadmill, jogging and laughing at the midday animated show playing on the screen. Lorna smiled, her resolve strengthening. *For kids like Sam, this is worth it,* she thought, heading to the locker room.

Lorna entered the locker room, the faint smell of gym disinfectant and sweat hanging in the air like a well-worn shroud. The space was nearly deserted except for the distant, muffled chatter of a few climbers preparing their gear. She quickly changed into her climbing attire, methodically securing her harness and double-checking her climbing hooks before heading towards the imposing indoor mountain wall.

The climbing area was quiet, almost eerily so, with only two others scaling the wall. Lorna glanced upward as she fastened her belay line, and then her stomach tightened. The blond man was back. Her heart skipped as she watched him move with an effortless grace up the wall.

He turned suddenly, catching her staring. Their eyes locked, and time seemed to halt, her breath caught in her chest. He gave her a warm smile. Lorna blinked, feeling her face flush under his gaze, and she raised a tentative hand to wave. But as she did, a new awareness hit her—it wasn't the enigmatic blond man from before. This climber looked remarkably similar but possessed softer features.

He waved at her, his expression friendly, and she waved back, her gesture clumsy and hesitant.

I am such an idiot, she thought, cringing inwardly. Just keep climbing.

Throwing herself into the climb, she concentrated on the rhythm of her movements, gripping the holds with determined tenacity. Yet, the awkward encounter lingered, her focus waning. Cutting her session short by thirty minutes, she retreated to the now-empty locker room, her thoughts troubled.

Once dressed and ready to leave, Lorna stepped out into the parking lot, her eyes instinctively scanning her surroundings. Nothing seemed amiss, but she couldn't shake the sensation of being watched.

Sliding into her car, she started the engine, deciding to treat herself to a smoothie. The thought of a refreshing strawberry-banana protein blend helped quell her nerves as she navigated the still streets.

As she approached the store, Lorna adjusted her rearview mirror—and freezes. A familiar gray sedan with heavily tinted windows catches her eye. Her pulse quickens as she narrows her eyes, trying to confirm what she's seeing.

The sedan is maintaining a steady distance, always lingering four to six car lengths behind her. She tests it, turning right at the next intersection. The sedan mirrors her movement, its deliberate pace unsettling her.

Lorna pulls into the parking lot of her favorite smoothie shop, parking near the large plate-glass windows at the front of the store. She waits, watching her peripherals for any sign of the car. To her relief, the gray sedan doesn't follow her into the lot. After a moment, she steps out of her car and heads inside.

The familiar hum of blenders greets her as she approaches the counter.

"Hey, Lorna," George Stevens, the store's owner, calls out with a grin. A fit and energetic 48-year-old, George is one of her favorite clients.

"Hi, Mr. Stevens," she replies warmly.

"George," he corrects, handing her the smoothie before she can place her order. "The usual. Strawberry-banana protein blend."

Lorna pulls out her wallet. "Let me pay you this time, Mr. Stev—George."

He waves her off with a firm gesture. "Put that away! You hooked me up big time with that property on Pine and Reever. This one's on the house."

Lorna tries again, offering him the money, but he shakes his head. "Eh, enough already! Just enjoy it. And tell everyone you know who makes the best smoothies in town!"

She laughs. "There's no doubt about it. Best smoothies in the country!" She grabs her drink and heads toward the door.

"Don't be a stranger now!" George calls after her. "Call ahead, and I'll have another one waiting for you!"

Back in her car, Lorna sips her smoothie, savoring the perfectly balanced flavors as she drives toward the Armstrong Library. Checking her rearview mirror, she scans for the gray sedan. It's gone. For now.

Pulling into the library parking lot, Lorna shuts off the engine and takes a moment to steel herself. She looks into the mirror and murmurs, "Ready to bang your head against the wall again?" With a resigned smile, she grabs her bag and heads inside, resisting the urge to glance over her shoulder as she crosses the lot.

Inside the quiet library, Lorna dives into her work, pouring over hospital birth records and registries. Hours pass as she painstakingly compares names and dates, her eyes scanning each document for anything that might unlock the secrets of her past.

But the longer she searches, the more intrusive her thoughts become. The familiar questions creep in, relentless and unyielding.

Were the Rittens hiding something? Could they know more about my adoption than they're telling me?

Lorna pushes the doubts aside, but they resurface with greater intensity.

Who am I? Where do I come from? What's my real mother's name?

Frustration builds as her search yields nothing new. Her heart aches with the weight of uncertainty, her unanswered questions swirling in her mind.

Eventually, Mrs. Velez approaches, her presence gentle and reassuring. She places a hand on Lorna's shoulder and says softly, "Time to lock up, sweetheart."

Lorna exhales, closing the folder in front of her. "Okay," she says, her voice tinged with exhaustion.

As Mrs. Velez turns to leave, Lorna calls out, "Mrs. Velez?"

The older woman stops and looks back. "Yes, dear?"

"Thank you. For always being so sweet to me. I really appreciate it." Lorna offers a tired but genuine smile.

Mrs. Velez steps closer, her motherly warmth evident. "Honey, I know you're looking for answers. I understand how frustrating it can be."

Lorna gives a small laugh, gesturing to her stack of papers and notes. "I guess coming to this section every night with my little notebook gave it away, huh?"

Mrs. Velez chuckles. "Sweetheart, I've been around the block a time or two. Believe me, if you keep at it, you'll find the answers you're looking for. It just takes time."

Lorna nods, her heart swelling with gratitude. "Thanks, Mrs. Velez. For everything."

"You're welcome, dear. Now get some rest." With a kind smile, Mrs. Velez walks away, leaving Lorna alone with her thoughts.

Mrs. Velez gives Lorna's shoulders a loving squeeze before walking away, her comforting presence lingering in the air like a warm embrace. As she heads toward the exit, her path intersects with Brian Highfill, the library's distinguished Art Collections curator. Highfill, ever the picture of polished sophistication, steps aside courteously.

"Pardon me," he says in his refined British accent, each word laced with the precision that only an elite upbringing could produce.

Mrs. Velez giggles lightly, her face momentarily brightened by the charm of his voice. She continues on her way, unable to resist the allure of a proper British gentleman.

Highfill stands momentarily, balancing a briefcase in one hand and a larger, leather-bound bag in the other. His gaze drifts toward Lorna, who has been observing the exchange with quiet curiosity. Their eyes meet, his expression cold and unreadable. The intensity of his stare unnerves her, and she looks away first, feeling oddly defeated.

With Mrs. Velez no longer blocking his path, Highfill strides purposefully down the corridor, disappearing behind a wall toward the elevators.

Not exactly the warmest guy in the world, Lorna muses. *I guess that's what years at Oxford or Cambridge or Hogwarts does to you.*

Shaking off the moment, she gathers her belongings, slipping her notebook and laptop into her bag, and makes her way outside.

16

Chapter Sixteen

The parking lot is sparsely populated, the once-bustling library now eerily quiet as the last patrons and employees trickle out. Most cars have gone, but a few remain scattered across the darkened expanse. Lorna realizes she parked near the back earlier in the evening, requiring her to cross several rows to reach her car.

As she walks, her footsteps echo faintly against the cool night air. She's two rows away from her vehicle when the sudden screech of tires breaks the silence.

The sound snaps her head up, and she turns toward the source—a car barreling through the lot at an alarming speed. Its shape is a blur, but as it draws closer, her stomach drops.

The gray car!

Her body freezes for an instant, her mind racing. The car's headlights pierce through the darkness, locking onto her like a predator targeting its prey.

Before she can react, a dark figure bursts into her peripheral vision, moving with impossible speed. The screeching tires grow louder, closer. Lorna squints her eyes shut, bracing for impact.

A powerful force jerks her body, pulling her sideways. The sound of metal grinding against something fills her ears, and then—NOTHING.

Time seems to slow as her body becomes weightless. Her eyes crack open for a fleeting moment. She's parallel to the ground, her surroundings a chaotic blur of motion. Her brain registers the fall, but her nerves haven't yet caught up.

The slope of an embankment looms ahead, rushing toward her. She braces for the impact, squeezing her eyes shut again, but it never comes.

Instead, everything fades to black.

When consciousness returns, Lorna's eyelids flutter open, allowing a sliver of light to invade her senses. The brightness is overwhelming, forcing her to squint as she struggles to orient herself. The blurry shapes above her slowly sharpen, revealing the sterile gleam of hospital instruments and other medical equipment.

Her vision clears, and she takes in her surroundings. She's lying in a hospital bed, the top sheet pulled up to her chest. The light blue of her standard-issue hospital gown catches her eye, and she instinctively brushes her hand over the fabric.

Sliding her legs over the edge of the bed, she rises slowly, her body still weak. She makes her way to a small bathroom nearby, flipping on the light switch. The mirror reflects a pale face with tired eyes – a shell of her normally vibrant self. The left side of her forehead is bandaged, the white gauze stark against her skin.

"I'm in the hospital?" she murmurs aloud, the words sounding foreign to her ears.

Fragments of memory flash through her mind—the gray car, the squeal of tires, the shadowy figure. The adrenaline rushes back as she recalls the dark silhouette standing just before the impact. A shiver runs down her spine, the room suddenly feeling colder.

"That car tried to hit me..." she whispers, her voice trembling. "I'm not safe."

The memories come in fits and starts, vivid but incomplete, like pieces of a broken puzzle.

Her thoughts are interrupted by a soft but firm voice. "Miss, please get back into bed."

Lorna turns, startled, to see a nurse silhouetted in the doorway. The woman steps closer, her expression a mix of concern and practiced compassion.

"Sweetheart, you need to rest," the nurse says gently, reaching for Lorna's arm to guide her.

Lorna nods, her legs wobbling slightly as she allows herself to be led back to the bed. "Yeah, that's probably a good idea. My head is killing me."

The nurse helps her settle in, adjusting the pillows and tucking the blanket around her. "There you go. Just relax, dear."

Lorna looks up at her, her voice soft but urgent. "How did I get here? What happened?"

The nurse hesitates for a moment, her kind eyes flickering with something unreadable. "Don't worry about that right now. You're safe here, and that's what matters. Just focus on resting."

As the nurse steps away, Lorna closes her eyes, her mind still racing. *Safe?* The word feels hollow. Whatever had happened in that parking lot, one thing was clear: someone had tried to hurt her—and they weren't finished yet.

The nurse's voice softened as she explained, "Miss Ritten, my name is Judy. You were found unconscious in the hospital waiting room around 10:33 p.m. last night. There were several people in the area when it happened. According to a witness, a man entered with you, approached a lady nearby, and asked her to get a nurse because the woman he was with—you—were unconscious and needed help. When the nurse arrived moments later, you were alone, sitting slumped in a chair. A note was in your lap, and that man was gone."

Judy's expression tightened with concern as she continued. "The note described your condition, detailed what had happened to you, and even included your name. It was unsettling, to say the least."

Lorna's mind reeled as she absorbed Judy's account. She stared blankly at the hospital room wall, fragments of the incident flashing in her memory: the gray car, screeching tires, the dark figure. The pieces refused to fit together into anything coherent.

"Miss Ritten?" Judy's voice broke through her haze. "Why don't you lie back down and get some rest? I'll be back in a few minutes with some aspirin." She placed a comforting hand on Lorna's shoulder.

Lorna nodded weakly, her gaze drifting toward her clothes hanging neatly in the open closet. Feeling a sudden and overwhelming urge to escape, she swung her legs over the side of the bed and stood. The cool hospital floor sent a jolt through her body as she moved toward her belongings, her focus fixed on the thought of getting out.

She quickly dressed, ignoring the mild dizziness in her head, and stepped into the hallway. The sound of Judy's voice calling after her reached her ears. "Miss Ritten! Where are you going?"

Lorna spotted the glowing red *Exit* sign at the end of the corridor and quickened her pace, nearly breaking into a run. "Miss Ritten!" Judy called again, her tone more insistent.

Lorna's fingers brushed the push bar of the exit door when Judy caught up to her. "If you're leaving, we just need you to sign some paperwork," Judy said, her voice calm but firm.

With a reluctant sigh, Lorna allowed the nurse to guide her through a brief administrative process. As she signed the forms, Judy offered one last piece of advice. "Would you like me to call the police? It might be a good idea to document what you can remember, even if it's just fragments. You never know what might come back to you later."

Lorna hesitated, the pen hovering over the clipboard. "I just want to go," she muttered, the exhaustion evident in her voice.

At 6:02 a.m., the hospital's glass double doors slid open, and Lorna stepped into the cold, dark parking lot. The sky was still an inky black, with no hint of the sun rising anytime soon. The chill in the air bit at her skin, and she instinctively shoved her hands into her coat pockets.

She froze as she realized something—her car was still at the Armstrong Library parking lot. Dread filled her as she considered the possibility of calling a friend or family member to pick her up. She glanced across the lot, scanning the rows of cars, and felt a twinge of relief that the area seemed empty.

Her relief was short-lived. A gray car entered the parking lot, its headlights slicing through the darkness. The familiar sight made her breath hitch as her pulse quickened. Her feet moved backward, step by cautious step, as the car approached. The vehicle turned down her row, its path eerily deliberate.

But as it drew closer, Lorna squinted and realized with enormous relief that this wasn't *that* gray car. She exhaled deeply, her breath forming small clouds in the crisp air.

As her hands remained buried in her pockets for warmth, her fingers brushed against something familiar. Pulling it out, she stared at her car keys dangling in her hand.

Her brow furrowed. *How did these get here?*

Pointing the keyless remote toward the sea of cars, she pressed the unlock button. A pair of headlights blinked in response from a distant corner of the lot. With a growing sense of unease, she trudged through the rows of vehicles, her eyes darting around the lot as if expecting someone—or something—to appear.

When she reached her car, she noticed skid marks leading away from it. A chill ran down her spine as she climbed inside. The driver's seat was slightly out of position, not where she usually left it. Her backpack and purse sat neatly on the passenger seat, as if deliberately arranged.

The faintest trace of aftershave lingered in the air. Lorna leaned closer, sniffing lightly, unsure if it was real or a figment of her imagination. Her unease deepened as she adjusted the seat, started the engine, and pulled out of the lot with a squeal of her tires.

Maybe Judy was right, she thought as she drove. *Maybe I should talk to the police.*

Moments later, Lorna arrived at the local police precinct. The building was quiet, its newly waxed floors gleaming under fluorescent lights. The only person in sight was a middle-aged, heavyset woman sitting behind the bulletproof glass at the front desk.

"Good morning, miss. Can I help you?" the clerk asked, her voice polite but clipped.

Lorna hesitated, the uncertainty evident in her eyes. "Uh... yes. I think I'd like to report something," she said, her voice trembling slightly as she wrestled with how much to reveal.

The clerk let out a faint sigh as she pulled out a clipboard, clipped a blank form onto it, and prepared to record Lorna's report. Her movements were slow and deliberate, betraying a lack of enthusiasm for what she seemed to expect would be a routine or nonsensical story.

"Name?" she asked, her voice monotone.

"Uh... Lorna Ritten," Lorna replied hesitantly.

The clerk arched a skeptical brow. "You sure about that?"

"Yes," Lorna said quickly, embarrassed by her hesitancy. "Sorry, I'm just really tired. I came straight here from the hospital."

The clerk jotted down Lorna's name, followed by her social security number and phone number. Then, without looking up, she asked, "So, what exactly are you reporting, ma'am?"

Lorna hesitated, her mind racing. How could she explain something so fragmented and bizarre when she herself could barely make sense of it? She took a deep breath and started. "Well... I was at the library—"

"Which one?" the clerk interrupted.

"The Armstrong," Lorna answered.

The clerk's pen scratched against the form as she nodded. "That's a nice library. Go on."

Lorna continued, fumbling over her words. "It was dark, and there was a car... and then I woke up in the hospital..."

The clerk stopped writing and peered over her glasses at Lorna. Her skeptical expression turned into one of thinly veiled concern. "Ma'am... are you alright? Would you like me to get someone to help you? Maybe take you back to the hospital? Perhaps to a place that's equipped to help folks... like you?"

The insinuation stung. *She thinks I'm crazy. Maybe I am,* Lorna thought, her frustration bubbling beneath the surface.

"I... I'm sorry for wasting your time," Lorna muttered, shaking her head. "I think I'm just overtired and confused." She stepped back toward the door. "I'm just gonna' go home and rest."

The clerk leaned forward, concern flickering across her face. "You sure, ma'am? I can get someone to help you—just give me a minute."

"No, really," Lorna insisted, holding up her hands. "I'm fine. I just need to sleep."

Without waiting for a response, Lorna turned and strode out of the precinct, her cheeks burning with embarrassment. *Why did I even come here?* she scolded herself. *I should've just gone home in the first place.*

By the time she got back into her car, the first hints of dawn were creeping across the Arizona sky. The faint light stretched long shadows across the desert landscape, creating shapes that seemed almost menacing. Lorna rolled down the windows for fresh air, but the atmosphere felt heavy, as though the world itself was pressing down on her.

The drive home, though less than twenty minutes, felt like an eternity. Every car she passed made her heart race, and she kept glancing in her rearview mirror, half-expecting to see the gray sedan following her again. The events of the past several hours replayed in her mind on an endless loop.

When Lorna finally pulled into her driveway, her home—a sanctuary under normal circumstances—felt cold and unwelcoming. She grabbed her things and stepped inside, dropping her bag and jacket carelessly by the door, a stark departure from her usually meticulous habits.

The faint smell of sweat and hospital lingered on her clothes. She grimaced, taking a quick sniff. *I'm dirty, my hair feels like it's coated in street grime, and I need a shower.*

She headed straight to the bathroom, shedding her clothes along the way. Under the scalding spray of the shower, Lorna let the water cascade over her, hoping it would wash away the tension gripping her body and mind. Normally structured and composed, she felt utterly disoriented and out of control.

A sudden crash shattered the silence, jerking her back to reality. It came from her bedroom, directly adjacent to the bathroom. Heart pounding, she quickly shut off the water, wrapped herself in a robe, and rushed out, leaving wet footprints on the tile.

In her bedroom, Lorna's lamp—an ornate find from a downtown furniture consignment shop—lay shattered on the floor in three pieces. Across the room, her cat, Tigger, stared at the mess with wide eyes, his expression practically screaming, *what just happened?*

Lorna clenched her fists, her frustration boiling over. The lamp was the least of her worries, but it felt like a tipping point. With a defeated sigh, she tossed a towel back toward the bathroom and muttered, "Great. One more mess to clean up."

She returned to the shower, finishing quickly this time, and wrapped herself in a fresh towel before collapsing onto her bed. Though her body screamed for rest, her mind refused to be quiet. Fragmented images of the gray car, the hospital, and the mysterious figure haunted her every thought.

After lying awake for what felt like hours, Lorna finally gave up on sleep. She threw on some casual clothes and headed downstairs, deciding to distract herself with coffee and real estate paperwork. The mundane tasks offered little comfort, and the suffocating weight of her solitude grew unbearable.

Unable to stay cooped up any longer, Lorna grabbed her things and left the house, battling lunchtime traffic until she arrived at Peg's Diner. The retro eatery was her go-to spot when she needed to clear her head.

17

Chapter Seventeen

With its shiny metal paneling and checkerboard floors, the diner looked like it had been plucked straight from a 1950s movie. It was shaped like a long rectangle, with a neon sign flickering cheerfully above the entrance. Inside, the smell of coffee and sizzling bacon wrapped around her like a warm hug.

She slid into a booth near the window, the red vinyl seat squeaking slightly as she sat down.

The inside of Peg's Diner oozed nostalgic charm, a throwback to a bygone era. The walls were lined with booths that had been around for over 60 years, their cushioned seats broken in just right, making them surprisingly more comfortable than those in modern eateries. Posters of vintage advertisements adorned the walls in a haphazard, endearing way. At the counter, a glass dome, slightly foggy from age, proudly displayed that day's homemade pies, each one a testament to the diner's dedication to authenticity.

The centerpiece of the establishment was the long, curved bar with its lip of 4-inch polished metal running around the edge. Perched along the bar were circular padded stools, bolted to the classic black-and-white checkered floor. They spun on their bases with a squeak that brought back childhood memories of simpler times. Peg's décor featured memorabilia from several decades—neon signs, tin soda ads, and even a jukebox—but nothing dated beyond 1975.

The place was bustling, though not uncomfortably crowded. Lorna sat in her usual booth near the back, equipped with a personal tabletop coin-operated jukebox. She traced her fingers over the worn edges of the menu, comforted by its familiarity. Peg's offered no culinary surprises—classic Americana diner food, simple and hearty. Servers bustled about in polyester uniforms, their pastel colors as timeless as the diner itself, smiling warmly at regulars and newcomers alike.

Lorna ordered her usual: a tuna melt on rye with chips, a dill pickle spear on the side, and endless coffee refills. While waiting for her food, she opened her laptop and connected to Peg's surprisingly modern amenity—free Wi-Fi. To anyone passing by, she appeared calm and collected, the picture of someone casually getting some work done over lunch. Even the small bandage on her forehead didn't detract from her composed demeanor.

But inside, her mind churned.

Why would anyone be after me? she thought, sipping her coffee absentmindedly. *All I've done is try to help some kids. What could I possibly have done to deserve...* She trailed off, unable to finish the thought.

The events of the last 24 hours kept creeping back into her consciousness. The gray car, the hospital, the fragments of her memory—they all pointed to something larger, something sinister.

Maybe Mr. Gronberg was right about politics and those powerful people. Maybe this is politically motivated. But would someone really try to kill me over helping orphans?

Her food arrived, but she barely noticed. She pushed through three emails, her attention fragmented as her thoughts kept circling back to the same troubling questions. Her focus was shattered completely when her phone buzzed loudly on the table, startling her enough to spill her coffee.

"Ugh," she muttered, reaching for napkins from the old-fashioned dispenser as her phone vibrated again. The caller ID read *Chelsea.*

"You have the worst timing," Lorna muttered into the phone, blotting up the mess.

"Well, excuse me," Chelsea quipped, unfazed by Lorna's irritation. "I just haven't heard from you since dinner the other night and thought you might want to catch a movie or something. Sorry for the bad timing."

Before Lorna could respond, she became aware of someone standing in front of her booth. She looked up, and caught her breath.

"Chelse, I'll call you back," she said quickly, ending the call before her friend could reply.

"Can I help you?" Lorna asked, her voice tinged with nervousness as she sized up the man before her.

The man appeared to be in his late-40s, impeccably dressed in a tailored gray silk suit that fit him like a second skin. His air of sophistication was undeniable, yet he carried himself with a surprising humility, as though he didn't want to draw attention.

"Good afternoon," he said in a low, authoritative voice. "My name is Phillip Mahoney. I'm an attorney, and I have information regarding your birth parents and other members of your biological family."

Lorna's mouth dropped open, her mind racing. She stared at him, searching his expression for a hint of insincerity, but his face remained unreadable.

After an awkward silence, Phillip placed a sleek business card on the table, his eyes darting subtly around the room as if scanning for something—or someone.

"How... how do you know I've been looking for my biological parents?" Lorna stammered.

Without making direct eye contact, Phillip replied, "Call me, please. We can't discuss this here. It's imperative we speak soon."

Lorna's initial shock gave way to suspicion. "Look, Mr... Mahoney," she said, glancing at the card for confirmation, "I have no idea who you are or how you know about me. Why should I even trust you?"

Phillip met her gaze for a fleeting moment, his voice calm but firm. "Because you've been searching for answers your entire life, and I can help you find them." He paused, glancing around again. "Please, just call me."

"This all sounds very mysterious," Lorna said, her tone skeptical. "Did Brianna put you up to this?"

Phillip didn't respond to the jab. Instead, he straightened his tie and said, "Your lunch is paid for. Good day." Without another word, he turned and walked briskly out of the diner.

Lorna sat frozen for a moment, then bolted to her feet to follow him. But by the time she reached the door, he was gone. The street outside was busy, but there was no trace of Phillip.

Returning to her booth, she sank back into her seat, staring at the card he had left behind.

The waitress interrupted her thoughts. "More coffee, Lorna?"

The question jolted her back to the present. "Uh, no, thanks, Linda. Just the check."

Linda gave her a puzzled look. "Your check's already paid for, along with a pretty generous tip. Anything else I can get you?"

"No, I'm good. Thanks," Lorna muttered, still dazed.

Gathering her things, Lorna headed out to her car. She sat in the driver's seat with the engine idling, gripping the steering wheel tightly as her mind raced. She stared blankly at the card in her hand, Phillip Mahoney's name and contact information printed in elegant, embossed lettering.

Who are you, Phillip? she wondered. *And what do you really know about me?*

After a moment, she took a deep breath, put the car into gear, and drove off, the card still clutched tightly in her hand.

Lorna hit the gas pedal with urgency, her car surging forward as she sped down the nearly empty stretch of highway. Every moment felt like a test of her nerves, the paranoia about the gray car following her still fresh in her mind. When she arrived at the Armstrong Library, she didn't immediately park but instead drove slowly through the nearly deserted lot, her eyes scanning every shadowed corner and glancing over each vehicle. She was on high alert, looking for anything—or anyone—out of the ordinary.

Finally, deciding there was nothing suspicious in sight, Lorna parked near the library's main entrance. She sat in her car for a moment, gripping the steering wheel tightly and taking a deep breath. She let her gaze wander across the rows of cars one last time before stepping out into the cool night air.

She jogged up the familiar stone steps, her heels echoing in the quiet as she made her way inside. Passing by the Art Collection room, she couldn't help but glance in, noting its usual emptiness. The sight of the shadowed sculptures and paintings gave her a slight chill, but she shrugged it off.

Lorna made her way to her favorite table in the lineage and biography section. The area was as silent and still as ever, the absence of other patrons only adding to the oppressive atmosphere. She set her book bag down, though with less force than usual, and began methodically spreading out her materials: notebooks, a laptop, and the familiar blue binder filled with her painstaking research.

Sitting down, Lorna opened the hospital ledger she had been combing through before everything went sideways. The numbers and handwritten notes stared back at her, but her focus wavered. Her head throbbed faintly, the weight of the day's events pressing heavily on her shoulders.

She tried to push through, flipping through more pages and attempting to decipher birth records, but her exhaustion was undeniable. Her eyelids grew heavy, and her head dipped lower and lower until it came to rest on her left forearm. Within moments, she drifted into a deep, dreamless sleep.

An indeterminate amount of time passed before a familiar voice pulled her from her slumber.

"Sweetheart," the voice said gently, accompanied by a light shake of her shoulder.

Lorna stirred, muttering incoherently.

"Lorna, honey, you need to wake up," Mrs. Velez said, her voice soft but insistent.

"Wha—Mrs. Velez?" Lorna mumbled groggily, blinking as her surroundings came into focus.

"Yes, it's me," Mrs. Velez said with a warm smile. "I hate to do this to you, but it's almost closing time again, dear."

Lorna stretched in her chair, yawning loudly. "Oh, man. I must've been out for hours."

"And snoring," Mrs. Velez added playfully. "You need to go home and get some proper rest. I'm heading out a bit early tonight. Goodnight, Lorna."

"Goodnight, Mrs. Velez," Lorna replied, managing a small smile.

As Mrs. Velez walked away, her footsteps echoed faintly in the vast emptiness of the library. Moments later, as if on cue, Brian Highfill appeared, his perfectly polished shoes clicking against the marble floor. He paused briefly to allow Mrs. Velez to pass, bowing slightly in his typically formal, British way.

Lorna watched the interaction from her seat. As Brian's gaze shifted to her, she felt a prickle of unease. His expression was unreadable, a neutral mask that somehow felt too calculating. She averted her eyes first, pretending to adjust the strap on her bag.

Once the echoes of footsteps had faded entirely, the library was deathly silent. Lorna stood, stretching her back and twisting from side to side to release the tension in her spine.

You should leave now while there are still people around, she thought, her instincts urging her to pack up quickly.

She hurriedly gathered her things, stuffing papers and notebooks haphazardly into her bag. Slinging it over her shoulder, she turned toward the staircase, only to freeze in place.

Standing at the far end of a nearby row of shelves was The Blond Guy. He was holding a book, but it was clear from his stiff posture and glances in her direction that reading wasn't his real intention.

Lorna's chest tightened, her breath catching as their eyes locked for a moment. She broke eye contact and began walking briskly toward the stairs. Behind her, she heard the soft shuffle of his footsteps.

Her pace quickened, and so did his. The sound of his pursuit grew louder. Lorna darted into a historical section, pretending to examine a random book on the shelf. She chanced a glance over her shoulder; he was closing in.

He's following me. This is actually happening! Her heart pounding in her chest.

Dropping all pretense, Lorna broke into a full run. She didn't dare look back this time, her heels clicking against the polished floor as she rounded a corner.

Her momentum caused her to slide slightly, and she realized with a sinking feeling that she had become disoriented. The rows of bookshelves blurred together, and she couldn't tell which direction led back to the staircase.

She slowed to a jog, trying to listen for any sound of pursuit. The silence was deafening.

Then, she rounded another corner—and there he was. The Blond Guy stood directly in her path.

Lorna let out a sharp gasp, stumbling backward.

"Stay away from me!" she shouted, her voice trembling as adrenaline coursed through her.

He didn't respond, but his intense gaze never left her.

Lorna bolted between two towering bookshelves, only to find herself at a dead end. The narrow aisle led to a wooden panel wall, offering no escape.

The sound of his footsteps grew louder. He was closing in.

Lorna almost has her back against the wall, her breathing shallow and rapid. Her eyes darted around desperately, searching for any way out.

Five feet away.

Four feet away.

Three feet away.

Two feet away.

The Blond Guy locks eyes with Lorna and then glances back toward the section of the library they had just come from, his movements deliberate, calculated. He shifts his gaze back to her, his expression unreadable.

One foot away.

Lorna backs up until her shoulder blades are almost against the wall. She has nowhere left to go. Or so she thinks...

Suddenly, she feels a strange absence behind her, an emptiness where there should be solid wood. Off balance, Lorna instinctively pivots to look over her shoulder, her hands searching for support. Instead of a wall, she sees a doorway swinging shut, sealing off the light from the library beyond. She stumbles forward, catching herself on her hands as the door clicks shut, leaving her in dim, unfamiliar surroundings.

Phillip Mahoney, the mysterious lawyer from the diner, stands just a few feet away.

"You?" Lorna breathes, her voice barely above a whisper.

Phillip's expression is calm, almost too calm for the bizarre circumstances. Behind her, the sound of the door sealing shut reverberates, and Lorna turns halfway, just in time to see the last sliver of light vanish. She notices a faint outline where the door had been, disguised by the intricate wood paneling. A framed picture now conceals what appears to be a one-way mirror, offering a covert view of the library beyond.

"What is this?" Lorna asks, her voice trembling as her gaze darts between the door and Phillip. Her fight-or-flight instincts kick in, her body tense, her pulse pounding in her ears.

Phillip raises his hands in a placating gesture. "Lorna, it's okay. I know how this must look, but I promise you, I'm here to help. Please, give me a moment to explain." His voice is steady, soothing, yet authoritative.

Lorna narrows her eyes at him. "I don't care how it looks. I want answers. Now!" she snaps, her anger briefly overpowering her fear. "You said you had answers at the diner, so start talking. Who are you? What's going on? Why is this happening to me?"

Phillip's calm demeanor doesn't falter. He gestures toward an oversized, brown leather chair positioned in front of a large, ornate desk. "I understand you're upset. Please, have a seat. I'll explain everything to the best of my ability."

Lorna hesitates, her gaze darting to the chair and back to Phillip. Her mind races, weighing her options. The room feels both foreign and oddly inviting, with its wood-paneled walls, renaissance-style paintings, and the kind of opulence she'd expect in a billionaire's private study.

Reluctantly, she steps forward and sits down, her movements slow and cautious. She doesn't relax, her posture rigid as she grips the arms of the chair.

Phillip takes his place behind the desk, settling into a matching leather chair. He clasps his hands together and begins, "I know you've been searching for answers for a long time. Who you are, where you come from, and most importantly, who your parents are. These are questions that have haunted you, and rightly so."

Lorna leans forward slightly, her eyes sharp. "And, you're saying you have those answers?"

"Some of them," Phillip admits, his tone measured. "Not all. But enough to give you clarity. Lorna, you are the granddaughter of Alfred Cypress."

Lorna freezes, her mind reeling. "Wait. Alfred Cypress? As in Cypress Industries? That Alfred Cypress?" Lorna thinks to herself, *That was the Alfred who wrote those letters.*

"Yes," Phillip confirms. "Your grandfather was more than just the founder of Cypress Industries. He was a man of vision, a pioneer. But his work—his legacy—has made you a target."

Lorna's voice rises. "Target? For what? Who would even care about me? I'm nobody!"

Phillip leans forward, his tone soft but firm. "You are far from nobody, Lorna. You are the last blood relative of Alfred Cypress, and that makes you a key player in a much larger game. There are factions—dangerous factions—who oppose everything your grandfather stood for. When they discovered your existence, you became a threat to them."

Lorna's breath catches. "Discovered my existence? How long have they known about me?"

Phillip hesitates, his gaze dropping for the briefest moment. "Roughly three months. Until then, we had taken every precaution to keep you hidden, to ensure your safety. But certain events unfolded that forced our hand."

"And my parents?" Lorna presses. "Who are they? What happened to them?"

Phillip sighs, leaning back in his chair. "I wish I could give you a definitive answer. Your grandfather rarely spoke about your mother, and I know little about your father. The details surrounding your mother's life are... complicated."

Lorna's frustration boils over. "Complicated? That's not an answer! You claim to know so much, but you don't even know who my mother is?"

Phillip remains calm. "I understand your frustration, Lorna. But I promise you, I'm telling you everything I can. As we navigate this together, more answers will come to light."

Lorna shakes her head, her hands gripping the arms of the chair tightly. "And what does 'navigate this together' mean, exactly?"

Phillip stands, pacing slowly as he speaks. "It means you're no longer a bystander, Lorna. The attacks on you—the one at the library parking lot, the one that landed you in the hospital—are just the beginning. You are now a central figure in a conflict that spans nations and industries."

Lorna's pulse quickens. "Attacks? You're saying someone tried to kill me? Do you know what happened?"

"Yes," Phillip replies, his tone grave. "You were targeted because of your lineage. These factions see you as a threat to their agenda, simply because of who your grandfather is."

"And what happened to him?" Lorna demands. "Is he alive? Is he dead? Where is he?"

Phillip pauses, his expression unreadable. "Your grandfather... is missing. And his absence has set off a chain of events that now places you in the crosshairs."

Lorna's stomach churns. "Missing? Since when?"

"Three months ago," Phillip answers quietly. "Right around the time they discovered you."

Lorna leans back in the chair, her mind racing. "So, I'm the last Cypress by blood. And because of that, I'm supposed to pick up where he left off?

Phillip nods solemnly. "In a sense, yes. But it's more than that. This isn't just about a company or a name. It's about a legacy. And it's time you understood what that legacy truly means."

Phillip folded his hands on the desk, his gaze steady as he studied Lorna's reaction. "There's one more thing you need to understand," he began, his voice carrying a tone of deliberate weight. "Your inheritance, the Cypress mansion, wasn't just a gift or a family heirloom. It was a test—your first real step into this world you've just discovered. When you chose to give it away to those in need, it told us something crucial about you."

He paused, letting the words settle. "You demonstrated compassion and a sense of responsibility, values your grandfather cherished deeply. That decision wasn't simply about the mansion itself—it was about proving that you're the kind of person who could carry the weight of this legacy. And you passed that test, Lorna." Phillip's words hung in the air, leaving her to grapple with their implications. The room seemed to grow smaller as Lorna tried to process what this meant for her—and for the dangerous world she was now entering.

Phillip leaned forward, his hands clasped together on the desk, his expression composed but sincere. "We've been observing you for some time, Lorna. We knew there were people who could benefit greatly from the resources you now hold. But we needed to be certain—certain that you'd choose to help, that you'd have the heart and the mindset for it. If you hadn't, we would have had to explore other options. Frankly, we didn't know what we'd do if you failed. But your decision to give up the estate proved us right. It's an incredible blessing, not just for those you've helped, but for us as well."

Phillip paused, letting his words settle before continuing more cautiously. "Still, there's so much we don't know, though we remain hopeful."

Lorna raised an eyebrow at the hint of uncertainty in his voice. Her tone was calm but pointed when she said, "For someone who seems so polished and educated, you don't sound very sure of much. Just shoot straight with me—do you believe my grandfather is alive? Yes or no?"

Phillip met her gaze without hesitation. "Yes, Lorna. I do."

His conviction brought a flicker of relief, but Lorna wasn't done. "Okay, why do you believe that?" she pressed.

Phillip's expression softened, a rare glimpse of emotion breaking through his otherwise composed demeanor. "Because your grandfather is the most extraordinary man I've ever known. I've traveled the globe, dealt with high-ranking officials, negotiated with four-star generals, and navigated some of the most complex situations imaginable. In every instance, Alfred Cypress stands out as someone unparalleled—someone who defies ordinary limits. I don't believe a man like that would simply vanish without a reason."

Lorna studied him carefully. "You really respect him, don't you? I mean, is he the kind of person you'd take a bullet for?"

Phillip's face remained steady, but there was a flicker of something unspoken in his eyes. "You assume that hasn't already happened," he said, his tone flat yet loaded with meaning.

Lorna froze, unsure how to respond to such a statement. The weight of his words added yet another layer of gravity to an already overwhelming situation. After a long pause, she finally spoke. "Alright. Then tell me more about what happened at the hospital. Do you know who tried to run me over? And, how exactly did I end up in that waiting room?"

Her voice was firm, laced with frustration but also determination. Phillip nodded, acknowledging her persistence. "Yes, we need to address that. Let me explain what we know."

Phillip reaches for a small, sleek device resting on his desk and presses a few buttons. "Take a look at this," he says, his tone measured but firm.

A wooden panel on the room's wall slides open with a soft mechanical hum, revealing a high-definition screen embedded within. The monitor, notably devoid of any corporate branding, flickers to life. Footage from the night Lorna ended up in the hospital appears on the screen. It shows her walking toward her car in the dimly lit parking lot of the Armstrong Library. Suddenly, the gray sedan screeches into view, barreling toward her.

Phillip pauses the footage and manipulates the perspective, zooming in with precision until Lorna can clearly see the driver's face. She catches her breath.

"Vin," she whispers, her eyes widening. "So, this guy—Vin—is he the mastermind behind the people opposing my grandfather?"

"Absolutely not," Phillip responds with a sharp edge to his voice. "*Vin* is a low-level operative in the larger scheme of things. He's competent, yes, but nowhere near CIA or GRU-level competent. He's a pawn, not a king. Keep watching." Lorna leaned in and asked, "GRU?" Phillip responded, "Elite, Russian military group. Ruthless, cruel and efficient. Pray you never meet them in a hostile condition." After sending a chill up Lorna's spine, she gestured, wanting more answers.

Phillip presses another button, and the footage shifts. This time, the screen displays hidden camera footage from earlier in the library. Lorna watches as she appears on-screen, walking toward her usual table with her backpack slung over her shoulder. She stops briefly to get a drink from the water fountain. In the background, a hand stretches toward her, but the focus shifts to reveal The Blond Guy lurking just beyond her line of sight, his body tense as he watches her every move.

The camera angle changes, showing Lorna perusing hospital journals in a quiet aisle. A shadowy figure enters from the other end of the row, unnoticed by her. Something slips smoothly from his sleeve into his hand—it's a syringe. Before the figure can approach her, Lorna walks away. The camera captures The Blond Guy peeking around the corner of a bookshelf, his gaze tracking the shadowy figure's movements.

Phillip switches to another clip, this one from the night Lorna was almost run over. The screen shows The Blond Guy tackling her to the ground, sending them both tumbling into an embankment. He scrambles to his feet with remarkable speed, pulling out an unusual, futuristic weapon—sleek, black, with glowing red accents.

He aims and fires, unleashing a burst of energy that looks like a blend of lightning and laser light. The shot crackles through the air, dissipating just before it makes contact with the gray sedan.

Lorna leans closer to the screen, her mouth agape. "What... what was that?" she asks, her voice tinged with awe and confusion.

"That," Phillip begins with a hint of pride, "is a plasma gun—one of the most basic weapons your grandfather developed. It's a testament to his brilliance."

Lorna processes this, her mind racing. "So, The Blond Guy... he's been protecting me this whole time?"

Phillip nods. "Yes. His name is Kyle. He's been assigned to follow you and neutralize any potential threats to your well-being. He's one of the few individuals we've entrusted with the truth about who you are and what you represent. You can trust him, Lorna, as much as you can trust anyone in this world."

Lorna exhales, her shoulders relaxing slightly. "Thank you for telling me that. I'll have to thank him myself if I ever get the chance."

Phillip's device beeps, drawing his attention. He glances at the screen and frowns. "It appears Vin has managed to slip past Kyle's surveillance for now. The good news is, with his cover blown, he's unlikely to reappear anytime soon."

Lorna lets out a breath she didn't realize she was holding. "That's a relief. Please let Kyle know I appreciate everything he's done."

Phillip nods. "Coming from a Cypress, that will mean a great deal to him. But Lorna, I need you to understand something important. For now, you need to return to your normal life as much as possible. At the same time, I will help you uncover your family's rich history and understand the responsibilities that come with being a Cypress."

Lorna looks around the room, overwhelmed but determined. "Phillip, I'm trying to wrap my head around all of this. I don't understand... all of this," she says, motioning to the ornate office and the unfolding revelations.

Phillip stands and gestures for her to follow. "Let me show you something," he says, leading her to a corner of the room where a stately bookcase stands beside a cozy reading area.

"What is it?" Lorna asks, her voice hesitant.

Phillip pulls a worn, brown leather journal from the shelf. Its edges are frayed, and its cover bears the marks of frequent use. He cradles it carefully, as if it were a sacred artifact, and walks back to sit across from Lorna.

"This journal belonged to your grandfather," Phillip explains. "It contains his thoughts, his inventions, and his vision for the future. It's time you started to understand what it truly means to be a Cypress." He places the journal gently in her hands.

Lorna stares at the journal, its weight both literal and symbolic. She looks up at Phillip, her determination growing. "I'm ready," she says, though her voice carries a mixture of resolve and uncertainty.

Phillip's expression softens. "Then let's begin."

Lorna is transfixed as she holds up the journal. Its leather cover feels heavy in her hands, not just in weight but in significance. Phillip places a burner phone in her palm. "This phone has a single pre-programmed number. When you're ready, call me, and we'll take the next steps together."

The enormity of the situation presses down on her, but Lorna nods. "Alright," she says softly.

18

Chapter Eighteen

Phillip radios for Kyle, who arrives moments later. He nods at Lorna, his expression calm yet vigilant. "Kyle will escort you out. You're safe with him."

Lorna follows Kyle through the library, the stained-glass depiction of Moses casting its kaleidoscope of colors across her path. Outside, the air felt thick and humid, uncharacteristic for Arizona. Kyle opened the driver's side door of her car, and Lorna hesitates.

"How did you get my keys?" she asks, her voice tinged with suspicion.

Kyle smirks. "I didn't. Your keys are still in your pocket." He steps back, allowing her to confirm the truth for herself. Yep, keys are in her pocket. "But, the door's open. How did you...? Never mind."

Sliding into the driver's seat, Lorna looks up at him. "Well, um... Thank you, Kyle. For having my back."

He nods. "It's what I'm here for."

As he turns to leave, Lorna calls out, "Kyle!" He turns to listen, and she continues, "I know this is an unfair question, but I gotta ask...." Kyle dutifully waits, "Can I trust Phillip?"

Kyle stops and looks over his shoulder. "Yeah. You can." She pushes, "And, why's that?" Kyle takes a moment and then sincerely says, "Because... he's my father and, I've never known him to break his word."

The revelation leaves Lorna speechless as she watches Kyle disappear into the night. Her grip tightens on the journal resting on the passenger seat. Questions swirl in her mind as she drives home under a vast, watchful sky, the journal a tangible link to the answers she's long sought.

When Lorna arrived home, the house felt more foreign than comforting. Normally her sanctuary, its familiar walls and meticulous organization now felt stifling and detached. Her structured world had been upended by the chaos of recent days, leaving her grasping for some semblance of control in a life that had become unrecognizable.

As she stepped inside, Tigger greeted her with his usual feline aloof enthusiasm. The irony of finding solace in the pet she once resisted wasn't lost on her. His presence, routine and grounding, was a small piece of normalcy in this otherwise recently turbulent existence.

"Hey, buddy. You hungry?" Lorna asked, her voice soft.

Tigger meowed loudly, curling around her leg, his answer unmistakable.

Lorna walked into the living room, setting the journal down carefully on the table beside the couch, as though it carried the weight of answers, she wasn't ready to confront. She moved to the kitchen, Tigger faithfully at her heels, and opened a can of moist cat food. As soon as the bowl hit the floor, Tigger dove in with gusto, devouring every morsel.

Lorna made herself a cup of hot tea, that simple act giving her something to focus on. She returned to the couch, set her tea on the table, and stared at the journal for a long moment. It seemed to call to her, but opening it felt like crossing an invisible threshold into an unknown world. Finally, she tucked her legs beneath her, settling into the couch. She picked up the journal, its worn, muted brown cover smooth under her fingertips.

It's just a book, she told herself. Yet holding it felt monumental, as if the answers to her deepest questions lay within its pages. Her grandfather's legacy, his essence, was captured in his own handwriting—a connection she had unwittingly sought for so long.

Lorna opened the journal gingerly, as if handling a rare and fragile artifact. The first page revealed elegant, meticulous script, each word a glimpse into the mind of Alfred Cypress. She lightly traced the ink with her fingertips, marveling at the precision of his handwriting.

For the first time, she felt a tangible link to her grandfather, a man she had only imagined. Her eyes drifted to the first entry.

Journal Entry - August 23, 1977

Today marks my first day at Eddington University. Settling in was exhausting, but saying goodbye to my dad was even harder. He gave me this journal just before he left for Gatwick airport, telling me it would help me track my progress and reflect on my journey. I don't fully understand how it'll help, but I trust his wisdom. Writing here makes me feel a little less alone. Losing Mom last year was hard for both of us, and now with me here and Dad back home, I know he'll feel the emptiness too. I'm thankful he has his faith to lean on, as do I.

Tomorrow will bring new challenges, especially as the youngest student here at just 16. Some of the older students didn't seem too thrilled to see me, and I know the road ahead won't be easy. But as I sit here tonight, nervous about what's to come, I am also filled with gratitude for this opportunity and the strength I draw from my faith.

Journal Entry - August 24, 1977

Wow, today wasn't as tough as I'd feared! I met my professors and got to see the incredible equipment I'll be working with. Some students were even kind, like Robert, who's older than me but treated me with respect and answered my questions. Still, I had an awkward moment with Dr. Brune, who questioned how I managed to get into Eddington at such a young age. He wasn't unkind, but it put me on the spot. I don't like talking about myself; it always feels like bragging. But Mr. Snowden, who recruited me, warned me that being exceptional would provoke curiosity. I know anything I have is a gift from God and really do not like it when it seems somehow, I am taking credit for it. Also, apparently, I have a "Southern accent," which also draws some attention. I mean, they're the ones with the accent!

Despite that moment with Dr. Brune, I can see so much potential here. I truly believe great things can be achieved in this place!

Journal Entry - August 31, 1977

It's been a few days since I last wrote, and things have been super busy. My projects are coming along well, but today something—or rather, someone—completely captivated me. A new student joined my French class. She had been delayed due to illness, and when she walked in, it was as if the room shifted. Vonya Zarene—her name is as beautiful as she is. I didn't get a chance to talk to her, but I can't stop thinking about her. There's something about her, something special. I can't wait for the next class.

Journal Entry – September 8, 1977

I must begin by saying how incredibly blessed I feel. Since my last entry, so much has happened. First, I finally had the chance to talk to Vonya! Though it wasn't the personal conversation I'd hoped for, it was still wonderful to speak with her. We've been placed in the same study group, which meets once a week. So far, our interactions have been brief, but they've been great. Even with my nerves, I don't think I've said anything too foolish yet. I may be shy, but it's going better than I could've imagined.

On a different note, I've been experimenting in the lab with a new branch of science that actually feels like science fiction – Robotics! Specifically, I'm working on programming a robotic unit to respond to my voice. I'm new to this, but I've made some progress. Seeing it begin to work, even on a small scale, has been incredibly exciting.

Lastly, I've taken up something new—fencing. I'm not the most athletic person, but I enjoy staying active, and the Eddington Fencing Club seemed intriguing. To my surprise, it feels somewhat natural to me, and it's been a great way to unwind. Life feels so full right now, and I am deeply thankful.

Journal Entry – November 23, 1977

Where do I begin? A few days ago, I had my first date with Vonya. Between my packed schedule and all the projects I've been working on, it felt impossible, but somehow, it just happened. I don't have much money, so we kept it simple—dinner and a long, peaceful walk. It was perfect. She looked stunning, and I was captivated by her kindness and grace. As we talked, I learned so much more about her. Like me, she only has one par-

ent—her father. Her mother passed away from cancer when she was just five years old.

On the project front, I've also had some exciting breakthroughs. I managed to get the robotic unit to respond to my commands. Watching it work was exhilarating! However, there's still a challenge with the power source—it's tethered to a wall plug, which limits its capabilities. I need to develop a more efficient energy source, but I'm optimistic about finding a solution.

Journal Entry – January 8th, 1978

Time seems to slip away so quickly these days. December was wonderful! Vonya and I are growing closer, and I even had the chance to meet her father. It went so well, and things between us feel incredible.

My friend Robert has also been helping me with some of my projects. Having someone to bounce ideas off of has been invaluable, and his assistance has been a huge help. Progress on the energy source is coming along. I feel like I'm on the cusp of something groundbreaking—something that could have a profound impact beyond robotics.

My father visited during the holidays. I've missed him so much. He's doing well and still working hard as an engineer. Hearing him say he's proud of me meant everything. I only wish he could have met Vonya, but our schedules didn't align. Even so, I feel hopeful and excited for what this year holds.

Journal Entry – April 27, 1978

Things just keep getting better. Vonya and I are spending more time together, and I love every moment of it. In the lab, I've been refining the energy source for the robotic unit. Inspired by a lecture from Dr. Whittmire on electromagnetism, I've been adapting and expanding on his ideas. Progress feels so close I can almost touch it.

Robert has been less involved lately due to personal issues within his family. I overheard that his family is struggling financially, and it seems to be affecting him. Despite his challenges, I'm grateful for the time he was able to help.

Journal Entry – June 28, 1978

Today has been devastating. My father was killed in a workplace accident. I know he's in Heaven, and I'll see him again someday, but the pain of losing him is overwhelming. I don't have the will to work on anything right now. Writing here was his idea, and I'm hoping it'll help me find some strength. I love you papa. One day, I'll see you again.

Journal Entry – July 3, 1978

The funeral is over, and I'm starting to feel a little more like myself. The realization that I'm now completely without family is hard to bear, but Vonya has been my rock through this. Her presence has brought me comfort, and I know I'm falling in love with her. I only wish my father could have met her.

Journal Entry – July 17, 1978

It's been a challenging few weeks, but Vonya reminded me of something I already knew: God makes no mistakes. That truth has given me peace and the push I needed to stop wallowing in self-pity. I am blessed beyond measure, and I want to live in gratitude for all that I have.

Lorna at this point could not hold back the tears. She could not help but relate to how he was feeling in some ways with her own life path and experiences. She also stopped and reminded herself of how blessed she had been as well.

Journal Entry – October 26, 1978

I did it! The energy source now works independently of a wall plug. The robotic unit runs on its own! I can't wait to share this news with Vonya tomorrow. This breakthrough has the potential to revolutionize so much. This is what God sent me across an ocean to do! Well, that and meet Vonya.

Journal Entry – November 5, 1978

I have significantly enhanced the power source for my robot to a level where I am now witnessing incredible potential for various practical benefits from all the work I've put into it. The excitement I feel is immense, but I am also beginning to notice a few drawbacks that concern me. Among some of the other students, I sense jealousy, while others have started discussing the financial implications of this project. These conversations don't sit well with me, and they raise serious concerns about the possible misuse of my work.

The work I'm doing could offer so much help to so many, but I am determined to ensure it doesn't become something that causes harm or division in any way. Reflecting on this, I can't help but think about Robert. His family has apparently made some unfortunate investments, which has put a strain on maintaining their estate and business. While it seems like he'll be able to finish school, I am genuinely concerned about him—he just doesn't seem like himself lately.

I find myself reflecting on the incredible diversity here—so many students from various backgrounds, cultures, and with their own unique challenges. Seeing this makes me realize how much potential my work has to bring positive change and relief to others. I feel deeply that this is what I want my invention to be: a tool to help and uplift people, not to create further problems or divisions. This commitment drives me forward, despite the complexities that may come.

Journal Entry – December 3, 1978

Tonight was truly unforgettable! I finally decided to propose to Vonya, and to my overwhelming joy, she said yes! Everything about the moment felt perfect—it couldn't have gone better. She loves painting, so I found her in the art room working on a new piece. I walked in, pretending it was just a casual visit to see how her latest art was coming along. After chatting for a few minutes, I gathered my courage, got down on one knee, and asked her to marry me.

Her reaction was priceless—she was completely surprised and started crying softly, her tears sparkling as she smiled and said 'yes.' I can't even describe the happiness I felt in that moment; it was as if the whole world had stopped just for us.

I wish I could give her a truly beautiful ring, but right now, I simply can't afford one. Instead, I found a few very thin, small metal washers I had been using on my robot project. I selected one that fit her finger size, polished it carefully to give it a unique shine, and used it as her engagement ring.

When I gave it to her, I told her how much I wished I could give her something grander. But to my surprise and relief, she said it was perfect—better than anything else I could have given her. She said it symbolized us and the way we always find meaning in the simplest things.

I'm bursting with joy and want to share this news with everyone, but there's hardly anyone I can tell. Regardless, I love her with all my heart, and I cannot wait to marry that British princess and start our life together. This is the happiest I've ever been!

It was 1:23 a.m., and Lorna, utterly exhausted, finally decided to crawl into bed. Despite the overwhelming events of the past few days, she knew she had a crucial meeting scheduled later in the day at the mayor's office to further discuss the Phoenix Children's Home project. This meeting was pivotal; if she failed to achieve her goals, the fate of the children's home would hang by a thread. Even with the weight of the new revelations about her grandfather and his legacy pressing heavily on her, Lorna knew rest was her best option for now.

By the time she woke up at 10:15 a.m., her phone was ringing incessantly. Half-asleep, she finally answered.

"Mmm..." was all she could manage.

"Lorna? It's Claire! Are you still coming to your 10:30? I figured you'd be here by now!"

The fog of exhaustion lifted just enough for Lorna to grasp the situation. She sat up with a start, her heart pounding. "Ahh! Jennifer Kresen!"

"Yep, that's the one. Should I have her wait or...?"

"Oh, no, no. Just...tell her I'm so sorry, something came up, and I need to reschedule. Got that?"

"Yep, got it."

Lorna hurriedly threw on clean clothes, her hair a wild mess, and barely had the energy to brush it into submission. There was no time for a shower. "Claire, when's my next appointment?" she asked, hurriedly grabbing her shoes.

Claire's keyboard clacked in the background. "You have an 11:00."

"Okay, stall them until I get there. I'll be as fast as I can."

"But, what if they don't want to wait around?"

"Claire, I love you, but you'll have to figure this one out. Stall them! Do something! Gotta go!"

Lorna tossed her phone onto the bed and glanced at the journal sitting on the nightstand. Memories of the past few days swirled in her mind, chaotic and overwhelming. A few days ago, she felt in control, her life orderly, with only unanswered questions about her origins. Now, everything felt out of place, like she'd been dropped into a foreign land with no guide and no sense of direction.

Traffic was mercilessly slow, but Lorna pushed her limits, weaving through it as fast as she dared. She burst into the lobby of Aztec Realty at 11:17 a.m., nearly breathless. A middle-aged couple waited for her. The wife seemed understanding, offering a gentle smile, but the husband glanced at his watch with clear impatience.

"Good morning, you two! I am so sorry for being late," Lorna said, her voice carrying genuine remorse. "I'll make it up to you by speeding through the initial paperwork!" She guided them quickly to her office, pausing briefly to give Claire's shoulder a grateful squeeze in passing.

Somehow, despite her frazzled start, Lorna managed to salvage the meeting. She charmed the couple, eventually even winning over the stone-faced husband. By the time they signed the paperwork, Lorna felt a small sense of victory, though her mind kept drifting back to the journal.

The rest of the afternoon flew by. She miraculously caught up on emails, paperwork, and phone calls before heading to her last meeting of the day—a last-minute summons by the mayor. Even the importance of this meeting couldn't keep her from longing to get back to the journal and the answers it might hold.

At the mayor's office, Lorna waited in his expansive corner room. The wait felt interminable, but finally, Mayor Brown entered, greeting her warmly. After pleasantries, he got straight to business.

"Miss Ritten, I'll be direct. I'm leaving for a much-needed vacation in Hawaii tomorrow. When I return, my calendar's booked solid, so I wanted to touch base about the Phoenix Children's Home project before I go."

"Thank you for making the time, Mr. Mayor. I appreciate your support for the project and the children," Lorna replied.

"Well, as I said in the meeting, I have a soft spot for that place. But here's the deal: if you can convince at least two of those business leaders to commit significant funding, I'll consider shifting some resources from the city's budget to add to the project. Can you make that happen?"

The weight of the mayor's request pressed heavily on her, but she forced herself to nod. "Yes, sir. I'll figure it."

"Perfect. Now, I have another meeting in a few minutes, so you'll need to let yourself out. Good luck, Miss Ritten."

Lorna left the mayor's office, her heels clicking briskly against the marble floor as she navigated the halls toward the exit. The abrupt conclusion of the meeting didn't bother her in the slightest. In fact, she felt a wave of relief wash over her as she realized that her obligations for the day were finally complete. The weight of the day's stress, the looming deadlines, and the pressure of convincing high-powered business leaders to support the Phoenix Children's Home project—all of it could temporarily be put aside. For now, there was just one thing on her mind: the journal.

As she stepped outside, the late afternoon sun greeted her, casting long shadows across the city streets. The warmth on her skin was soothing, a reminder that even amidst her chaotic life, there was still beauty in the world. She reached her car, climbed in, and took a deep breath before starting the engine. The journal rested on the passenger seat beside her, its aged leather cover a quiet reminder of the secrets it held within. Her fingers itched to pick it up, to flip through its pages right then and there, but she knew better than to rush. This was something to savor.

The drive home felt longer than usual, even though the traffic was mercifully light. Every red light, every slow turn, and every pedestrian crossing felt like an eternity. Her mind was already racing ahead, imagining what insights and revelations the journal might contain. She found herself wondering about her grandfather, Alfred Cypress, the man who had seemingly orchestrated so much in her life without her even knowing it. What kind of person was he? What drove him to create the technologies and estates that were now so intricately tied to her?

Journal Entry – January 10, 1979

Today, Vonya and I made one of the most exciting decisions of our lives: we officially set the date for our wedding—April 27th. I can hardly contain my excitement! Knowing that in just a few short months, I'll get to call Vonya my wife fills me with a joy I never knew possible! She truly is the love of my life, and I feel like the luckiest man alive to have her by my side. Every step we take toward building our future together feels like a blessing.

The wedding planning itself has been a wonderful adventure. It's been fun to sit down with Vonya and envision how we want our special day to unfold. From choosing a venue to picking out flowers, we've shared so many laughs and moments of inspiration. But as much as we've enjoyed planning the celebration, what excites me even more is how we've decided to start our married life together: by giving back to others.

Over the past few months, Vonya and I have been deeply involved with the youth group at our church, working on ways to support our local and global communities. It's been such a fulfilling experience. We've spent hours brainstorming and organizing fundraising efforts, doing everything from car washes to bake sales—British people thought fundraising car washes was a little funny, but hey, it kind of worked!

There were moments we joked about standing on street corners with signs asking for donations—thankfully, we didn't need to go that far! The hard work has paid off, and we've finally raised enough money to participate in the church's upcoming mission trip.

In just a few weeks, we'll be joining the youth group and several pastors on a journey to a remote part of the Amazon River. The trip's mission is simple yet profound: to bring much-needed medical supplies, educational materials, and, most importantly, the gospel to communities who may never have heard it before. The thought of reaching out to people in such need, not just with material support but with the hope and love of Christ, is humbling.

I can already sense that this trip will be transformative—not just for the lives we'll touch but for us as well. Vonya and I have talked at length about how this experience will shape our perspective and strengthen our bond. We both believe that starting our marriage with a commitment to serve others is the perfect foundation for our future. I'm eager to see how God will work through us and what lessons we'll learn from the incredible people we'll meet along the way.

There's so much to look forward to in the months ahead—our wedding, the mission trip, and all the new adventures that come with beginning a life together. I feel blessed beyond measure and can't wait to see what's next.

Journal Entry – March 17, 1979

Vonya and I went on that missions trip to the remote Amazon River tribe, The Outzaln village and I had never seen so much poverty and primitive conditions in my life, from bad drinking water to food shortages, power, but I also saw the relief we brought those beautiful people as we helped with passing out medical supplies. They were very receptive to the gospel and without overstating it, the trip was an unmitigated success!

I left England as one person and returned as another. I've always thought of myself as a compassionate person, but now, I feel a calling to help people; especially people who are less fortunate like those beautiful tribal people. I know Vonya feels the exact same way and when we were on the plane flying back to Heathrow, we agreed that God has blessed us both with abilities that we need to use wisely and that our lives will be dedicated to helping others.

The trip not only helped us in seeing direction for our lives and philanthropic future, but also gave even more energy to pursue science as a means to provide tools that would help the Outzaln tribe and many other such places around the world.

Lorna pauses for a few moments after finishing her reading, then gently places the journal down.

19

Chapter Nineteen

It was now 9:02 p.m., and the room was bathed in the soft, amber glow of the nearby floor lamp. Lorna leaned back into the plush cushions of her couch, sinking into their familiar embrace. A soft smile crept across her lips as the weight of the day seemed to momentarily lift. She let her head rest against the back of the couch, her eyes drifting to the ceiling as her mind replayed the words she had just read. For the first time in what seemed like an eternity, she felt a faint but undeniable sense of connection—a small piece of the puzzle in her quest for answers had finally fallen into place.

The room was quiet, save for the faint hum of the refrigerator in the kitchen and the rhythmic ticking of the clock on the wall. She turned her gaze to Tigger, who had claimed the oversized armchair across the room as his throne. The contrast between the serene scene before her and the chaos of the last few days was striking. The whirlwind of revelations, near-misses, and unanswered questions had left her drained, yet here, in this still moment, she felt a fleeting sense of peace. It was a rare and precious reprieve.

Her thoughts wandered back to the journal resting beside her on the couch. It was incredible how the simple act of reading her grandfather's words, written decades before she was born, could evoke such a profound sense of connection. Her fingertips brushed the worn leather cover, and she felt the weight of its significance. But tonight, she wasn't ready to dive back in. There was something else she needed to do.

Taking a deep breath, Lorna leaned forward and reached for her backpack, which rested against the coffee table. She rummaged through it until her fingers found the small burner phone Phillip had given her. The device felt foreign and impersonal in her hand, a stark contrast to the tactile warmth of the journal. She flipped it open, the screen lighting up with an unassuming green glow. As promised, the phone dialed itself, emitting a soft series of tones before connecting.

Lorna's pulse quickened slightly as she waited. The line clicked, and Phillip's calm, measured voice came through almost immediately. "Yes?" he said, his tone carrying a blend of anticipation and reassurance.

Lorna hesitated for just a moment, her mind briefly racing with all the questions she wanted to ask, the doubts she still harbored, and the uncertainty of what came next. But then, she exhaled slowly, grounding herself in the knowledge that this was just another step in the journey she had already committed to. She cleared her throat and began to speak.

"When can I come in?"

"Be at the library, 10am tomorrow morning. Here's how you get to my office..."

Phillip explained the procedure on how to gain entry into his secret office within the library. Per Phillip's directive, she went into her garage, pulled a hammer out of her small toolbox, and smashed the burner cell phone to pieces, sending little chunks of plastic circuitry flying. Why a hammer? Melting it down seemed more final, but whatever.

She walked back and sat down on the couch to gather her thoughts and what needed doing in preparation for what may come next, trying to feel some sense of organization after these last several days. She picked up her phone and dialed the main number for Aztec Realty. Claire's voice chirped out the message, "Hello, and thank you for calling Aztec Realty, where we make real estate buying a pleasure. If you know your party's extension, please dial it now..."

Lorna hit zero and after the operator message and beep...

"Hi Claire, it's Lorna. I just wanted to let you know that I won't be in the office for a few weeks. I'm working on a project and I really need to focus on it, so I won't be checking emails and voice mail every day. As soon as I come back, I'll bring you a baker's dozen of those bagels you love so much. Bye."

Lorna carefully picked up the journal, opening it gently, mindful of the history contained within its pages. Her eyes scanned the text as she flipped through the entries, each one a snapshot of a life she longed to understand. Finally, she came to the last written entry—the final thoughts her grandfather had chosen to record in this particular journal – she assumed there would be more journals Phillip would distribute to her when he saw fit to do so.

She paused for a moment before reading, her mind swirling with anticipation and questions. The handwriting, so meticulous and deliberate, seemed to hold a rhythm of its own, as if every stroke of the pen had been intentionally implying more than the obvious, every word a clue. The remaining blank pages stretched before her like an unfinished story, their emptiness stark against the vibrant life depicted in the previous entries. Why had he left so many pages unused? Was it a deliberate choice, or had something interrupted his writing?

She lingered on this thought, the possibilities branching out like roots. Had he intended to fill these pages but been unable to? Did he believe the journal's purpose had been fulfilled, or had he set it aside for a reason she could not yet comprehend? Perhaps the gaps were meant for her, an unspoken invitation to continue what he had begun.

Lorna leaned back against the couch, the journal balanced on her lap, and let her eyes drift to the ceiling. The weight of the unknown pressed against her, an unspoken mandate to push forward. She glanced back down at the blank pages and then to the final entry, her curiosity sharpening. Whatever the reason for the journal's incomplete state, she knew one thing with absolute certainty: she needed to understand what had been left unsaid.

Journal Entry – April 12, 1979

Today was one of those days that felt pivotal, even though it began like any other. I spent most of the morning immersed in the intricate details of programming the robot, making adjustments and testing its responsiveness. The progress was steady, and I felt closer than ever to achieving full functionality for the robot. The sense of anticipation was thrilling—it felt like standing on the brink of something monumental.

As I was deep in my work, Robert walked in and greeted me with a broad smile and genuine applause, praising the strides I had made so far. I couldn't help but feel encouraged by his recognition, even though his visits have been sporadic lately. I started explaining how close I was to getting the robot to work properly, sharing the excitement that had been building within me.

Then, as we often do, the conversation drifted, and I began talking about the missions trip Vonya and I had gone on to the Outzaln village. I described the faces of the villagers as they received medical supplies, the gratitude in their eyes as they heard about the gospel, and the profound impact it all had on me. I explained how it had reshaped my perspective and fueled my desire to use technology for good—to address real-world problems like clean water access, better medical care, and education in underserved areas.

But before I could finish, Robert cut me off. "Hold on a minute," he said, holding up a hand. His tone shifted abruptly, and what followed left me completely taken aback. He began talking in a way that mirrored some of the other students on campus—the ones who viewed the world through a lens of power, influence, and greed.

"You have this amazing opportunity," Robert said, his voice carrying an almost rehearsed enthusiasm. "The ability to make a huge impact on the world. Do you even realize what you're sitting on here? This isn't just about helping a few people in some remote village. This could be global. It could be revolutionary. Think about the kind of power and money this could generate!"

I was stunned. This wasn't the Robert I thought I knew—the friend who had supported my work, shared meals with me, and spoken so earnestly about wanting to help others. His words felt hollow, driven by ambition that didn't align with the vision Vonya and I held for my work.

I took a deep breath, steadying myself before I responded. "Robert," I began carefully, "any ability or opportunity I have is a gift from God. It's not about power or money—it's about using what I've been given to make the world better, to help those who can't help themselves. To me, it would be beyond wrong to ignore that."

He didn't like my answer. His expression darkened, and he shook his head in visible frustration. Without another word, he turned and walked out of the lab, leaving a heavy silence in his wake. I sat there for a long time after he left, staring at the robot's unfinished frame, trying to process what had just happened. I couldn't shake the sadness I felt—not just because Robert disagreed with me, but because his words seemed to reflect a deeper disconnect from the values I hold dear.

In the past year, so much has come into focus for me. The questions that used to loom large— "Who am I?" and "What is my purpose?"—no longer feel so insurmountable. Attending Eddington has given me the clarity to see that my purpose is multifaceted yet deeply connected: to strive to be the best Christian I can be, to push the boundaries of science and technology, and, most importantly, to use my gifts to help people in need.

These realizations haven't come easily, but they've grounded me in a way I never thought possible. I know the path I've chosen won't always be easy—there will be challenges, disagreements, and moments like today when my convictions will be tested. But I also know that staying true to my purpose is the only way forward. I can only hope that one day, Robert—and others like him—will come to understand what I'm trying to do and why it matters.

Lorna laid the journal back down and then was trying to organize her thoughts on what to do next and how to plan the next morning. Although the previous week's events were altogether depleting, her mind was firing on all cylinders, feeling unorganized and completely out of her normal rhythm, but she comes to the conclusion...

I may as well get organized for tomorrow and then try to get some sleep.

Lorna glanced at the open journal, almost making sure it hadn't moved at all. She took one step toward the hallway, but then doubled back picked up the journal and carried it to the bedroom. Somehow having it close, this made her feel a little closer to her grandfather. She carefully started packing, while the journal lay at the foot of her bed.

When she finished packing, she carried her luggage to the front door ready, so everything was good to go first thing in the morning. She went back to her bedroom and sat down on her bed. She could not help but feel a little anxious and excited. Even though she had just put the journal down a little while before, she picked it up and started reading through some of it again and finding herself smiling and feeling compassion in all the same places.

When she had finished re-reading some of the journal entries, she examined the journal closely. There were various nicks, scrapes and scratches indelibly marked in the leather binding. She focused on one particular gash on the lower end of the journal's spine and wondered...

That's a particularly nasty looking gash. How'd that happen. Looks like Grandpa blocked a sword attack with it or something. And, how about this little scratch?

Random thoughts like these wafted in and out of Lorna's imagination. She clutched the journal close to her chest. She knew that the journal didn't possess some sort of strange magical power, but it did make her feel better. However strange her past and her family might be, she was finally on the road to really finding answers!

She sat and reflected on the last few days and thought to herself that maybe keeping a journal of her own may not be a bad idea. Just like Grandpa! She thought about stopping and picking one up on her way to meet Phillip. Tigger had been sitting in a chair for most of the night and now decides it is a good time for a petting. He jumps on the bed next to Lorna and for the first time out of all the recent events she is relaxed and with Tigger calmly purring beside her she finally laid down and fell asleep.

Lorna was awake before her alarm let her know it was time to get up. She offered a good morning to the journal, which rested next to her on the opposite pillow. She quickly showered and dressed, got her last bag that she needed, grabbed the journal off the bed and walked toward her front door.

She paused in the very center of her home. For a moment, she just stood there, letting the stillness envelop her. Today felt unlike any other—a pivotal day, charged with anticipation and a weight she couldn't fully articulate. She closed her eyes briefly, inhaling deeply, and then opened them to let her gaze travel over the familiar surroundings. It wasn't just about leaving this house -- HER HOUSE. It was about stepping into a new chapter of her life, one brimming with uncertainty and significance.

The moment reminded her of the odd thrill that comes when you're heading off on vacation midweek while everyone else is still working. Except this wasn't just a break—it was something far greater, far heavier. Her lips curled into a soft, almost involuntary smile, but a nervous energy pulsed just beneath the surface.

After the brief pause, she turned her attention to Tigger, who was already watching her intently, as if sensing the shift in her demeanor. She crouched down, scooped him up gently, and placed him into the travel cage with a reassuring pat. "You're coming with me, buddy," she murmured softly. She double-checked the journal, tucked securely into her bag, feeling its reassuring weight as she adjusted the strap over her shoulder. With everything in place, she opened the door and stepped outside, the crisp morning air hitting her skin like a subtle jolt of clarity.

As she approached her car, her eyes flicked across the street, where Kyle's sedan remained stationed. The sight brought a surprising sense of comfort, a quiet reminder that she wasn't navigating this alone. Sliding into the driver's seat, she secured Tigger's cage on the passenger side and started the engine. Slowly backing out of the driveway, she maneuvered her vehicle toward where Kyle's car was parked. Rolling down her window, she leaned out the window toward him, her expression warmer than it had been in days.

"Good morning," she said, her voice steady but tinged with gratitude. "I'm glad to see you're still here this morning."

Kyle's face softened into a reassuring smile. "Good morning to you as well. And I'm glad to be here." He raised his coffee thermos as part of his salutation–that coffee helped him watch her place all night.

"I'm stopping by my mom's first, I just need to see her before going," Lorna explained, her tone shifting to something a little more practical. "So don't think I'm trying to shake you off. You're welcome to follow me, but please don't get too close to the house. I don't want to worry her."

Kyle nodded, his easy demeanor putting her at ease. "No problem. You won't even know I'm there. Let's get going." Lorna smiled again, this time a touch more softly, and said, "Okay." She eased her car forward, glancing at Tigger in his cage, who seemed surprisingly calm for all the commotion. As she pulled away from the curb, she caught sight of Kyle's sedan in her rearview mirror, following at a discreet distance.

For the first time in days, she felt a small sense of control returning. The chaos of the last week had left her reeling, but this morning, with her plans set and the journal close, there was a hint of organization creeping back into her life. The sun had just begun to rise higher, casting long shadows over the road ahead, and for the first time in a while, she felt a glimmer of hope that she might just be ready for whatever came next.

After visiting her mom, Lorna found herself on a familiar main road. Tigger, safely tucked in his cage and riding shotgun, seemed unusually content for a cat in transit. His green eyes tracked the passing landscape with what Lorna imagined to be a feline mixture of boredom and curiosity. The sky overhead was unusually bright, its few scattered clouds painting wispy streaks across the pale blue expanse. The scene should have felt tranquil, but Lorna's mind was anything but. Each passing mile seemed to hammer home the enormity of what lay ahead.

Fifteen minutes later, she pulled into the driveway of a house that had become something of a refuge for her—a place where the people inside, Susan and her husband, were trusted pillars in her life. As Lorna stepped out of her vehicle, she felt a welling of gratitude for the stability they represented, especially now when everything else seemed to be spiraling into uncertainty.

Carrying Tigger's cage up the front walk, she knocked gently on the door. Susan answered with her usual warmth, her smile a small but reliable comfort in Lorna's chaotic world.

"Thanks for watching him," Lorna said, handing over the cage. "I know it's short notice, but this project I'm working on really needs my attention. And, someone's got to feed this little numbskull."

Susan took the cage, tilting her head slightly in curiosity. "I don't mind pitching in and helping, but it's kind of last minute. Everything okay?"

"Yeah," Lorna replied, though her tone betrayed the truth: things were far from okay. "It's just... important. To me. This project could really help a lot of people. I can't get into it right now, but I'll keep you updated when I can."

Susan nodded, her expression softening. "Don't you worry about Tigger. He and I get along just fine. I hope everything goes smoothly for you. Call when you get a chance, alright?"

"I will," Lorna promised, though she knew her time would be tightly constrained. Before turning to leave, she added, "One more thing. There's a little girl named Sam—she's ten, from the Phoenix Children's Home. She's a sweet kid but shy. If you see her at the gym, could you introduce her to some of the other kids? Help her feel a little more comfortable?"

Susan's smile widened, and she placed a reassuring hand on Lorna's shoulder. "Of course. I promise."

Lorna felt a wave of relief wash over her. Knowing Sam would be looked after lightened her emotional load just a bit. She leaned in for a quick hug, said her goodbyes, and made her way back to the car. As she climbed into the driver's seat, she glanced back at the house, her hand waving absentmindedly even after the front door had closed.

As Lorna merged onto the highway, the morning sun cast long golden rays over the landscape. She couldn't help but reflect on the weight of her next steps. Dropping Tigger off had felt like more than a practical errand—it was a symbolic farewell to her normal, structured life. The road ahead wasn't just uncertain; it was potentially life-altering. For the first time, she truly considered the possibility that she might not return the same person—or worse... might not return at all.

She reached for her phone and dialed Chelsea. After a few rings, her friend picked up. "Hey! What's up?"

"I just wanted to apologize for being short with you the last few days," Lorna said, her voice filled with genuine regret. "Things have been... really crazy. I'm sorry."

"No worries," Chelsea replied easily. "We all have those days... Weeks." They share a chuckle.

Lorna hesitated for a moment, wishing she could share more, but knowing that wouldn't be a good idea. "I just wanted to let you know I'll be out of town for a few weeks on a project. Probably won't have much phone access. Can you let Brianna know, too?"

"Sure thing," Chelsea said, her tone light. "Good luck with everything. And when you're back, we're hitting that climbing wall. You owe me a rematch."

Lorna chuckled softly, grateful for Chelsea's easygoing nature. "I'm not gonna take it easy on you, you know. Be ready." Chelsea appreciated the parting challenge.

After hanging up, Lorna spotted a small convenience store and decided to make a quick stop for supplies. She motioned to Kyle, parked a few spaces over, to signal she wouldn't be long. Kyle gave a subtle nod but kept a watchful eye as she entered the store. Though she felt somewhat secure knowing he was there, she couldn't shake the unease that had become her constant companion. After making her purchases, she returned to her car, noting Kyle back in his car, ready to follow. She offered a quick wave of acknowledgment before continuing on her way.

By the time she arrived at the Armstrong Library, it was 9:54 a.m. She parked and began unloading her luggage. As she reached to close the car door, her eyes fell on the old blue binder that had once been her constant companion. It now seemed like a relic from a different life—a time when her quest for answers was limited to scraps of information and endless frustration at this library. Holding it for a moment, she realized how far she'd come. She had pieces of her history now, but with them had come more questions than she ever anticipated. Hopefully, that all changes starting today.

Following Phillip's instructions, she made her way inside and navigated to the hidden office. Phillip was seated at his desk, his back to her as he meticulously reviewed video footage from the library. Each screen showed clips of Lorna's near abduction by Vincent. The sight of herself on the screens sent a chill down her spine. To make her presence known, she let her luggage drop to the floor with a deliberate thud.

Phillip turned slowly, his expression serious. "You're here," he said simply, his tone carrying a weight that matched the gravity of the situation.

Lorna nodded, her jaw tightening as she gestured toward the screens. "So, what now?"

Phillip stood, smoothing the front of his jacket as he crossed the room. "Now, we prepare."

He gestured to the screens, the images flickering with ominous clarity. "Each one of these clips is a reminder of the danger you're in. You need to stay vigilant, Lorna. This is just the beginning. It doesn't get easier or safer moving forward."

As his words sank in, Lorna squared her shoulders, her resolve hardening. "Let's get started."

Phillip paused, his sharp gaze settling on Lorna with the kind of scrutiny that seemed to pierce through her exterior and into the very core of who she was becoming. There was something different about her now, something he hadn't quite seen before. It was in the way her shoulders squared just slightly, the way her eyes no longer darted with uncertainty but instead locked onto his with quiet resolve. She still carried the weight of her confusion, the endless questions swirling in her mind, but beneath it all was a budding strength—a quiet resilience that spoke of a woman stepping into the unknown with purpose.

When he finally spoke, his voice was calm but layered with a gravity that underscored every word. It wasn't just what he said—it was how he said it. Each syllable carried the weight of everything they had been through, the urgency of what was still to come, and the unshakable belief that this moment was pivotal. This was a turning point, and Phillip wanted to ensure Lorna understood it as much as possible.

"There is one overriding principle in all of this, Lorna," he began. "It's the reason you've been monitored by multiple parties over the past few months, why you ended up in the hospital, and why you're standing here with me this morning in a hidden room that only a handful of people in the world knows exists."

"And what principle is that?" Lorna asked, her voice steady despite the tension in the air.

"You're a Cypress," Phillip stated, each word said with deliberation. "That name carries far more weight than you understand—yet. It's not just about wealth or social influence; it's about responsibility. It means you are tied to a legacy, a network of secrets, and, yes, enemies. Your presence changes everything."

Phillip paused, letting the significance of his words settle over her. He then asked, "Did the journal you read help you gain any clarity?"

Lorna hesitated, recalling the whirlwind of emotions she'd experienced while reading the entries. "It gave me some insight into my grandfather's character, yes," she admitted. "But it also raised more questions than it answered."

"That's to be expected," Phillip replied. "The journal you've read is just one of many. Your grandfather wrote extensively, chronicling his life, his inventions, and the challenges he faced. These journals, scattered across the globe, are critical. Together with the hard drives we're tracking, they contain the keys to understanding everything—his work, his disappearance, and, most importantly, the next steps."

"What's on those hard drives?" Lorna asked, her curiosity piqued.

Phillip's expression tightened. "That's a discussion for later. For now, we need to focus on what's directly in front of us."

He walked to his desk, pressing a button hidden beneath its polished surface. A section of the wall slid aside, revealing a brushed steel elevator embedded in the far end of a short corridor. Its polished, industrial design stood in stark contrast to the more traditional library setting she had just come from.

Lorna blinked in astonishment but quickly composed herself. "What's this?" she asked.

Phillip motioned toward the elevator. "You'll see. Grab your bag.

20

Chapter Twenty

She trailed behind him into the corridor, her bag slung tightly over her shoulder, its weight a subtle reminder of everything she was carrying—both literally and figuratively. They arrived at the elevator, and as the doors slid open, Lorna felt her breath shorten for a moment. The elevator was sleek, its walls crafted entirely from tempered glass that glinted faintly under the corridor's soft lighting. The design seemed pulled straight from the pages of a sci-fi epic; its futuristic aesthetic more advanced than anything she had seen before. She hesitated for the briefest moment, then stepped inside.

The doors closed with a whisper, and the elevator began its smooth descent. As it moved downward, the world beneath her unfolded in an awe-inspiring display. What had initially seemed like an ordinary underground space quickly transformed into something extraordinary. The first thing that struck her was the sheer size of the cavern below—it was massive, a sprawling expanse that stretched farther than she had imagined. The bluish light emanating from the walls and floor cast an ethereal glow, giving the entire area an otherworldly atmosphere.

Her eyes widened as the control center came into full view. Rows of high-tech consoles lined the space, each one covered in a dazzling array of buttons, touchscreens, and blinking indicator lights. Towering server racks stood like silent sentinels, their surfaces shimmering faintly with the heat of their inner workings. Intermittent pulses of light traveled along intricate wiring systems, creating a faintly hypnotic rhythm. A soft hum filled the air, a low-frequency buzz from the machinery, occasionally broken by the gentle beeps and whirs of monitors flickering to life.

Lorna pressed her hand against the cool glass of the elevator, leaning slightly forward to get a better look. The closer they descended, the more details emerged—small teams worked at some of the consoles; their faces illuminated by the glow of their screens. It was a blend of cutting-edge technology and meticulous organization, a place where everything seemed to serve a purpose. Large holographic displays hovered above the main consoles, displaying real-time data feeds, maps, and diagrams. The movement of the data seemed alive, as though the very room were breathing with intelligence.

She turned to Phillip, her voice barely above a whisper, tinged with disbelief. "This... this is incredible. What is this place?"

Phillip allowed himself a faint smile, his eyes scanning the scene as though seeing it anew through her wonder. "This is the Cypress control center—one of the most advanced hubs in the entire world. It's been dormant for some time, but with you here, it's beginning to awaken."

Awaken? The word struck her as odd, almost surreal. She turned her attention back to the view, noticing that some of the inactive monitors and systems seemed to flicker briefly as the elevator passed. As though reacting to her presence.

"What do you mean, awaken?" she asked, her voice tinged with curiosity and a slight edge of nervousness.

Phillip glanced at her, his tone steady but deliberate. "Your grandfather designed this place with specific safeguards. It was built to recognize only one thing—a Cypress. An actual blood relative Cypress. Without one present, much of its full functionality remains inaccessible. But, with you here... it's as though the system is recognizing its purpose again. And now, so must you."

The words hung in the air as the elevator slowed to a gentle stop, the glass doors parting with seamless precision. Lorna stepped out onto the polished metallic floor, her shoes making soft clicks against the surface.

The atmosphere was cooler than she expected, the air tinged with the faint metallic scent of advanced machinery.

She stood there for a moment, taking in the enormity of the space before her. The weight of Phillip's words settled heavily on her shoulders, but there was also a flicker of something else—possibility. Whatever lay ahead, she was beginning to realize, was far beyond anything she had ever imagined. And there was no turning back.

As Lorna descended deeper into the cavernous facility, Lorna's gaze was drawn to a curious phenomenon. It began subtly at first—an array of dormant screens suddenly flickered to life in her peripheral vision, their monitors emitting soft glows. Machines stationed along the walls, previously lifeless, started humming gently, their indicator lights blinking in sequence as though heralding her arrival – almost saying hello.

The illumination rippled outward like a wave, each system waking up just as the elevator moved closer to its destination. It was mesmerizing, but also unnerving.

Lorna turned to Phillip, her brow knit with both awe and concern. "Are these systems... responding to me?" she asked, her voice barely above a whisper.

Phillip glanced at her, his expression calm but resolute, as if he had been anticipating the question. "Yes, they are. The facility is keyed to respond to the DNA signature of a Cypress. Without a member of your family present, the majority of these systems remain dormant, conserving their resources. Your presence has triggered a reactivation sequence. In other words -- It's been waiting for you."

Her pulse quickened at his words, the gravity of her connection to this place sinking in deeper. She turned her attention back to the sight before her, unable to look away as more machines lit up in her path, their hums of activity growing stronger.

Lorna stopped in her tracks, turning to face Phillip with a mixture of trepidation and disbelief. "You're telling me this entire facility is... mine to control?" Lorna didn't even like the way that left her mouth, but it was direct and to the point.

Phillip's gaze was steady. "In essence, yes. But, control comes with responsibility. This base contains technology and information that can change the course of industries, governments, even the world. That's why your grandfather was so meticulous about who could access it. It's not just about inheriting the legacy—it's about proving you're worthy of it."

Her breath caught in her throat as she looked around the cavernous space, the weight of Phillip's words pressing down on her. She walked toward one of the consoles, her fingers brushing lightly against its edge. The screen flickered to life, displaying a cascade of data that was both alien and fascinating. She could feel the hum of energy beneath her fingertips, as if the machine was waiting for her command.

Taking a deep breath, Lorna straightened her shoulders and turned back to Phillip. "What's next?"

Phillip's expression softened slightly, a glimmer of approval flickering in his eyes. "Next, we take you to the briefing room. There's much to discuss and little time to waste. The world outside may not wait for you to decide who you are, Lorna, but this place—this legacy—needs you to decide and quickly."

With that, he motioned for her to follow him down a long corridor that branched off from the control center. Lorna glanced over her shoulder at the systems behind her, their faint glow still pulsating as if watching her retreat. She felt both dwarfed and emboldened by the enormity of what lay before her.

Phillip led her down a wide corridor lined with more machinery. The walls bore faint scars of use, and the air smelled faintly of ozone. "This facility was built by your grandfather decades ago," he explained. "It extends five stories underground and connects to an elaborate network of tunnels that go on for miles. It was created not just as a base of operations but as a sanctuary and, if needed, a last line of defense."

Lorna absorbed his words, especially the last line of defense part, feeling both awe and unease. They reached a door that slid open as they approached, revealing a large briefing room. Rows of chairs faced a massive monitor, and a sleek podium stood off to one side. Phillip gestured for her to take a seat.

She hesitated, glancing at the robotic figure seated beside her. It was humanoid in design, its metallic surface polished to a reflective sheen. Its "eyes" glowed faintly, and it sat with an eerie semblance of human composure.

Phillip caught her staring. "That's C.E. One. It's one of your grandfather's first prototypes—a testament to his work and the level of advancement we're dealing with. Don't be alarmed; it's here to assist."

Lorna took her seat, her mind racing with questions, but before she could voice them, Phillip began. "What I'm about to show you is critical to understanding the task at hand."

He tapped on the podium's control panel, and the monitor lit up with a satellite image of a small island nestled within a large lake. He zoomed in, revealing a sprawling mansion surrounded by dense foliage, two helipads, boat docks, and subtle signs of movement.

"This island," Phillip said, "is one of your grandfather's estates. It's heavily fortified and houses some of the most advanced technology ever developed. However, it has also become a focal point for those who oppose everything your grandfather has stood for."

Lorna's jaw dropped slightly. "You're telling me he owns an island like that?"

"Yes," Phillip said matter-of-factly, as if it were the most natural thing in the world. "It's where we'll find answers—and potentially, the key to everything your grandfather left behind."

Lorna couldn't help but inject a touch of sarcasm into her tone. "Well, of course. Everyone has a secret high-tech island in their back pocket."

Phillip smiled faintly, appreciating her attempt to stay grounded despite the overwhelming revelations. "It's not just an island, Lorna. It's a symbol of what your family has built—and what's now at risk."

Lorna leaned back, the weight of his words pressing down on her. "So what's the plan?"

Phillip's expression grew serious. "The plan, Lorna, is for you to lead the way. You're a Cypress, and this is your legacy."

Phillip, maintaining his laser-sharp focus, pressed on. "The issue at hand is that the AI on the island has inexplicably powered up. Not only that, but based on our observations, it appears to be moving autonomously and attempting to establish a protective strategy."

Lorna raised a hand, interrupting with disbelief. "Wait, wait—what do you mean by 'a protective strategy'? And... moving AI? What are you talking about?"

Phillip paused, his tone steady but his expression firm. "The way Alfred designed the systems, everything was built to prioritize the protection of a Cypress. The AI was programmed not to harm anyone unless directly ordered to do so in the context of a specific mission. However, in the absence of a Cypress for an extended period, all systems were designed to shut down as a safety measure."

He stopped pacing and crossed his arms, staring intently at the interactive table in front of him. His brow furrowed as if searching for an answer hidden within the grain of the polished surface. Taking a deep breath, he spoke again, his voice carrying a faint trace of unease. "What's troubling is that we can't determine why the AI has reactivated on its own."

Lorna, who had been watching Phillip's every movement, tilted her head. "What do you mean, 'unclear'? What could cause something like this to happen?"

Phillip exhaled heavily and finally met her gaze. "There's really only one explanation that we can come up with at the moment. Your grandfather would have had to come into the area."

Her eyes widened, and her voice rose slightly. "You're saying my grandfather is there? He's on the island right now?"

Phillip shook his head slowly. "I don't know for certain. But if the AI has powered up, it suggests he was either there recently or... he might still be there."

Lorna leaned forward, her body tense, her voice trembling between hope and dread. "If he's there, then what's the problem? Why not just find him?"

Phillip's shoulders dropped slightly, as if the weight of the situation was pressing down on him. "The problem is twofold. First, most of the Pentagon officials we've worked with are cooperative and reasonable. But there are a few politicians who see this technology as something they must either control or destroy. They're pressuring us, and their patience has run thin. Now, with no certainty of what is going on and no communication, they've already issued a directive: we have less than 72 hours, before they're going to bomb it into oblivion."

Lorna's jaw dropped, her voice barely above a whisper. "Bomb it? The Pentagon? But, what if my grandfather is there?"

Phillip tried to soften his tone, but his words carried no comfort. "From what we've gathered, there's no indication he's currently on the island. However, we cannot take anything for granted. That's why it's imperative we act quickly. We need to retrieve the data and confirm his presence—or absence—before it's too late."

Lorna stood up abruptly, pacing a few steps before turning back to Phillip. "What do you mean by 'retrieve the data'? How am I supposed to do that?"

Phillip walked to a chair, sat down across from her, and gestured toward the monitors. "You're the only one who can retrieve it, Lorna. The AI systems are programmed to recognize and protect a Cypress. They won't harm you, but they may attempt to stop you if the systems aren't fully online or updated."

Lorna narrowed her eyes. "Wait. 'May not harm me'? What do you mean by that? Shouldn't I be safe?"

Phillip hesitated, standing and pacing again. "You should be. But there's always a margin of uncertainty. The AI was built to adapt, and in its current state, we can't predict how it will react."

Lorna threw her hands in the air, frustration dripping from her voice. "So let me get this straight: I'm going to an island full of rogue robots that *probably* won't hurt me, to search for data I don't know how to find, all before the place gets blown to bits in 72 hours, with the clock already ticking?"

Phillip straightened, meeting her exasperated gaze head-on. "Yes."

Lorna's laugh was dry, almost bitter. "And I suppose you're going to tell me not to worry?"

Phillip's lips curved into the faintest hint of a smile, though his eyes remained serious. "Yes, because you've already overcome so much. I believe in you, Lorna. This isn't just about the technology or the island. It's about you stepping into the legacy that's been waiting for you your entire life."

She sighed deeply, pinching the bridge of her nose in consternation. "This feels like a bad action movie script, Phillip."

"And yet," Phillip replied, his tone firm but understanding, "it's your reality. And I have every confidence you'll succeed."

Lorna stood frozen for a moment, the weight of the situation pressing down on her. She felt trapped—forced into a scenario she barely understood but knew she couldn't walk away from. There was a mix of disbelief and resignation swirling inside her. Finally, she stood up, pacing the room, her eyes flickering to the screen displaying the island as she made laps around the conference room.

She abruptly stopped, turning to Phillip with a steadying breath. "Okay," she said, her voice tinged with frustration and resolve. "There's really nothing else I can say but... okay."

Phillip didn't let it show, but a wave of relief washed over him. He knew how critical her cooperation was. For a brief second, he allowed himself a small nod of approval before responding in his usual calm tone, "Good. We'll move quickly but let me assure you—there are still people in the Pentagon who are on our side. They've confirmed that the timeline I've given you is accurate. They want us to succeed, Lorna. They want us to continue the work Alfred began and, if possible, uncover what happened to him."

Lorna's brow furrowed. "What's stopping them from just going to the island themselves and taking what they want?"

Phillip didn't hesitate. "The AI is the primary deterrent. It's programmed to defend the island and its resources at all costs. If an unauthorized party were to attempt to access the estate, it would perceive them as a threat and respond accordingly."

Lorna's eyebrows knitted together as unease settled in. "Respond accordingly? You wanna' walk me through what that means exactly?"

Phillip's expression remained firm. "The AI is capable of neutralizing any perceived threats. That could mean isolating intruders, disabling their equipment, or something more... forceful. And if it determines that the integrity of the island or its systems is compromised beyond recovery, it has a failsafe."

Her stomach churned, her voice tightening as she asked, "Failsafe? What kind of "failsafe" are we talking about?"

Phillip's tone grew heavier, matching the gravity of what he was about to reveal. "The AI is programmed to ensure that nothing—absolutely nothing—falls into the wrong hands. If it comes to it, the AI will initiate a self-destruct protocol of its own to destroy the island and everything on it."

The words hit Lorna like a punch to the gut. She stared at Phillip, trying to process the enormity of what he had just said. "Destroy the island?" she repeated, her voice barely above a whisper, the weight of the statement bearing down on her.

Phillip nodded gravely. "Yes. That's why your role is crucial. As a Cypress, the AI recognizes your DNA. It's programmed to prioritize your safety above all else and won't harm you intentionally. That gives you an advantage no one else has."

Lorna shook her head, her voice tinged with incredulity and frustration. "Wait—so you're saying I'll be safe, but then you turn around and tell me it might try to stop me? Our government wants to blow up the island and so does the island's AI? This is supposed to inspire confidence, Phillip?"

Phillip's gaze softened, but his tone remained resolute. "I understand how this sounds, but the AI is a complex system. While it won't actively harm you, its current state is... incomplete. Without Alfred's presence, certain systems may not function as intended, and its protective measures could interfere with your mission. It's not about trust—it's about understanding the risks."

Phillip exhaled slowly, clearly measuring his words, "You're not going into this blind. We'll equip you with the tools you'll need, and the AI's primary directive is to safeguard a Cypress. That alone puts you in a unique position to succeed."

She stopped pacing and fixed him with a sharp glare. "That's not exactly reassuring, Phillip. I feel like I'm being sent into a lion's den and told, 'Don't worry, the lion might just be in a bad mood.'"

Phillip looked at her with a rare flicker of sympathy. "Your grandfather wanted to protect you for as long as possible. This wasn't the life he wanted for you. But now, circumstances have forced us all into action. He left behind the tools, the technology, and the knowledge for you to step into this role when the time was right."

She looked away, her emotions warring between frustration, fear, and a reluctant sense of purpose. "And, you really believe I'm the only one who can do this?"

Phillip nodded without hesitation. "Yes. The AI will only allow a Cypress to retrieve the data. No one else can access it without triggering the failsafe. You're not just the best choice, Lorna—you're the only choice."

Lorna let out a slow, shaky breath. "And if I fail?" she asked, her voice barely audible.

Phillip's eyes locked onto hers, the weight of the situation evident in his tone. "You won't fail. You can't fail. If you don't succeed, everything Alfred built—his work, his legacy, and possibly even the chance to find him—will be lost forever."

Her heart pounded as the enormity of the mission pressed down on her. She looked back at Phillip, determination flickering in her eyes.

"Fine," she said, her voice steadier now. "I'll do it. But you better be right about this, Phillip."

Phillip gave her a small, approving nod. "I am right, Lorna. You'll see that soon enough. Now let's get you ready."

He sighed, walking to his desk and retrieving a small box from a secure safe. "You'll be as safe as we can ensure, Lorna. But this will help." He opened the box, revealing a sleek bracelet-like device with a small, embedded screen. It glimmered faintly in the room's low light, its design both intricate and futuristic.

"What is that?" Lorna asked, eyeing it with a mix of curiosity and caution.

Phillip held it out to her. "It's a locator and interface device your grandfather designed specifically for you. It will help you navigate the island and mansion, identify important data points, and—if all goes well—facilitate your access to the information we need."

Lorna hesitated before taking it, her fingers brushing against the cool metal. "He designed this... for me?" Her voice was softer now, almost disbelieving.

Phillip nodded. "Your grandfather believed in you, Lorna. He always planned for this moment, even if he hoped it wouldn't come to this."

Her throat tightened. She slipped the bracelet onto her left wrist, fastening the latch. Instantly, it powered up, small lights flickering to life and the embedded screen displaying a stream of data. She watched in awe. "Well... that's a thing."

Phillip allowed himself a small smile. "Remarkable, isn't it?"

The moment of levity was brief. Phillip quickly transitioned back to the matter at hand. "Here are your instructions. You'll head to the dock where a boat, coded specifically to your DNA, is waiting for you. It will take you to the island. Once there, the bracelet will guide you. The bracelet will also project a bit of a cloaking device to the AI's."

Lorna's eyebrows furrowed as she followed up, "Cloaking? Sorry, I'm not up on my sci-fi terminology. This makes me invisible...?"

Phillip smirked and responded, "Not invisible, but it will give you enough of a cover to allow you to sneak around quietly without being detected. Make noise or knock something over and they will probably find you. Do be careful."

Lorna stared at him, the enormity of the task sinking in. "I'll do my best."

Phillip's expression turned deadly serious. "Lorna, we need that data. You can do this."

She nodded. "Got it."

As she left the room, a lingering tension hung in the air. It was as though both of them knew the stakes were impossibly high, and failure wasn't an option.

21

Chapter Twenty-One

Lorna got into a van with only windows in the driver's area, making it impossible for anyone to see her riding in the back. Kyle sat silently in the back of the van with Lorna; she found his presence comforting. Lorna's thoughts twisted and turned as she wondered if this was the day she would meet her own demise. After a drive that seemed both long and short, she finally arrived at her destination.

At the dock, Lorna made her way to the boat Phillip had directed her to. It looked unassuming, its sleek design more practical than flashy. She stepped aboard, and as soon as she approached the console, the controls powered on, illuminated by a soft glow. A calm, mechanical voice spoke from a small speaker. "Please untie this boat from the dock to begin your journey."

Caught off guard, Lorna hesitated for a moment, but then followed the instruction. She unfastened the ropes securing the boat, and as she returned to the console, the boat began to move. It picked up speed, cutting through the water with an almost eerie precision.

Sitting at the console, Lorna glanced around the lake. The boat's automated nature unnerved her.

As if on cue, Phillip's voice crackled through the bracelet on her wrist. "Lorna, is everything okay?"

Startled, she jumped slightly, her heart racing. "Phillip! Could you warn me next time?" she snapped. "You almost made me jump out of the boat!"

Phillip chuckled softly. "Apologies. I wanted to check in. The boat will take you directly to the island. Just stay near the console, so it looks like you're steering—it'll attract less attention."

Lorna rolled her eyes. "Sure, I'll pretend I'm in control," she muttered under her breath, feeling anything but in. control.

"You're doing fine," Phillip reassured her. "Trust his technology. Trust yourself."

As the boat cut swiftly across the lake, Lorna couldn't help but feel the weight of her mission pressing down on her. She stared ahead at the horizon, where the shadow of the island was beginning to form. Her mind raced with questions. What would she find? Could she truly do this? And more importantly, what if she couldn't?

The boat surged forward, and Lorna gripped the console tightly. "Here we go," she whispered to herself.

As the boat cut smoothly through the water, Lorna's nerves heightened with every passing moment. The journey had taken approximately twenty minutes, and by now, she expected to see some indication of an estate or dock ahead. Instead, as the island loomed closer, it appeared completely uninhabited. There were no visible structures, no signs of life—just dense foliage and rugged rock formations lining the shore. Her pulse quickened. *Was this the right place? Had something gone wrong? Did this crazy AI boat take me to the wrong address?*

She reached for her wrist bracelet device, prepared to contact Phillip for reassurance, but before she could press a button, a deep mechanical groan reverberated through the air. The sound was so powerful it seemed to vibrate through her chest. Directly in front of her, two enormous sections of rock—what she had assumed were part of the island's natural formation—began to separate with a low grind. The concealed doors moved with an eerie smoothness, revealing a massive cave-like tunnel leading straight into the island's core.

Lorna's mouth parted slightly in astonishment. These weren't ordinary doors—they blended seamlessly with the natural stone, expertly disguised. If she hadn't witnessed them moving, she would have sworn they were solid, immovable rock.

The boat's engines slowed almost instinctively, shifting into a gentle idle as it glided forward, guided automatically into the tunnel's entrance. The doors behind her silently sealed shut, plunging her into an enclosed space of dim, flickering light. Small lanterns were embedded in the rock walls at precise intervals of about ten to fifteen feet, their soft glow casting shadows across the blackened water. The passageway was narrow, approximately twenty feet in width, with a ceiling just as high, giving it a slightly claustrophobic feel.

Lorna's grip tightened on the edge of the boat as it continued forward, her senses hyper-aware. The water beneath her was an inky void, its surface barely disturbed by the boat's quiet motion. Though the tunnel felt enclosed, there was an eerie vastness to it—like something unseen could be lurking just beyond the dim glow of the lanterns.

After about three minutes, the tunnel took a slight turn, revealing a docking area. Concrete steps led up from the water to a platform that appeared man-made, and large metallic doors stood at the far end, waiting – *Now, those are unmistakably doors*. The boat eased up to the edge of the platform with precise control, coming to a smooth stop before shutting down completely. It was as if the vessel had been trained to arrive at this exact spot, as though it had done so countless times before and it knew when to cut the engines for a smooth stop.

Lorna exhaled slowly. She had been so focused on the ride through the tunnel that she hadn't fully processed what awaited her beyond those doors. She reached for her wrist device, checking for a signal. Nothing. Figures. She was deep inside an island surrounded by rock—communication with the outside world was probably impossible.

With hesitant but steady steps, she disembarked, her boots tapping lightly against the stone platform. It was a relatively small dock, roughly twenty feet by twenty feet, but well-constructed. The craftsmanship of it all was remarkable and was smooth and seamless. Despite being hidden underground, the space was pristine and well-maintained. The air was cool and still, filled with the faint scent of mineral-rich stone.

As she approached the large double doors, she reached out to grasp one of the handles—only for both doors to swing open on their own before she could touch them. The motion startled her, but she quickly reminded herself that this entire place had been designed with advanced technology. Automatic doors should be the least surprising thing she encountered here.

Still, she muttered under her breath, "Pretty cool."

Beyond the doors stretched a corridor, extending about forty feet before curving slightly to the right. The walls were lined with metallic panels, interspersed with control panels and embedded lighting strips that flickered to life as she passed. It was an unsettling yet fascinating effect, as though the island itself was aware of her presence. It wasn't terribly different from the underground lair Phillip took her to when she was first being introduced to this fascinating world of the future.

At the end of the corridor, another door awaited her. It too slid open without prompting, making a subtle whooshing sound as it moved out of the way. She stepped inside and was immediately struck by the sight before her.

She had entered what could only be Alfred Cypress's laboratory.

The sheer scale of the space left her momentarily breathless. The walls soared at least forty feet in height, with towering shelves, suspended platforms, and mechanical arms lining various workstations. Several sections of the lab were designated for different types of research, each one filled with a dizzying array of equipment, blueprints, and prototypes.

Lorna's eyes were drawn to a massive monitor on the far wall, displaying a digital map of the estate. Several small blips moved across the screen, marking the patrol patterns of what she assumed were the AI-controlled security units—most likely the first iteration of the Cypress Elite, or the Knights, as they had been called. Though they didn't appear to be in full activation mode, they were moving.

Her gaze then fell on something else—a cylindrical chamber positioned near the back of the room. It stood about seven feet tall, sleek and metallic, with various cables and data ports attached. A sinking feeling formed in her gut. It looked eerily similar to descriptions she had read about.

Her breath caught in her throat as she approached the chamber, her mind racing. If this was some kind of stasis pod, meant to house an AI or humanoid entity—then where was it?

A soft chime broke her thoughts, and she turned abruptly to see an elevator built into the far side of the lab. Without hesitation, she walked over, and as expected, the doors slid open upon her approach. She stepped inside.

A smooth, neutral voice asked, "What floor, please?"

The sudden sound made her flinch, though she quickly recovered. She pursed her lips together before muttering, "Main floor... I guess."

The elevator began its ascent, gliding upward with a seamless motion.

The elevator doors gently whooshed aside and Lorna stepped out onto the main floor. She was met with a vast hallway, its walls lined with intricate molding and towering windows overlooking the estate grounds. The mansion was stunning—every detail carefully designed with elegance and grandeur. This wasn't just a high-tech fortress; it was a home.

As she moved through the halls, something outside caught her eye. *Movement.*

She tensed, her breath hitching. Was it one of the AI guards? She pressed herself against the wall, peering carefully through the glass. Whatever it was, it was moving with slow, deliberate purpose. She forced herself to keep going, staying as quiet as possible.

She soon found herself in the great room, a massive space with an even grander fireplace. Above it hung a stunning portrait of a woman—regal, poised, and heartbreakingly familiar from what she had read, it was Vonya.

Lorna's breath caught. She stared at the painting, realization dawning upon her. This wasn't just any woman. This was her grandmother. And as she looked at the features, she realized just how much she resembled her. She reflexively touched her face as she recognized the family resemblance.

Emotion swelled in her chest. She had spent her entire life wondering about her biological family, and now here she was, standing face-to-face with a piece of her history. For a brief moment, she allowed herself to feel that connection—until a noise in the distance shattered the moment.

Her body tensed, instincts kicking in. Her breathing quickened.

Someone—or something—was inside the mansion with her.

Lorna's pulse sped up as she quickly moved into another room. A study, judging by the large desk and scattered notes on the surface. One note in particular caught her attention—it wasn't a completed letter, but rather scribbled fragments of thoughts, as if someone had been trying to piece something together.

She didn't have time to dwell on it.

A door opened somewhere in the distance.

Her breath hitched. Footsteps.

Someone was coming.

She bolted down the hall, scanning desperately for a place to hide. Her heart pounded as she ducked into what appeared to be an enormous library, quickly tiptoeing over a large, oriental area rug and slipping under one of the large desks.

The footsteps grew closer.

She held her breath, her pulse thudding like a drum in her ears.

Someone was here. Walking through the room.

She clenched her fists, her mind racing.

She had walked into something far bigger than she had anticipated, and now, she had no choice but to see it through.

Lorna remained frozen under the desk, heart pounding so loudly she feared it might give her away. She listened intently as the faint whirring sounds—electronic in nature—faded slowly down the hall.

Whoever, or whatever, had been in the room was now moving away. She exhaled as quietly as possible, still not daring to shift her position. Her muscles ached from being tensed for so long, but she dared not move. Not yet.

She strained her ears, counting the seconds, waiting for complete silence. A minute passed, then another. Only then did she carefully inch out from under the desk, rising to a crouch. Her fingers grazed the edge of the polished wood for balance as she slowly straightened, her eyes scanning the dimly lit library for any sign of movement.

Every step forward was hesitant, her body on high alert. She felt like a rabbit creeping across an open field, waiting for a predator to strike. With her back to one of the massive wooden shelves, she surveyed the grand space. The library was breathtakingly beautiful, two stories high, with intricate molding along the ceiling and towering bookshelves that reached to a stunning second-floor balcony. A spiral staircase wound upward, its gold-accented railing gleaming in the dim light.

For a moment, she allowed herself to take it in. The sheer elegance of the place was overwhelming. This had been her grandfather's private library, filled with books, knowledge, and secrets. But right now, she had no time to appreciate its grandeur—she needed to stay focused.

Her eyes flicked up toward the second floor. Something about it called to her, as if instinct was guiding her toward an answer. With a cautious but steady pace, she made her way up the spiral staircase, each step creaking slightly beneath her weight.

When she reached the top, she walked along the balcony, her fingers brushing lightly against the spines of leather-bound books. About midway down the row, her eyes landed on something unusual—an open section of shelving that wasn't filled with books. Instead, various objects sat neatly arranged, as if waiting for her.

Lorna's pulse quickened as she stepped closer. Among the items on the shelf, her gaze locked onto something eerily familiar.

The sparrow.

22

Chapter Twenty-Two

It was the same intricate mechanical sparrow that had led her to her first discovery back in the mansion she had been given; or at least an identical one. The realization sent a chill through her.

She hesitated only for a second before stepping closer, slowly reaching out toward the small mechanical bird. As soon as her fingers came within inches of it, the eyes of the sparrow flickered to life with a soft golden glow. But this time, something different happened.

Instead of revealing a hidden book, the entire bookshelf trembled slightly, then with a barely audible hiss, the entire case swung open like a secret doorway. A dark corridor yawned before her, shrouded in mystery.

At that exact moment, her wrist device blinked to life, a small light pulsing faintly.

Lorna swallowed hard. She was onto something. Something big.

Taking one last glance behind her to make sure she wasn't being followed, she stepped inside. The moment she crossed the threshold, the bookcase swung shut behind her with a muted thud. The vast nature of the library had now changed to a very quiet and confined environment.

The corridor was narrow, lined with old stone walls that gave it an almost medieval feel. The air was slightly cooler here, carrying a faint metallic scent. The path sloped gently downward, and after about twenty feet, she emerged into a dimly lit room.

Her breath caught in her throat.

The room was filled with information in every form imaginable.

Maps, diagrams, and sketches covered the walls, pinned up in a seemingly organized chaos. Shelves lined with large binders and rolled-up blueprints filled the space. Tables were stacked with papers, and in the center of it all stood a massive desk covered in scattered notes, as if someone had been working here recently, not unlike the organized mess she passed moments ago in the large study.

But what truly captured her attention were the monitors on the far wall.

They flickered, struggling to power up, but never quite making it. Whatever controlled them wasn't fully functional.

Lorna took a cautious step forward, unsure what to do next. As she scanned the room, her eyes landed on something even more familiar—the sparrow.

It perched on a small pedestal near the far corner. Unlike the other one, this one had no bookcase to open—at least, not that she could see. Instead, as she approached, a hologram in front of the pedestal flickered to life before her eyes.

She gasped.

The hologram displayed a top-down view of the island, its entire layout mapped in intricate detail. Several locations flashed intermittently, each marked with a different color. To the left, a smaller projection appeared, acting as a legend to decode what the markers meant.

Her eyes widened as she realized what she was looking at.

These were the locations of the key hard drives.

Her grandfather had hidden them in various lockboxes around the island, likely to prevent anyone from easily finding them. The thought made her heart race. If someone had come looking for this information, they would've had an impossible time retrieving all the drives without this precise data. But, as Phillip keeps saying, she's a Cypress.

Just then, her wrist device buzzed again. A prompt appeared on the small screen, offering her the option to download the hologram's data. With a smile borne from relief, she pressed the confirmation button. The screen flashed, and within seconds, the map transferred onto her device, causing a small version of the hologram to form over her wrist device.

A relieved smile touched her lips. This was it. This was exactly what she needed. With this information, all she had to do was locate the key drives, retrieve them, and get off this island of extreme danger and overall weirdness.

Lorna turned quickly, already making her way back toward the secret entrance. Confidence surged through her—this was going to be easier than she'd thought.

She stepped carefully, retracing her path down the narrow corridor, her boots barely making a sound against the cool stone floor. The dim overhead lights flickered slightly, casting eerie shadows that elongated her movements against the walls. As she reached the end of the passageway, she hesitated, pressing her hand against the smooth wooden panel that had seamlessly hidden this secret room from the rest of the mansion.

With a soft click, the bookcase shifted once more, silently swinging open to reveal the second floor of the grand library. The warm glow of the antique sconces lining the walls was a stark contrast to the sterile, metallic coldness of the hidden room she was leaving behind. She stepped through quickly, and the moment she was clear, the panel quietly sealed itself shut behind her, once again disguising its existence among the countless shelves of books.

Lorna exhaled sharply, taking in the vast space of the library. It was even more imposing now that she had returned with the weight of new information pressing against her mind. Her eyes darted instinctively toward the spiral staircase, remembering the path she had taken earlier. If she retraced her steps, she could make her way back down to the main floor and hopefully find an exit that would take her outside without drawing any attention.

She moved swiftly, descending the staircase with controlled urgency. Each step felt deliberate; each breath measured. The massive portrait of her grandmother still loomed over the grand fireplace watching her, but she didn't stop to take it in this time. Every second mattered.

As she reached the first floor, she immediately searched for an exit. The grand double doors that led to the main foyer were tempting, but she dismissed them just as quickly as the thought entered her mind. Too open, too exposed. If anyone—or anything—was lurking nearby, it would be the first place they'd expect her to go.

Instead, she turned down a narrower hallway, moving past towering shelves of ancient texts and personal journals. In a place that had hidden rooms and was dripping with secrecy, she was certain there had to be another way out.

Her hands skimmed along the edges of the bookshelves as she moved, feeling for any hidden mechanisms—just in case there was another secret passage her grandfather had built into the structure.

Then, just as she neared the far end of the library, she spotted it. A door.

It was unassuming, tucked between two tall bookshelves as if it had been an afterthought in the mansion's design. It wasn't the kind of grand, elaborate exit she might have expected in a place like this—it was simple, wooden, and without ornamentation. A small, narrow window next to it gave a glimpse of what lay beyond. The glass was slightly dusty, but through it, she could see the faint glow of moonlight filtering through the trees.

This was it!

Lorna reached for the handle, her pulse quickening. The cold metal met her fingertips, and for a brief second, she hesitated, pressing her ear against the door to listen for any movement on the other side. Silence.

She turned the handle.

The door opened smoothly, revealing a short, enclosed landing with a narrow staircase leading down. The air was cooler here, slightly damp, carrying the scent of moss and aged wood. She carefully stepped onto the first stair, making sure it wouldn't creak under her weight. The last thing she needed was to alert anyone—or anything—to her presence.

As she descended, the passage grew darker, and she instinctively reached up to adjust the brightness on her wrist device. The small screen glowed faintly, casting just enough light to make out the steps ahead of her.

Finally, she reached the bottom, where another door stood waiting. This one was sturdier, reinforced with iron hinges and a thick wooden frame. A gust of crisp night air whispered through the cracks, sending a shiver down her spine.

Taking a steadying breath, she pushed it open.

The night enveloped her immediately. The sounds of the mansion faded behind her, replaced by the rustling of leaves and the distant lapping of water against the shore.

She had made it outside.

Relief washed over her for only a moment before she froze. A heavy, mechanical sound rumbled through the air.

Footsteps.

Lorna's breath caught in her throat. Whatever was out here, it was big.

Without thinking, she darted into the wooded area just beyond the mansion, pressing herself tightly against the trunk of a tree. The dense foliage offered some cover, but the open space between the trees wasn't enough to truly hide her if whatever was approaching had enhanced vision—or worse, heat sensors. As Phillip indicated, the wrist device could only provide a small amount of cloaking but wouldn't completely hide her.

She held her breath, gripping the rough bark as she listened.

The footsteps were slow but deliberate. Metal shifting against metal. A low, almost rhythmic hum accompanied each step.

Something was hunting the island.

And now, she was caught right in its path.

She pressed herself against the rough bark of a thick tree, every muscle in her body tense.

The sound of heavy footfalls approached. They were rhythmic, deliberate... mechanical.

Lorna held her breath.

Something big WAS hunting the island and she had just stepped into its territory.

The air was thick with moisture, the scent of earth and lake water blending together as Lorna moved cautiously through the dense jungle-like foliage to evade it. The night sky was vast above her, the sliver of the moon casting just enough silver light to guide her way.

She glanced down at the small glowing display on her wrist device. The map of the island flickered on the screen, indicating five different locations where the encrypted hard drives were hidden. One was somewhere close—just beyond a rocky outcrop near the shore. She took a slow, measured breath.

Keeping low, she crept through the underbrush until she reached the jagged cliffs that overlooked the water. The terrain was uneven, the rocks worn smooth by the tide that lapped against them far below. Her boots crunched softly against the gravel as she climbed over a large boulder, scanning the area.

Her wrist device beeped softly. She was close.

Lorna crouched, running her hands along the base of one of the large stones, searching for something out of place. Then, just under the lip of the boulder, she felt it—a small, square indentation. Brushing away the loose debris, she found the first lockbox embedded into the rock itself.

She pressed her thumb against the biometric scanner, and with a quiet *click*, the panel slid open. Nestled inside was a slim, matte-black hard drive slightly smaller than her palm. She snatched it up, securing it in the small pouch strapped to her belt.

Before she could let out a relieved breath, movement in the distance caught her eye.

A humanoid figure, tall and sleek, its metallic frame gleaming under the dim moonlight, was patrolling the ridge above her. One of the Cypress AI guards. Its head swiveled from side to side, scanning the landscape with glowing red optics. Lorna flattened herself against the rock, barely breathing as she watched the robotic sentry pause, as it sensed something nearby.

Her pulse pounded against her ribs.

The machine lingered for a moment, then resumed its steady patrol, disappearing into the shadows of the trees. The sounds of crickets and other night critters helped Lorna's own sounds blend into the overall wall of night sounds.

Lorna exhaled slowly. *One down. four to go.*

The second location brought her to the remnants of what looked like an abandoned storage shed, its walls long since collapsed, leaving only a skeletal frame of rusted metal beams. This had to be a leftover from a long time ago and Alfred just never bothered to get rid of it. According to her wrist device, the lockbox was underground.

She crouched down, brushing aside a layer of leaves and dirt, and found a concealed metal hatch. She gripped the handle and heaved it open with a groan, revealing a dark, musty hole lined with old maintenance tunnels.

Lorna lowered herself carefully, her boots landing on a metal walkway below. The air was stale, thick with dust. Guided by the soft glow of her wrist device, she found the lockbox tucked into the base of a support column.

As she retrieved the second hard drive, a sound made her freeze.

A metallic *clang* echoed through the tunnels. *Wonder where this thing goes...? Are there other tunnels here? Where would they go and why were they built?*

Lorna's heart leapt into her throat. She turned slowly, peering down the length of the tunnel, her grip tightening on the hard drive. A faint red glow pulsed from deeper within.

A patrol bot was here, scanning the area with a beam of reddish light.

She had only seconds.

She backed away, watching as the red glow flickered in the distance before eventually fading.

She didn't wait to see if it would emerge. Two down. Three left.

With careful, silent movements, she slipped out of the tunnel, hoisting herself back onto the forest floor. She shut the hatch as softly as she could, scattering dirt and leaves over it to hide any sign of her presence.

Lorna's next destination was a walled-off courtyard behind the mansion, overgrown with ivy and surrounded by thick stone barriers. The area was eerily quiet, save for the occasional rustling of leaves in the night breeze.

The lockbox was hidden beneath an old marble fountain in the center of the courtyard. She knelt beside it, running her hands along the edge until she found a small removable tile. She pried it open, revealing the third drive nestled within.

Just as she secured the drive, a sound made her stomach drop—mechanical whirring and approaching footsteps.

She turned her head slowly. *Uh oh!*

Two AI sentries were entering the courtyard from opposite ends, their glowing optics sweeping the area.

Lorna's breath hitched.

They were closing in.

She pressed her back against the fountain, assessing her options. There was no way she could outrun them in the open courtyard. She needed to move—fast.

The only way out was back through the mansion.

23

Chapter Twenty-Three

As quietly as possible, she slipped toward a side entrance, ducking into the shadows. She crept along the outer wall, barely daring to breathe as one of the sentries passed just feet from her hiding place.

When she reached the door, she pushed it open just enough to slide inside, closing it silently behind her.

Her hands were trembling as she exhaled.

That was too close. But she wasn't done yet.

According to her wrist device, there was one in the large kitchen and one in Alfred's office.

Since the other hard drives had been hidden well, she knew retrieving these last two wouldn't be easy.

Bracing herself, Lorna slipped deeper into the mansion, her heart pounding as she moved toward the kitchen.

The hallways were eerily quiet, the only sound being the faint hum of the AI systems embedded in the walls. Even the massive chandeliers that hung above cast only a dim glow, giving the grand corridors an otherworldly feel. Shadows stretched across the marble floors, shifting as she moved carefully through the expansive space.

She hugged the walls, keeping herself pressed against the cool surfaces of wood paneling and expensive wallpaper, as she advanced, her ears straining for any sound that would indicate movement. She knew she wasn't alone in the mansion—the AI patrols were moving, scanning, watching.

Lorna paused at the intersection of two hallways. A long corridor stretched to her left, the heavy scent of oak and aged paper suggesting that it led to the library. To her right, a series of tall arched windows cast thin beams of moonlight onto the floor. And straight ahead—where she needed to go—was another hallway leading to the mansion's enormous kitchen.

Her wrist device pulsed softly, indicating that she was heading in the right direction.

She took a careful step forward.

A sudden mechanical *click* echoed in the distance.

Lorna froze. The sound wasn't close, but it was close enough.

She crouched slightly, peeking around the corner. Down the hall, past an open doorway, a silhouette moved—tall, rigid, unmistakably mechanical.

An AI sentry.

Its humanoid frame glowed faintly, the metallic plates on its body catching the dim light as it scanned the area with slow, deliberate movements. Red optics flickered, casting a soft glow on the walls as it turned its head methodically from side to side.

Lorna gritted her teeth.

She could try to slip past it, but the hallway was long and open—too much of a risk. If she got caught in the open, she wouldn't stand a chance against something designed for protection and efficiency by the greatest inventor of the 21st Century.

Her only option was to find another way around.

She carefully backtracked, moving through a side passage that led toward the mansion's service corridors. These were the pathways used by house staff back when the estate was operational, narrow and discreet, designed for movement without intrusion. The walls here were plainer, with exposed beams and dimly lit sconces lining the way.

The air was cooler here, carrying a faint metallic scent.

Lorna crept through the passage, checking her wrist device for navigation. It wasn't a direct route, but if she could snake her way through these hidden corridors, she might be able to get around the AI patrols undetected.

She reached a small alcove where an old wooden door stood slightly ajar. Beyond it, she could see a sliver of the main hallway—the path leading straight to the kitchen.

Taking a deep breath, she pushed the door open just enough to slip through.

The moment she did, her blood ran cold.

Standing halfway down the hallway, barely twenty feet away, was another AI sentry.

It hadn't seen her yet, but its head was scanning in slow, rhythmic motions.

Lorna flattened herself against the wall, back into the shadows, her breathing shallow, pushing her wrist device against her forehead in case that helped with the cloaking – it was worth a shot. What she needed was a distraction.

Slowly, she reached into her pocket and pulled out a small ballpoint pen she had collected from her office weeks ago. It wasn't much, but it would do.

She waited, heart pounding, until the AI turned slightly in the opposite direction. Then, with a flick of her wrist, she tossed the pen down the corridor, letting it clatter against the floor a good distance away.

The AI's head snapped toward the sound.

Lorna didn't waste a second.

She darted forward, staying low, moving as quickly and silently as she could. The kitchen doors were only a few steps away.

The AI remained fixated on the noise for a moment longer before resuming its patrol.

Lorna slipped through the doors and exhaled, pressing her back against the cool wood and finally seeing the place where elaborate meals were made back in another time.

The kitchen was enormous—restaurant-sized, just as Phillip had said. Stainless steel countertops stretched across the room, reflecting the dim glow of emergency lighting. Rows of shelves lined the walls, filled with dishes, utensils, and long-expired dry goods. A massive island sat in the center, and above it, a hanging rack still held pots and pans.

But Lorna wasn't interested in the kitchen's grandeur—she was looking for one thing...

The lockbox.

Her wrist device pulsed, guiding her toward the far end of the kitchen, near what appeared to be an old walk-in refrigerator.

Moving swiftly but carefully, she crossed the room, scanning every surface for something out of place.

Her device pinged softly as she neared the far counter.

Then she saw it—a small, embedded panel in the cabinetry beneath the counter.

She crouched down, brushing her fingers over the smooth surface. No visible seams. It was perfectly hidden.

In the absence of a biometric reader for her to place her thumb against, Lorna exhaled in frustration and thought about this new challenge. Then, inspiration hit her. She pressed her thumb against her wrist device, and the gamble paid off. A quiet *click* sounded from the panel. It slid open, revealing the small lockbox inside.

She grabbed the hard drive, tucking it safely into her pouch.

But, before she could even rise to her feet, a metallic *clank* rang out from the hallway just outside the kitchen.

Lorna's stomach clenched.

The AI sentry was moving again—this time, toward the kitchen.

She had only seconds.

Her eyes darted around the room. There was no back exit. The only way out was the way she had come in and that wasn't an option.

Then, her gaze landed on the walk-in refrigerator. It was risky, but she had no other choice.

She sprinted toward the heavy door, slipping inside just as the kitchen doors swung open, hopefully, undetected.

The inside of the fridge was icy, the lingering chill from long-deactivated cooling systems still present. The glow from her wrist device revealer shelves of empty bins and expired containers filled the space, giving her limited options for hiding.

She squeezed into a corner, pressing herself against a row of shelving, peering through the narrow crack between the door and the frame.

The AI entered the kitchen, its heavy footsteps echoing against the tile floor.

It moved slowly, scanning the room.

Lorna's breath was shallow, her heartbeat hammering in her ears.

The sentry's glowing red optics swept across the kitchen, lingering for a moment near the cooking prep island.

Lorna remained perfectly still.

Then, after what felt like an eternity, the sentry turned and walked back toward the hallway.

She waited, counting the seconds.

When she was sure it was gone, she exhaled, and pushed the refrigerator door open just enough to slip out. Lorna let out a shaky breath.

One last hard drive and it was in Alfred's office.

This has been far from easy, but she was accomplishing her mission. Perhaps Phillip's trust in her wasn't misplaced after all. She had come too far to fail now.

Steeling herself, she slipped back into the shadows and began making her way toward the final destination – her grandfather's office.

Lorna steadied herself in the dimly lit kitchen, her fingers still curled around the latest hard drive she had retrieved. She could still feel the icy chill of the walk-in refrigerator clinging to her skin, but she didn't have time to dwell on it. She slipped the latest hard drive into her pouch and gathered her resolve.

One more hard drive and then, let's get out of here!

The last hard drive was in Alfred's office, and that meant navigating through more of the mansion's labyrinth-like halls, avoiding the ever-present AI sentries.

Lorna pressed herself against the kitchen doorway, carefully peering down the hallway. The glow from an AI patrol bot flickered against the darkened walls as it methodically scanned its surroundings. She took a slow breath, counting the seconds between its movements.

Five... four... three... two...

The sentry turned away, moving further down the hall.

Now was her chance.

She slipped out of the kitchen, keeping her steps light and quick. The long corridors stretched before her like veins through the mansion, the polished marble floors eerily silent beneath her careful footsteps. The grandeur of the estate was undeniable—gold inlays traced the borders of the ceilings, and ornate sconces cast long, shifting shadows as she moved.

She turned a corner and paused, pressing herself against a column. Another AI stood further down the hallway, blocking the direct path to her grandfather's office. Its posture was rigid, its red optics glowing steadily as it processed its surroundings.

No way past it. She'd have to take a longer route.

Doubling back, Lorna ducked into one of the side corridors, this one much narrower and lined with old wooden panels instead of marble. It had an older feel—almost like an old servant's hallway or passage used for discreet movement.

She crept through, passing what looked like a gallery of paintings—portraits of various figures she assumed were past members of the Cypress family. Their eyes, painted with meticulous detail, seemed to follow her as she moved past them.

She reached an intersection and hesitated.

Left or right?

She glanced at her wrist device, but the mapping was hazy—perhaps due to the AI interference in the mansion. *Can nothing be easy here?*

She chose left.

The air grew heavier, tinged with a faint scent of aged books and worn leather. That had to be a good sign. Her grandfather's office must be filled with bookshelves, a space where knowledge and history surrounded him.

The corridor opened into a vast sitting room—high ceilings, velvet drapes, and a grand piano resting near one of the tall windows.

Then...movement.

Lorna barely had time to react before she saw an AI sentry positioned near the far end of the room.

Heart pounding, she dropped to the floor, rolling underneath a long table covered with an embroidered cloth. She pressed herself flat against the ground, her breath coming in shallow bursts.

The AI's footsteps were measured, slow but heavy, as it patrolled the area.

She needed a distraction.

Her eyes darted to a small decorative vase sitting at the edge of the table above her.

Carefully, she reached up and nudged it—just enough to let it wobble and eventually teeter too much and crash to the floor.

The porcelain hit the floor with a sharp crash. *Sorry Grandad, hope that wasn't expensive!*

The AI immediately turned toward the sound, its optics flickering.

As soon as its attention was diverted, Lorna slid out from beneath the table and darted toward the next doorway.

She pushed through and—finally—she was in Alfred's office.

The room was massive.

Floor-to-ceiling bookshelves lined every wall, stretching up at least twenty feet, filled with worn tomes and leather-bound volumes. A grand oak desk sat near the center, adorned with scattered papers and an old globe. An enormous fireplace stood on the far side, a portrait of Vonya, her grandmother, hanging above it.

For a moment, Lorna stood still, absorbing the atmosphere of the space.

This was where Alfred had spent so much of his time and now, she's breathing the same stolid air.

The weight of history surrounded Lorna, pressing against her like an unseen force.

Her wrist device pinged softly, pulling her back to the task at hand. The lockbox was somewhere in this room.

She approached the desk first, running her hands over the surface, checking for hidden compartments. But nothing.

She moved toward the bookshelves, scanning the rows upon rows of books. If Alfred had hidden something here, it wouldn't be in plain sight.

Her wrist device pulsed faster as she neared the far-right section of shelving.

Lorna's fingers skimmed along the spines of the books, looking for anything out of place. That was when she saw it—a slight gap between two books, a space that shouldn't be there.

She reached up and carefully pulled at one of the books.

It didn't budge.

A mechanism.

She searched for a lever or latch, something that could release the hidden compartment. Her eyes landed on a small brass sparrow figurine nestled among the books.

Lorna hesitated.

Then, slowly, she pressed down on the sparrow's head.

A soft click sounded, and the bookshelf lurched forward.

The movement caught her off guard. She instinctively reached up to steady herself, but the entire shelf suddenly tipped. She then saw the hard drive within reach – it jostled free after touching the sparrow.

The weight of the bookshelf was too much.

The bookshelf collapsed forward.

The bookcase crashed onto the desk—and onto her.

Pain exploded through her legs as they became pinned under the weight of the fallen shelf and she hit her head, opening a cut and a trickle of blood. Dust filled the air, the scent of old paper and aged wood surrounding her as she struggled to move.

She barely had time to react before the entire structure came crashing down on her, books tumbling in every direction.

"Uhh... that hurts. Nicely done, Lorna. Uggh. What did you do?"

As she slowly regained consciousness, she realized that climbing this large bookcase to find the final hard drive, led to this disastrous result.

Now, with several of the books that it held splayed on top of Lorna, she realized that her legs were completely trapped under the massive structure, leaving her unable to move.

She pushed on it with a grunt and tried to lift it just enough so she could slide out.

"Come on!"

Predictably, she could barely move it at all. This was a dense, heavy, old, lacquered shelving.

"Way to go, Lorna."

After a couple of wiggling attempts that only resulted in exhausting herself, she took a second to stop pushing and just breathe.

She was trapped and it didn't look like she could do anything about it.

Time was running out. She remembered that the island is basically going to destroy itself if the U.S. Military doesn't strike first and do the job with a couple of Tomahawk missiles. This reminder was not a comforting one.

As she lay there, struggling to regain her composure, her mind drifted back—thinking about the events that had led her to this present predicament.

She pushed again against the bookcase with all her might, but it was impossible. It was too heavy. Her fingers ached as she clawed at the floor, trying to shift her legs free, but the crushing pressure held her firmly in place.

"Can't believe this." She muttered through clenched teeth.

She closed her eyes for a moment, trying to suppress the rising panic. Lorna was running out of time. Her wrist device blinked erratically—it was partially damaged. That meant she was cut off from Phillip. There would be no one coming to rescue her.

You can't just lie here. Get out of this!

She turned her head, scanning the floor. Her heart nearly stopped when her eyes landed on a small, black object lying just inches away from her—the last hard drive!

"Got you! Now, how do I get out of here?"

Relief and urgency flooded her simultaneously. She reached out, snatching it up and shoving it into her backpack. But she was still trapped, and the seconds were slipping away.

Just as she was about to attempt shifting the weight again, a shadow moved in front of her.

Lorna's breath came in short, uneven bursts as she lay pinned beneath the massive bookcase. Her muscles burned from the effort of trying to shift the heavy weight off her legs, but it wouldn't budge. Panic crept up her spine as the reality of her situation set in. She was trapped, and there was no telling what lurked in the shadows of the abandoned mansion.

The rhythmic pounding crescendos, accompanied by an unsettling noise, like garbled communication in a language she cannot understand. Then, they appear. Not one, but three massive, metal-clad figures emerge from the shadows. They look like futuristic knights, their armor sleek and reflective, their forms towering and menacing. Each holds a rifle, the barrels gleaming under the faint hallway lights, and all three raise their weapons in unison, pointing them directly at her.

The tension was unbearable. Lorna braced herself, convinced this was the end. The silence between the heavy thumps of her heartbeat is deafening. Just as it feels like they're about to fire, a commanding voice cuts through the air with startling clarity.

"STOP!"

24

Chapter Twenty-Four

The voice, firm yet feminine, holds undeniable authority. From behind the armored figures steps a strikingly beautiful woman. Her appearance is unlike anything Lorna has ever seen. She was dressed in a sleek, futuristic jumpsuit that clings to her form, clearly functional yet elegant, with subtle panels and illuminated lines suggesting advanced technology. Her poise was confident, her movements fluid and purposeful.

The knights lower their weapons immediately, snapping to attention as the woman strides past them. Without hesitation, she approached Lorna, who is still pinned beneath the heavy bookcase.

"Hello...?" she rasped, her voice hoarse from exhaustion.

The woman, the AI, didn't immediately respond. Instead, she bent down, grasping the bookcase with one fluid motion. Without any visible strain, she lifted it and tossed it aside as if it weighed nothing. Lorna barely had time to react before strong, unyielding hands closed around her arms and hauled her up with shocking ease.

She winced, her bruised body protesting. "Easy! I do break!" she grumbled.

The AI barely acknowledged the remark, adjusting Lorna in her grasp as if calibrating the best way to hold her. Then, in a voice both calm and calculated, she finally spoke.

"My name is Vonya."

Lorna's blood turned ice cold.

She blinked, momentarily stunned. "Wait—you mean *Vonya Cypress*? Alfred's Vonya?"

For the first time, Vonya's expression flickered, a momentary shift in her otherwise emotionless demeanor. She looked away, her jaw tightening, but she didn't answer.

Lorna barely had time to process before Vonya moved, carrying her like a child as effortlessly as if she weighed nothing. The metallic hum of the AI's exosuit echoed softly as she strode forward, exiting the dusty library and into a corridor Lorna hadn't noticed before.

She realized something then—Vonya wasn't just an AI. She was the guardian of this island. And Lorna had no idea whether she was being rescued or taken prisoner.

She simply turned on her heel and carried Lorna down a narrow corridor, her movements eerily smooth, unnaturally precise.

Lorna, still cradled in Vonya's arms, struggled to process what was happening. The walls of the corridor blurred past her in a mixture of metallic panels and low, recessed lighting. She caught glimpses of computer monitors embedded into the walls, flashing strange symbols and diagrams that she couldn't quite decipher.

Then, the space opened up into a massive, circular control area.

Lorna's breath caught.

The room was enormous, stretching in every direction. The ceiling was high, lined with dim blue lighting, casting the area in a cold glow. Around the perimeter, stations were manned by dozens of humanoid figures—Cypress AI. The Cypress Elite.

Just like the ones on the island.

They moved in perfect coordination, carrying out tasks with mechanical precision, their glowing eyes flickering as they worked. The entire room was like a living machine, every part moving in sync, directed by an unseen force.

Vonya carried her toward a small room on the edge of the control center. The moment they crossed the threshold, the door slid shut behind them with a soft hiss.

Lorna was set down onto a small cot, her injured leg immediately sending another wave of pain through her body. She winced, trying to sit up, but Vonya was already moving.

Without a word, she knelt beside Lorna and began tending to her leg. Her movements were efficient and methodical.

Lorna, watching her closely, noticed something—small, tattered sections of Vonya's forearms, a tear on her thigh. The synthetic material covering her body had been damaged in places.

Lorna hesitated, then finally asked, "Does that... hurt?"

Vonya didn't break her concentration.

She continued scanning Lorna's leg, adjusting it with a precision that made it clear she wasn't just guessing—she knew exactly what she was doing. After a moment, she finally spoke.

"You have a minor fracture," she said. "You will be okay."

Lorna exhaled slowly, strangely comforted by the certainty in Vonya's tone.

Then it hit her.

This was an android, but most importantly - a synthetic version of her grandmother.

The thought sent her into a spiral of emotions. She had spent so much time wondering about her past—about her family, about her mother—and now, here she was, face-to-face with a being who was both familiar and completely unknown to her.

She had so many questions.

But before she could ask any of them, a sharp, robotic voice interrupted the silence.

One of the Cypress Elite appeared in the doorway, speaking in a series of coded sounds. Lorna didn't understand them, but Vonya did.

She stood immediately, her posture shifting.

Whatever had been said, it changed something.

Vonya turned, issuing a single, firm command, motioning toward one of the tunnels leading out of the room.

The Cypress Elite obeyed, vanishing down the hallway.

Vonya turned back to Lorna, her expression unreadable.

Lorna watched as she finished securing her leg, but something about her movements seemed... different now. More urgent.

Lorna hesitated before asking, "Where are you going?"

Vonya didn't answer.

She stood, turned toward the door, and began to leave.

Lorna's pulse quickened. The realization of where she was, of how vulnerable she was, hit her all at once. She was in a room, underground, surrounded by AI.

Panic set in.

"Wait! You can't just leave me here!" Lorna's voice cracked with desperation.

Vonya paused in the doorway but didn't turn back.

Then, the door slid shut.

Lorna slammed her fists against the cot, frustration and fear mixing into a single, overwhelming sensation.

Her breathing quickened.

Then—alarms.

Loud. Blaring. Deafening.

A voice, smooth but urgent, echoed through the facility.

"Evacuate. Inbound threat detected."

Lorna's blood ran ice cold. *They're early!*

Her heart pounded violently against her ribs. The sound of rushing footsteps—mechanical—filled the corridors outside.

She struggled to sit up, her injured leg sending sharp pain up her body.

This was bad. Really bad.

She didn't know what to do.

The only thing she could do was plead for help.

"Vonya! Please! We need to get out of here!" Lorna shouted, panic rising in her throat.

Nothing.

The room shook slightly, the deep tremor of something approaching rattling through the walls.

Then—just as suddenly as she had left—the door burst open.

Vonya stood there.

Two Cypress Elite flanked her, their glowing eyes locked onto Lorna.

But Vonya... Vonya's expression was different.

Something had changed.

She didn't hesitate.

She crossed the room, grabbed Lorna, and lifted her effortlessly.

Lorna, despite everything, felt a strange sense of security in that moment.

For the first time since arriving on the island, she felt like she wasn't entirely alone.

But she also knew—the real danger was just beginning.

Vonya moved with calculated urgency, cradling Lorna in her arms as she carried her out of the small room and into the chaos of the underground base. The air buzzed with tension, a symphony of rapid footsteps, mechanical whirs, and blaring alarms echoing through the tunnels. The red emergency lights pulsed along the walls, casting sharp, flashing shadows that flickered with each movement.

Lorna barely had time to process what was happening before Vonya shifted her weight effortlessly and sprinted forward, the two Cypress Elite keeping pace at either side. The corridors were a maze of steel and concrete, dimly lit and narrow, branching off in multiple directions. They twisted and turned so quickly that Lorna struggled to keep track of where they were going.

She tried to steady her breath. "Vonya—where are we going?"

Vonya didn't answer at first. She moved with precision, turning sharply down another corridor as a deep, thunderous rumble shook the floor beneath them. The alarms blared even louder. A sharp voice came over the intercom, the AI's calm yet firm tone sending a chill down Lorna's spine.

"Hostile approach confirmed. Security countermeasures engaged."

Vonya finally spoke, her voice steady but edged with something close to urgency. “Extraction point.”

Lorna’s mind reeled. “Extraction? What extraction? Who’s coming for me?”

Vonya made another turn, her grip on Lorna unwavering. “You are no longer safe here.”

That answer did nothing to ease Lorna’s pounding heart.

Ahead, a heavy steel door slid open, revealing a large industrial corridor, lined with thick support beams and crates of equipment stacked against the walls. But what caught Lorna’s attention most were the figures moving through the space. More Cypress Elite—at least ten of them—were stationed at various points, their glowing eyes tracking Vonya’s approach.

Then, in the distance, a low, deep boom rattled the walls, shaking dust loose from the ceiling.

Lorna felt it more than she heard it, the pressure of the explosion rippling through the underground structure. The AI’s voice crackled through the intercom again.

“Outer perimeter breached.”

Vonya didn’t slow. She moved through the corridor like a ghost, silent and fast, weaving between the Cypress Elite as if they weren’t even there. Lorna, despite the pain in her leg, tried to twist slightly in Vonya’s arms to get a better look at the situation around her.

“Who breached the perimeter?” she asked, gripping Vonya’s shoulder. “Who’s attacking the base?”

For the first time, Vonya hesitated. Not long, just for a fraction of a second, but Lorna noticed.

Then Vonya spoke, her voice unwavering, but with something else behind it.

“An enemy.”

Lorna’s breath caught.

Another explosion rocked the underground structure, this time closer. The walls groaned under the pressure, and for the first time since she had arrived, Lorna felt the true weight of the danger pressing down on her.

She wasn't just in over her head anymore.

She was in a war she didn't understand.

Before Lorna could question further, alarms blared through the base.

Red emergency lights bathed the walls in an eerie glow, and a deep mechanical voice reverberated through the space:

"WARNING. IMMINENT STRIKE DETECTED. EVACUATE IMMEDIATELY."

Lorna's stomach dropped. This was no longer the stuff of sci-fi movies and such. It was real. The threat was imminent, and Lorna was in actual mortal danger.

Lorna barely had time to register what was happening as Vonya continued to make her way through the area.

Vonya's grip was unshakable, her movements precise, almost inhuman in their speed and efficiency. The world around them blurred as she charged forward, her footfalls barely making a sound against the hard ground in the tunnels.

Lorna, who was being carried as if she were a baby, struggled to keep up with what was happening, her head bouncing slightly with each powerful stride. "Wow, you are fast!" she grumbled, her voice muffled by the sheer speed at which they were moving.

The corridors were a labyrinth, twisting and turning in ways that made Lorna's head spin. She caught only fleeting glimpses of her surroundings—tall; servers lined the corridors. Workstations with large monitors, crates with all kinds of supplies and what appeared to be large aviation parts, were stored in this area. It was clear there was a lot going on with all that was here. The grandeur of the mansion and this underground area barely registered now; all she could focus on was the distant, thunderous rumble of approaching destruction.

The ground beneath them shuddered.

A deep, mechanical voice echoed through unseen speakers.

"WARNING. IMMINENT STRIKE DETECTED. EVACUATE IMMEDIATELY."

Lorna's breath caught in her throat. It was happening.

Vonya didn't stop.

She swiftly pivoted, kicking open a panel on the wall with such force that it shattered inward, revealing a concealed passageway. Without a moment's hesitation, she darted inside, sprinting through the dimly lit tunnel with unwavering speed. The ceiling was low and arched, adorned with wires and old pipes along its length. The air was cool and damp, carrying the pungent scent of stone and earth within the confined space.

Vonya's breathing remained remarkably steady, as if effortlessly carrying a fully grown woman through the winding, underground corridor.

Lorna, on the other hand, was feeling increasingly disoriented and a little nauseas.

They rounded a sharp corner, descending a steep metal staircase that led deeper underground. The metallic clang of Vonya's boots echoed sharply, bouncing off the narrow walls.

Then—another TREMOR.

Dust and loose gravel showered down from above, and for the first time, Vonya's pace faltered, just for a moment.

"Vonya, this place is coming down on us!" Lorna's voice rose in urgency.

Vonya tightened her grip around Lorna and pressed forward, pushing harder, moving faster, taking giant loping strides.

The passage opened up suddenly into a massive tunnel that stretched forward into darkness. At the far end, Lorna could make out the faintest glimmer of light—the outside. The dock – thank God!

Almost there...

Vonya didn't slow down. She carried Lorna through the last stretch, her movements like clockwork. The walls vibrated, a distant explosion rumbling through the island's foundation.

Then—fresh air.

The tunnel opened into the hidden dock, the cavernous space just as Lorna remembered it. The lake's dark waters lapped against the smooth concrete, the boat still waiting, perfectly positioned. The small, mounted lanterns along the walls cast long shadows, giving the entire dock an eerie, almost unnatural glow.

Finally, Vonya stopped running and jumped onto the boat with agility and smoothness. Vonya placed Lorna down onto the boat with surprising gentleness, her arms uncoiling from around her like a machine completing a task.

Lorna swayed on unsteady legs, her breath ragged. Her body ached from the rough escape, being carried at high speeds like a sack of potatoes wasn't without some bodily consequences, but she was alive.

25

Chapter Twenty-Five

Vonya wasting no time, turned on her heel, sprang back onto the dock, and moved to the control panel embedded in the cavern wall. She input a series of rapid-fire commands, fingers moving as a blur with a precision that was both elegant and mechanical.

Lorna, still catching her breath, watched Vonya with growing alarm.

The boat's engines roared to life.

A sharp hum filled the space as the vessel began to shift, drifting slowly away from the dock.

Lorna's stomach dropped.

"What are you doing?" She demanded.

Vonya didn't respond. She simply placed one foot against the edge of the boat and gave it a firm push.

The boat lurched backward, moving faster now.

"No!" Lorna lunged forward, nearly losing her balance. "You can't stay here! The whole place is going to be blown up!"

Vonya stood unmoving, her silver eyes reflecting the dim light of the cave like twin mirrors.

Lorna reached toward her, desperation clawing at her chest. Remembering the prime directives of her grandfather's AI's, she tried a new tactic, "I need your help!"

Still, Vonya didn't move.

The boat was now several yards away, the entrance of the cave coming into view.

And then—

Lorna saw them.

The jets made the sonorous engine propulsion sound they are famous for which was followed by jet trails.

High above the island, sleek, black military aircraft sliced through the sky. Their lights flashed ominously in the distance, circling like predatory birds preparing to strike.

Her blood turned ice cold.

"NO! NO!" Lorna screamed, but she knew—it was too late.

The jet's underbelly flashed.

Twin missiles soared aggressively from the body of the jet.

They streaked through the sky with deadly precision, their glowing trails like burning scars against the night.

Lorna's breath caught as she watched a missile strike the mansion.

The explosion was instantaneous.

A fireball erupted, sending a shockwave through the water, nearly knocking Lorna off her feet. The second missile followed, hitting the subterranean entrance with devastating force.

The cave shook violently, sending debris cascading down into the lake.

Lorna stared, her heart pounding out of control.

Her eyes searched desperately for Vonya.

But she was gone. Swallowed by the flames.

Or had she escaped? Lorna didn't know for sure.

She could only watch helplessly as the island was consumed by fire; its secrets reduced to ash.

Then—

The radio crackled to life.

"LORNA! LORNA, CAN YOU HEAR ME?!"

Phillip's voice was frantic.

Lorna swallowed hard, forcing herself to find her voice. "I'm here."

"Are you okay? Where are you?"

She took a shuddering breath, still watching the distant plumes of smoke rise into the night sky.

"A little banged up. I'll be fine," she said urgently. "I'm on my way back." She reached inside her bag and pulled out the last hard drive that she retrieved from Alfred's office, making sure she had accomplished her mission.

She told Phillip that she was fine, but as the boat carried her away from the wreckage, she knew—

This was a new chapter in her life and a point of no return.

As Lorna pressed forward, focused entirely on her escape, the destruction behind her, and the uncertainty ahead, she remained oblivious to what was happening on the far side of the island.

Beneath the surface of the dark water, hidden by shadows and the remnants of the burning gigantic estate, a nearly silent craft slipped from a concealed underwater exit. The vessel, sleek and unmarked, moved with deliberate precision, cutting through the water like a phantom, its presence unnoticed by the chaos that had unfolded above.

But not everyone was blind to it.

Roughly 400 yards away, a small yacht floated, motionless, against the gentle lapping of the waves. Its elegant silhouette blended into the night, its presence seemingly unremarkable in the vast expanse of water. The boat's running lights were dimmed, making it almost indistinguishable against the backdrop of the distant fires still smoldering from the island's destruction.

On the upper deck, beneath a darkened overhang, a man stood, still as a statue, watching through a pair of high-powered binoculars. His posture was relaxed but purposeful, his stance unwavering as he tracked the craft's movement with an almost unnatural precision. The subtle glow of distant flames reflected off the lenses, flickering like tiny embers on the glass as he adjusted the focus.

The small craft continued to glide away from the island, disappearing slowly into the horizon. The man did not follow its path with his own boat. He merely observed, taking in every detail, his expression unreadable.

After a long moment, he lowered the binoculars, his grip on them firm yet unhurried. A slow, measured breath escaped him, the night air cool against his skin.

A smirk crept across his face—one of understanding, of amusement, and perhaps something more calculated and sinister.

"Hmmm."

The sound was barely audible, more of a whisper to himself than anything meant for the empty water around him. Then, without another word, he turned away from the railing and disappeared into the shadows of the yacht's cabin, leaving only the rhythmic sound of the waves against the hull as the vessel remained adrift, its purpose—whatever it may be—left unanswered.

Lorna clutched the side of the boat, her knuckles white from the pressure. The roaring engines beneath were the only thing keeping her tethered to reality as the craft sped across the water, slicing through the waves with a smooth, unnatural precision. She felt the cool spray of the lake on her face, but it barely registered.

Her mind was still trapped on the island—on the explosions, on Vonya, on the hard drives in her backpack that she clung to like a lifeline.

She had escaped, but the weight of what she had just witnessed clung to her like a second skin. The mansion, the hidden technology, the AI guardians that had nearly caught her—none of it seemed real. And yet, the bruises on her body, the burning ache in her muscles, and the sheer exhaustion pressing down on her told her otherwise.

As the boat neared the dock, she could see movement on the shoreline. Blurred figures stood waiting, their forms growing clearer with every second. As the vessel slowed, cutting through the last few feet of water before drifting to the edge of the dock, her breath caught in her throat.

They were there waiting for her.

A three-man team had been sent ahead, their sharp gazes scanning her as though assessing for injuries before she had even fully arrived.

And there, standing a step ahead of the others, was Kyle. His stance was firm, his expression unreadable, but his eyes told a different story—sharp, focused, scanning her like a soldier assessing a battlefield for casualties. His dark clothes were dusted with hints of dirt, as if he hadn't left the dock since she departed, as if he had been waiting, watching the horizon for any sign of her return.

The tension in his shoulders was unmistakable, but the moment his gaze locked onto hers, something flickered across his face—relief, concern, something unspoken yet palpable.

For a second, Lorna felt like she was tethered to something real again. The storm inside her, the adrenaline, the exhaustion, all of it momentarily quieted at the sight of him. It was strange. They hadn't known each other long, and yet, seeing him there, unwavering, made her feel safer than she had since leaving the dock for the island.

Then Kyle moved.

Without hesitation, he stepped forward, closing the space between them in long, purposeful strides. The rest of the team stood ready, but Kyle was the first to reach her, the first to extend a steadying hand as the boat came to a stop. His fingers wrapped around her wrist, gentle but firm, as if he was afraid, she might disappear if he didn't hold on.

"Lorna," he said, his voice low, controlled—but there was something beneath it, something raw. "Can you stand?"

She tried to nod, to reassure him, but the moment she shifted, her legs wobbled beneath her, drained of any strength they had left. Kyle reacted instantly, stepping onto the boat with practiced ease, his arm sliding around her waist to support her weight. She felt his strength, solid and unwavering, as he held her up.

"It's okay, I've got you," he murmured, his voice softer now, meant just for her. "Let's get you out of here."

And for the first time since leaving the island, she let herself believe she was safe.

She wanted to tell him she was fine. That she could walk without wobbling. But, that would be a lie, and right now, lying felt like far too much effort. Instead, she simply nodded weakly, letting him guide her as the others moved in to help.

They led her toward a waiting vehicle—a sleek, black ambulance that was anything but ordinary. Reinforced panels lined its exterior, and the tinted windows suggested that whatever was inside wasn't meant to be seen by just anyone. The moment they reached it, the back doors swung open, revealing a stark but well-equipped medical bay inside.

Kyle helped her inside, settling her onto the gurney. The moment her body hit the cushioned surface, she felt the last of her energy drain away. She exhaled, long and slow, and then, without warning, the tears came.

Silent. Unstoppable.

She wasn't even sure why she was crying, because she wasn't a crier. But with the weight of everything she had just been through and the sheer relief of making it back, she couldn't help it. Also, the lingering uncertainty of what had happened to Vonya—the image of her standing on that dock, watching her leave, burned into her memory like an imprint she would never shake.

Kyle sat beside her, his presence grounding. He didn't say anything at first, just placed a reassuring hand on hers. The simple gesture nearly broke her.

"You did great," he said softly.

Lorna turned her head slightly to look at him. Despite everything, she managed the faintest smile before letting her gaze drift upward. The last few hours felt surreal, but one thing was certain—this was far from over.

They had the hard drives. But what they contained, what they meant, and what came next... she wasn't sure she was ready to find out.

The vehicle rumbled to life beneath her, and as it pulled away from the dock, Lorna finally let herself close her eyes.

The events of the last evening played like a fragmented dream in her mind—Vonya, the mansion, the hard drives, the explosions. And yet, despite all of that, she still had more questions than answers.

What happened to Vonya? Did she escape? Was she even meant to escape? And if not... why?

The vehicle moved swiftly through the darkness; the low hum of the engine barely audible over the sounds of Lorna's labored breathing. Every bump in the road sent jolts of pain through her battered body, but she clenched her jaw and focused on the rhythmic motion, letting it lull her into a state of exhaustion rather than agony. Kyle sat beside her just as he did on the first leg of their trip, his presence helping her feel grounded; his arm resting within reach should she need it.

As the vehicle sped through the empty streets, Lorna barely registered the passing city lights. Her mind was still reeling from the mission, the island, the AI, and most of all—Vonya. The weight of exhaustion pressed down on her, but she fought to stay alert, gripping the edge of the seat as the vehicle took a sharp turn.

The library came into view, its familiar stone façade bathed in the soft glow of streetlamps. To any passerby, it was nothing more than a historical landmark, a quiet sanctuary of books and knowledge. But Lorna now knew the truth—it was so much more. Beneath its foundations, buried deep underground, lay the operations facility—the nerve center where Phillip had been preparing her for everything to come.

The vehicle slowed as it approached an inconspicuous alley behind the library, where a shadowed entrance blended seamlessly into the old brick wall. No signs, no markings—just an unremarkable service door that hid an entire world beneath it.

Kyle was the first to step out. He scanned the area, eyes sharp, muscles tense. Satisfied that they hadn't been followed, he signaled to the others. The back doors of the vehicle swung open, and a wave of movement followed.

Lorna felt multiple hands reaching for her, firm yet careful, as she was eased out of the vehicle. Her legs were weak from the bookshelf smashing on top of her in Alfred's office, and for a moment, she felt as if she might collapse. Kyle was there instantly, wrapping an arm around her waist to steady her.

"You're almost there," he murmured, his voice low but reassuring. "Just a little further."

With Kyle's help, she shuffled toward the door. One of the operatives swiped a key card through a near-invisible slot embedded in the brick, and a mechanical click echoed in the silence. The door swung open, revealing a dimly lit corridor that stretched into darkness.

Lorna swallowed hard as she was led inside. The air was cool, sterile, and the scent of aged books mixed with the faint hum of hidden machinery. The door shut behind them with a soft thud, sealing them away from the outside world.

The corridor sloped downward, the walls subtly shifting from aged brick to sleek metal. She hadn't noticed this entrance before—when she first met Phillip, she had entered through the main library doors, completely unaware of the hidden passages beneath her feet. Now, she could see how seamlessly the old and the new had been woven together. The deeper they went, the more the atmosphere changed. The warmth of the library above faded, replaced by the cool precision of technology.

Finally, they reached a security checkpoint. A reinforced steel door, flanked by two armed guards, blocked the path forward. One of the operatives accompanying them stepped forward, pressing his hand against a biometric scanner. A green light blinked, and the door slid open with a hiss.

Beyond it, the underground training center stretched before them—vast, sophisticated, and alive with quiet activity. Rows of monitors flickered along the far wall, displaying maps, schematics, and surveillance feeds. A handful of AI operatives moved with practiced efficiency; their voices low as they worked at various stations.

The sight of it sent a wave of relief through Lorna. She had made it. She was safe.

Or, at the very least, safer than she had been.

Kyle helped her toward the infirmary, where a small medical team was already waiting. The moment they stepped inside, she was gently eased onto an examination bed. The sterile white lights above made her squint, her head pounding from the sudden brightness.

"Let's get you checked out," one of the medics said, already reaching for a medical scanner. "Looks like you've been through it."

Lorna let out a breath she didn't realize she had been holding. She had made it back. But as the medics worked, her mind drifted back to the island, to Vonya, to the hard drives she had retrieved.

Inside, the air was sterile, crisp with the faint scent of antiseptic. The infirmary was brightly lit, a stark contrast to the dim corridors and eerie silence of the island. Lorna squinted as her eyes adjusted. She was led to an examination bed, and the moment she sat down, the adrenaline that had been holding her together began to wear off. The exhaustion hit her like a tidal wave.

The medical team moved quickly, assessing her condition with quiet efficiency. A woman with sharp blue eyes and a crisp uniform pressed cool fingers to her wrist, checking her pulse. Another, a man with graying temples, crouched beside her and gently examined her shoulder.

"You took a pretty nasty hit here," he murmured, his voice professional but not unkind. "Did you fall?"

Lorna gave a weak, breathless laugh. "More like... had a bookcase fall on me."

The woman arched an eyebrow. "A bookcase?"

"A big one," Lorna muttered, wincing as the medic rotated her shoulder.

The bruising along her ribs was more severe than she had realized, deep purples and blues spreading across her skin like a storm rolling in. She inhaled sharply as they probed gently at her side, determining whether any bones had been fractured.

"Looks like you were very fortunate," the older medic noted. "No bad breaks, your legs are bruised up pretty good, and also a minor fracture, it will take you a little time to heal."

Her hands, scraped raw from climbing and her frantic escape, were cleaned and wrapped in fresh bandages. The gash on her arm, which had been bleeding sluggishly since she left the island, required a few stitches. She barely registered the needle as it worked through her skin. The pain had faded into a distant blur, drowned out by exhaustion.

She was just beginning to drift, her mind threatening to shut down completely, when the last medic finished up and stepped back.

"She'll need rest," the woman said, addressing Kyle. "But nothing serious enough to keep her under observation."

Kyle gave a single nod, his gaze flickering to Lorna with something that looked suspiciously like relief.

The door opened, and the presence in the room shifted.

Phillip stepped inside.

Lorna blinked up at him, her body too heavy to sit up straight.

Phillip's sharp gaze swept over her, taking in every detail—her bandaged hands, the bruises along her arms, the way she sat slightly slumped against the bed. His expression remained unreadable, but she caught the subtle tightening of his jaw, the way his fingers flexed at his sides.

"How are you feeling?" he asked, his voice calm but carrying that ever-present weight of authority.

Lorna stared at him for a long moment, then exhaled a slow, exhausted breath.

"I'm too tired to give an explanation that would actually make sense."

Phillip chuckled softly, shaking his head. "Well, at least you still have your sense of humor."

Lorna pushed herself up a little more, groaning as her muscles protested. "Not really that funny."

He studied her for a beat longer before stepping closer, hands slipping into his pockets. There was something different in his stance—something not quite as rigid as usual.

"I still feel like I just came out of a dream," Lorna admitted, her voice quieter now. "I mean, the mansion and everything I had to do was one thing, but… seeing her. Vonya."

Phillip nodded, his gaze steady. "It's a lot to process."

"That's an understatement," she muttered, rubbing a hand over her face.

He sighed, glancing toward the window as if gathering his thoughts. "Your grandfather has always had an incredible mind—brilliant beyond his years. But more than that, he has a heart for people. That's why we had to be so careful with you. He needed to be sure you had that same heart before bringing you into all of this."

Lorna frowned. "You keep saying that. That it had to be me. That I had to prove something. Why? What is so dangerous about what he built?"

Phillip held her gaze, weighing his words. Then he began pacing slowly, hands still in his pockets, his tone measured.

"There are things in this world that most people never see. Technologies, discoveries, advancements that could change everything. Your grandfather was one of the few who had access to that kind of power—true power. And not everyone who wants it has good intentions."

Lorna's stomach twisted. "You mean people like... the Pentagon? The ones who ordered the island to be destroyed?"

Phillip's lips pressed into a thin line. "Not all of them. There are still people in the government who believe in what we're doing, who are on our side. But there are others who would rather see Alfred's work in their control—or wiped from existence—than risk it being used in a way they can't regulate. Or profit from."

Lorna swallowed, her mind racing despite the exhaustion. "And I'm part of that equation now."

Phillip nodded. "You are."

The weight of it settled over her like a lead blanket. The mansion, the AI, Vonya... the past few days had turned her world upside down, and now she had to figure out where she stood in all of it.

She looked back at Phillip, her brows furrowing. "So, what happens now?"

Phillip studied her for a long moment. Then, with a small, almost reluctant smirk, he said, "Right now? You rest."

Lorna groaned, rolling her eyes. "You have got to be kidding. All of that, and now I just have to wait?"

Phillip's smirk deepened slightly as he turned toward the door. "Trust me. You're going to want to be at full strength for what comes next."

Lorna furrowed her brow. "So, this was all some kind of test?"

Phillip nodded. "In a way, yes. What Alfred has developed—and what you have only just begun to uncover—can be a tremendous asset to the world. But if mismanaged, if placed in the wrong hands, it could become a weapon of unimaginable consequence. Your grandfather would rather see everything he's created destroyed than allow it to be used for harm."

Lorna let that sink in, but it still didn't answer everything. "I get that he was brilliant. I get that he was careful. But why are there so many... threats?" Her voice was edged with frustration. "Why does it seem like every move I make, there's someone in the shadows waiting to pounce?"

Phillip, still pacing, sighed. "As you continue down this path, things will become clearer. And yes, there will be more dangerous moments ahead. You need to understand that the world you've stepped into isn't the same one most people live in.

The mainstream world—the one where people go about their daily lives, oblivious to what really keeps things in motion—exists because there are forces constantly at work behind the scenes, working thanklessly on their behalf."

He stopped and looked at her. "Your grandfather has adversaries. People who want what he built. People who would twist his work into something unrecognizable. And one man in particular, one with vast resources, is undoubtedly aware of you by now."

Lorna straightened. "Who?"

Phillip held her gaze for a moment, then sighed, shaking his head. "That's a conversation for another time. Right now, you need rest."

Lorna groaned, rolling her eyes. "You've got to be kidding. You drop all that on me and then just tell me to wait?"

Phillip smirked. "Yes. Because for what comes next, you'll need to be at your best."

Lorna sighed, sinking back into the bed. She hated it, but she knew he was right. She wasn't done—not even close. And whatever was waiting for her outside the safety of these walls was only going to get more dangerous.

But now, at least, she had a direction.

And she wasn't going to stop until she found out the truth. All of it.

As Phillip stepped toward the door, he hesitated for just a moment, glancing back at Lorna. She was sitting up in bed, still bandaged and sore, but with a fire in her eyes that hadn't been there before. She had changed—whether she fully realized it yet or not. With a small smirk, Phillip finally turned away, stepping through the doorway.

Just as he disappeared into the corridor, Lorna threw up her hands. "Really? You're just leaving me with a cliffhanger?!" Her voice echoed off the walls, her frustration plain. She leaned back against the pillows, exhaling sharply as she stared up at the ceiling. Then, after a moment, she muttered under her breath, "I don't think so, Phil."

26

Chapter Twenty-Six

And then, Lorna swung her legs off the bed and sat forward, her determination solidifying. She wasn't going to sit around and wait for things to be handed to her. There were too many unanswered questions, too much left for her to discover. She pushed herself up to her feet, testing her balance before gathering her things.

She exited the infirmary and followed the path Phillip had taken earlier. The underground facility was massive, stretching far beneath the old library, and she was still getting used to the sheer scale of it. After a few minutes of winding through dimly lit corridors, she finally caught up to Phillip, who was waiting at the entrance to a large staging area.

The space before her was vast—large enough to accommodate at least fifty people standing shoulder to shoulder. Its walls were lined with sleek metal paneling, and there was an eerie quiet, save for the occasional hum of unseen machinery. Lorna glanced around, momentarily disoriented. The entire room looked like something straight out of a futuristic subway station, which made absolutely no sense.

"Hey, Phillip!" He turned around and she continued, "What is this place?" she asked, stepping closer.

Phillip didn't answer right away. Instead, he simply gestured toward the far end of the chamber.

A soft rumbling reached her ears. Then, she saw it.

A tram car—sleek, metallic, and moving with seamless efficiency—was approaching at an impressive speed. Unlike any train she'd ever seen, this one glided in quietly. As it neared, the doors hissed open with precision, revealing an interior lined with polished seating, touch screens, and monitors embedded into the walls.

Phillip turned toward her and nodded. “Couldn’t sleep, huh? Alright, let’s go.”

She stepped forward hesitantly, feeling as though she had just been transported into the set of some high-tech espionage film. The tram’s interior was not what she expected—plush seating, intuitive interfaces, and a level of craftsmanship that made commercial trains look like relics from another era.

Setting down her luggage, Lorna took one of the seats and ran her fingers across the smooth armrest. “My grandfather... he built this?” she asked, still trying to process everything.

Phillip took his seat beside her and activated the control panel in front of him, placing his hand on a palm scanner. A soft beep confirmed his identity before he spoke into a microphone embedded into the screen. “Phillip Mahoney, voice recognition.”

The system acknowledged him, and the doors slid shut. The tram smoothly accelerated forward.

“Yes,” Phillip finally answered, keeping his gaze on the monitors. “But with some help.”

Lorna frowned. “Help? I thought he worked alone.”

Phillip shook his head. “Not exactly. He was never one for traditional partnerships, but collaboration was necessary at times. Construction projects like this were often just a means to an end for his larger vision.”

Lorna let that sink in. “So, he wasn’t in the construction business, but he built entire underground transit systems?”

Phillip turned in his seat, studying her. “Your grandfather has been involved in more industries than you could possibly imagine. He designed and built facilities like this one because they were necessary for protecting his work. Over time, he became involved in everything from energy solutions to communication advancements.”

He leaned back slightly. "Your grandfather is more influential than most people will ever know. He's been burned before—betrayed by people he trusted. That's why he keeps so many of his projects hidden. Even something like this monorail system... He never wanted credit for it. He just wanted to make sure that those who needed it could use it."

Lorna's mind reeled. "So... he's been secretly consulting on major technological advancements for years? Example?"

Phillip nodded. "The miniaturization of cell phones, long-range missile guidance systems, advancements in modern refrigeration—your grandfather played a role in all of them. He's been a ghost consultant for some of the biggest breakthroughs of our time."

Lorna sat in silence for a moment, staring out the window as the tram sped through a long, dimly lit tunnel.

Phillip glanced at her and smirked. "I'm glad you decided to come." Lorna retorted, "You expected it, didn't you?" Phillip looked forward and grinned.

Lorna let out a breath and looked down at the floor. She wasn't sure what she could do yet, but she wanted to know more. If she had even a fraction of her grandfather's determination, his vision, then maybe she could help in some way. Maybe she also could make a difference.

Phillip's voice cut through her thoughts. "We're approaching the base."

In the distance, the tunnel lights shifted. The lighting ahead was different, arranged in a precise pattern. As the tram approached, a massive chamber came into view, dimly lit but expansive. She could see a large open space beyond the monorail windows—several levels of machinery, workstations, and storage bays filled with equipment.

Lorna pressed closer to the window. "People actually work down here?"

Phillip didn't respond.

The tram glided to a stop, and the doors opened with a quiet hiss. Lorna grabbed her things and stepped onto the platform, which led to a large entranceway.

Beyond it, an enormous hangar-style space stretched before her, the ceilings soaring at least a hundred feet high. The high-tech design mirrored that of the control room, but the atmosphere here was different—more active, more urgent. Military-style vehicles lined one side of the chamber, and in the distance, she could make out what appeared to be a hangar filled with aircraft.

Everything felt somehow... unfinished.

She noticed that many of the workers moved in a sluggish, almost mechanical fashion. Clad in uniformed gear, they worked at various stations, but there was something robotic about the way they moved. They weren't Cypress Elite, but they certainly didn't carry themselves like regular personnel either. Not quite human.

As she took it all in, the weight of the moment settled over her. She wasn't just visiting a facility—this place was a stronghold. A hidden world her grandfather had built, one that she was now stepping into.

As Phillip and Lorna walked to the edge of the platform, the sheer enormity of the facility below fully hit her. It was vast, stretching far beyond what she had initially perceived, its depths layered with intertwining catwalks, towering structures, and dimly glowing control stations. The entire scene was bathed in a muted, bluish light, giving the space an otherworldly feel.

Lorna's gaze swept across the landscape of technology and machinery. Every level had its purpose, from monitoring stations lined with blinking consoles to maintenance bays filled with dormant vehicles. A few tunnels stretched out into the distance, hinting at an even greater underground network beyond what was immediately visible.

She squinted as her eyes locked onto the soldiers below—only they weren't exactly soldiers. Humanoid figures, standing rigidly, moving with unnatural precision, carried out tasks in their designated stations. Their synthetic movements reminded her instantly of the AI guards from the island. Her pulse quickened.

"Wait..." she muttered, turning toward Phillip with growing apprehension. "These... these are like the ones on the island. What are we doing here?" She took an involuntary step backward.

Phillip glanced at her, his expression calm yet calculated. "No," he corrected. "These are not the same. Not at all. The ones on the island were doing their job, fulfilling their directives as best they could in Alfred's absence. But these... these have been left to function in a void. Without a Cypress to guide them, there have been changes. They weaken over time." His voice was steady, but there was an undercurrent of concern.

Lorna looked back down at them. Now that she was paying closer attention, she saw it—the subtle glitches in their movements, the occasional pause before executing a task, the slight wavering in their posture. They were not as seamless, as controlled as they had once been.

And then, as if reacting to Phillip's very words, one of the Cypress Elite units below abruptly stopped what it was doing. The movement was fluid but precise, as if suddenly shaken from a trance. Slowly, it straightened to a full upright stance. Then, without a word or signal, it turned... and faced her.

Lorna's breath caught in her throat. It was less than 24 hours ago when she thought creatures like this were going to attack her.

One by one, across the massive facility, every single Cypress Elite halted their work. The clang of metal against metal, the soft hum of mechanical limbs, the steady sounds of tasks being executed—everything fell away into eerie silence.

Then, as though responding to an unseen command, they each turned in perfect synchrony, standing at attention, their glowing artificial eyes locked onto her.

The energy in the room shifted. The air was suddenly charged with a palpable electricity, a moment suspended in time where even the humming of computers seemed to recede into the background. The room, once filled with activity, now stood still.

Lorna swallowed hard. Her muscles tensed, every instinct telling her to take a step back, to move, return to the futuristic subway car that brought her. To do something; anything. But instead, she stood frozen, feeling the weight of hundreds of robotic gazes locked onto her.

She leaned toward Phillip, barely able to breathe, whispering as cautiously as possible, "Why are they looking at me?"

Phillip didn't move at first. He kept his eyes trained on the silent sea of Elite units, his expression unreadable. But there was something behind his gaze—a flicker of deep satisfaction, of understanding.

Then, with deliberate slowness, he turned to her, his voice laced with a quiet reverence.

"You're a Cypress."

The words hit Lorna harder than she expected. It wasn't just a statement—it was a declaration, a reminder, an undeniable truth she was still struggling to fully grasp. She felt a shift in the atmosphere, an unspoken acknowledgment from the machines below. They knew. Somehow, they had always known.

Phillip let the words settle for a moment before taking a breath and addressing the vast assembly before them.

"Cypress Elite," his voice carried, strong and unwavering. "This is Lorna. Alfred's granddaughter."

The response was immediate.

A surge of energy rippled through the space, like a dormant force suddenly being reignited. The dim lights seemed to glow just a little brighter, the hum of machinery deepened, and the collective presence of the Elite shifted ever so slightly, as if they had all just been... reawakened.

Lorna swore she felt something—an odd sensation of recognition, a sense of being welcomed without words.

She stood motionless as the realization settled deep in her core.

They had been waiting for her.

Phillip turned to her, his expression calm but unmistakably pleased. "Let's continue," he said, gesturing toward the grand staircase that led down to the main floor.

Lorna hesitated for only a moment before stepping forward. Together, they descended into the massive hangar, moving deeper into the heart of the facility. As they walked through the silent ranks of Cypress Elite, Lorna could feel their presence surrounding her, their attention unwavering.

Lorna stood at the edge of the platform, gazing out over the vast underground facility, the glow of dim overhead lights casting long shadows across the towering machinery and the ranks of Cypress Elite standing at silent attention. The air carried the low hum of energy, as if the entire base had been waiting for something—for her.

She had spent weeks chasing the past, unraveling a mystery that had nearly cost her life, but here, standing in the heart of her grandfather's legacy, she understood something with crystal clarity—this wasn't the end of her journey. It was only the beginning.

The answers she had fought for, bled for, were not the final truths she had imagined. Instead, they had only led to more questions, deeper mysteries buried beneath the surface of everything she thought she knew. The Cypress Inheritance was more than an estate, more than a company, more than technology beyond anything the world had seen. It was a responsibility. A destiny.

And it was now hers.

The weight of that realization settled over her, but for the first time in her life, she didn't feel burdened by the unknown—she felt alive!

As the hum of the facility seemed to grow, almost in anticipation, she glanced at Phillip, who watched her with measured patience, as if he, too, knew that there was no turning back from this moment.

Lorna took a breath, steadying herself. Whatever came next—whatever secrets were still hidden, whatever dangers lurked beyond this underground world, and the countless unanswered questions —she knew this was where she needed to be.

Because this was not just about uncovering the past anymore, but a much larger world...

ACKNOWLEDGE

I thank God for all He has done for me, for His grace, mercy and for His Son Jesus Christ. I am very thankful for the opportunities He has given me. God has always been faithful and loved me, even with how I have failed Him. So again, I want to say, thanks to God!

I also thank God for America, to have the freedom to write a story and to put that story out to read.

Lastly, thanks to some very special people who have been great friends along the way!

ABOUT THE AUTHORS

C.E. One Cypress has never sought the spotlight. Deeply dedicated, he thrives behind the scenes. Fulfillment comes not from recognition, but from telling the story. With a talent for elevating complex ideas, CE One blends innovative insights with timeless themes, ensuring the narrative is thought-provoking and immersive while he orchestrates the details with precision and passion.

Dave DeBorde is an award-winning filmmaker and screenwriter whose work spans theatrical features, television, and reality series. He was a producer on the acclaimed romantic drama Old Fashioned, and wrote the theatrical family adventure Camp Hideout (Roadside/Sony). Now, Dave brings his cinematic storytelling to the page as co-author of Cypress Inheritance The Beginning, writing alongside the Cypress Inheritance saga's original creator. This book launches an ambitious narrative universe filled with mystery, science fiction, and emotional discovery. A regular speaker at international film festivals including Cannes and Sundance, Dave balances his creative pursuits with his favorite role: devoted husband and father to four energetic kids.

www.ingramcontent.com/pod-product-compliance
Lightning Source LLC
Chambersburg PA
CBHW060804310726
48980CB00002B/229
9798998836008